"You left w̶i̶t̶h̶o̶u̶t̶

Andria whirled a̶ ... ...ave the decency to say good-bye to Bridget, and you never wrote."

Rafe saw her fists balling and barely had time to protect himself as she started pounding his chest.

"I hate you, Rafe!" she shouted. "I hate you so much, I would like to kill you. You ruined everything; you ruined my life."

Tears clogged his throat as he tried to digest all that she'd told him. He caught her wrists and held her tightly. Her chest rose and fell rapidly in the storm of her wrath, and her blue eyes spewed venom. They did not lie. He groaned as he searched her face, seeing nothing but her anger and her rejection. Something in him yearned fervently to end the pain, to put a stop to the gloom of the past. He didn't know how to do it, what to say. Would there be any right words?

She fought to get out of his grip, but he only hauled her closer until their arms and locked fists were pressed between them. His chest expanded as if he would burst. He cried out and gathered her into his arms, quieting her struggle by folding his arms tightly around her and holding her until she stopped fighting.

Her hair held the fresh scent of roses; her skin, the sweet, elusive odor of femininity. His senses reeled. Some part of him recognized her unique scent intimately, but she was a stranger in his arms. . . .

Dear Romance Reader,

Last year, we launched the Ballad line with four new series, and each month we'll present both new and continuing stories set everywhere from medieval England to the American West—the kind of passionate, romantic stories you love best, written by the most gifted authors. At the back of each book, we'll tell you when you can find subsequent books in the series that have captured your heart.

This month, Cindy Harris returns with the second installment of her celebrated *Dublin Dreams* series. When a penniless miss decides to become a "modern" woman, she must decide if the dashing sea captain who agrees to help her is a **Wolf at the Door**—or the man of her dreams. Next, travel back to the lush intrigue of Georgian England with Maria Greene, as a man returning from war with no memory of his past faces the alluring woman who was his wife with **A Stranger's Kiss.**

In the third entry of the century-spanning *Hope Chest* series, talented Karen Fox introduces an art historian hired to restore a royal portrait—until she travels back in time to meet the prince himself. Is love part of the **Grand Design?** Finally, reader favorite Linda Lea Castle concludes the uproarious *Bogus Brides* trilogy with **Lottie and the Rustler,** as the cowboy one woman chose as her "husband" from a wanted poster arrives in town with mischief in his heart—and temptation on his lips. Enjoy!

Kate Duffy
Editorial Director

Midnight Mask

A
STRANGER'S
KISS

MARIA GREENE

ZEBRA BOOKS
Kensington Publishing Corp.
http://www.zebrabooks.com

ZEBRA BOOKS are published by

Kensington Publishing Corp.
850 Third Avenue
New York, NY 10022

First Printing: August 2001
10 9 8 7 6 5 4 3 2 1

Printed in the United States of America

PROLOGUE

Flames of black candles flickered uneasily in the draft from the ancient stone walls. Silence hung heavy, a drugged, syrupy kind of silence during which only one flicker of alertness jumped—in the eyes of the leader. Evil resided there, a deep-seeded evil that touched everyone. His black velvet hood had been drawn forward to conceal his identity, but Derek Guiscard knew him by that icily burning glance. It came to him in his dreams.

He would never dare to utter the name of the leader, or death would meet him on the moor or in his bed. The same rule applied to the others around the oblong stone table. The five hooded men sat silent, their heads bent as if in prayer.

It would be a prayer not to God but to the Devil.

An icy shiver rippled up Derek's spine. At one point, this had been a club of gentlemen meeting for a night of punch and card games. But everything had changed as a new force started driving them: the desire for ultimate power.

He glanced at each man in turn, carefully weighing the words of resignation in his mind. A restlessness ate at him.

He wanted out, to tear the bonds of this suffocating circle and return to what he loved most, painting. He had to be free, or he would not be able to breathe. Fear clenched his gut.

"Gentlemen," he said hoarsely, testing the air before continuing. Heads shifted in his direction. "Hear me." He paused until he had everyone's undivided attention. He had to continue before he lost his courage. "I have to speak my truth. Due to increased responsibilities at home, I regret to inform you of my decision to terminate my membership in this club. I will of course always keep my vow of silence as sworn at the time of my initiation."

The silence densified, sticking like glue to his face. He could barely breathe, and cold sweat trickled down his neck. The sweet odor of blood from the altar behind the leader nauseated him, and the cold from the stone floor seeped up his legs, numbing him.

"Really?" the leader snapped. "You find us no longer worthy of your support?"

"It's not that. . . . I have family obligations that take all of my time. My mother's recent illness—"

"Yes, but the renovation of your ancestral pile costs a mint. Through our efforts, we have helped you bolster your finances so that you could embark on these projects. You owe us something for that. You owe us your unstinting loyalty."

The leader's words lay like whiplashes on Derek's face. "You'll always have my loyalty. I have followed the rules; I accomplished the duties allotted to me, including my help to ruin powerful people. Without me, you wouldn't have the financial success that you now enjoy. I did my share exceptionally well, as you well know."

"That is true." The leader looked at each member in turn. "What do you say? Shall we let him resign? Let's take a vote."

Feeling light-headed, Derek listened to the muttering

sweeping through the room. Hands were raised, and Derek could breathe a little easier. Three against two in his favor. He wished he knew who had voted against him.

"As I said, my loyalty remains. You know that you can trust me. I won't breach the secrecy of the club." He rose, pushing back his chair a bit too quickly.

The leader's voice purred. "No . . . you won't breathe a word. Because if you do, we shall pay a swift visit to your mother."

The next morning, Derek was found in the village lane badly beaten, the fingers of his right hand, his painting hand, crushed.

ONE

A year later, 1749.

Andria Saxon wasn't sure it had been such a good idea to accept this handsome commission to paint the portrait of her husband's aunt. Her *estranged* husband, she corrected herself. Her return to Yorkshire had dredged up all the painful memories.

But perhaps it was time to face the past, put it behind her, and let the pain and guilt that still crusted her heart dissolve and flow away on the icy waters of the River Fynn.

She kicked the thick carpet of golden leaves lining the riverbed. Water gurgled at her feet, and the river resembled a sheet of silky obsidian, beckoning and dangerous at the same time. The middle held treacherous depths and currents, as she knew from her childhood.

Derek had saved her once from drowning then, and she owed him all the support she had to give now. Since the crime against him, when some vagabonds had attacked him, mutilated him, and stolen all of his valuables, he had lost his will to live. The local constable had never found the culprits, and Derek never spoke of the night when it had happened.

Somehow she would have to help him find that flame

to live again. Derek was more of a brother than the one she'd had. Whereas Ruddy had been domineering and cold, Derek was kind. Ruddy had been dead ten years now; such a long time. One's entire life, one's values, changed in a decade.

Thoughts of Ruddy brought back other memories she'd fought to keep at bay ever since she came up to Yorkshire. *Rafael.*

"I can't think of Rafe, or I will surely fall apart," she whispered to herself. Her lips felt stiff and awkward, and she realized that the cold, dank air had crept through her fur-lined cloak and sneaked up her ankles. Her toes had turned to pebbles of ice, and her fingers were stiff despite her kid gloves.

Rafe had been everything she'd dreamed of as a young woman—virile and handsome, somehow a bit dangerous in his recklessness to do forbidden things, as young men were wont to do. He had always climbed the highest fell and ridden the most untamed horses, he'd gambled and won, he'd stolen kisses and more, and she'd known about the wenches who'd adored him to distraction until he came directly across her path.

He'd always claimed that he adored her.

She had believed that until her whole world fell apart and turned her heart to ice.

She hurried back toward the inn where she'd left Lady Stowe to confer with the local seamstress, who lived next door. New gowns and fripperies did not interest Andria, not since she had lost all that mattered to her. She had lost Julian and her beloved, sweet Bridget. And she'd lost Rafael.

How that name still caused pain after two whole years. Rafael Howard, Lord Derwent, her husband, the son of the Marquess of Rowan. She had believed Rafe had died in battle in Flanders, but no, he lived. She had found that out at their one and only chance meeting in London. The arrogant scoundrel had neglected to inform her of his return, and he had looked straight through her as if she were a stranger. *A pox on him.*

She kicked a moss-covered rock in her path, and pain shot through her foot. "Damnation," she swore, jumping on one leg to the nearest bench. She wiggled her toes in the tight boot and found to her relief that they had not been broken.

Father had always said she was resilient, a sturdy, pliable yew growing tough at her core despite her frail appearance. Perhaps he was right. Her losses had not broken her completely.

She was a branch of the proud old Saxon family tree, and she'd rather wear her maiden name than live with humiliation as Lady Derwent, a woman whom everyone whispered about after she'd been abandoned by her husband. Everyone also knew that he'd accused her of having a liaison with another man, with Derek.

"It wasn't my fault," she said to herself. *"Rafe* left me." She could kick another rock, but it would not ease her frustration. Gossips had set out to slander her name and had succeeded beyond their wildest dreams. Were their lives so barren that they had to live vicariously through someone else's misfortune? The defamation was untrue, of course, but her peers and the entire village of Rowan's Gate *enjoyed* believing the worst about her.

Andria closed her eyes and tried to avoid the train of thought that would only send her into a steep decline from which there was no way out. She'd been in that black pit before. *Never again* would she go there.

As the pain left her foot, she hurried back to the Quail and Hare Inn. A nasty wind began to stir, finding its way through every seam of her garments. She swung her hooped skirt through the narrow door and drew a sigh of relief as the warmth from the fire in the taproom closed around her.

She peeled back the fur-edged hood from her head and noticed the knot of local gentlemen by the fireplace, all known to her. They were drinking ale and talking. She would have to pass them to enter the private parlor where Lady Stowe had arranged to see the seamstress on their way back home to Stowehurst. Walking quickly, with her head held high, she passed the group. Most of the locals still treated her with contempt, she'd noticed when she returned, but she had nothing to be ashamed of.

"Lady Derwent," someone said, a deep, smooth voice she would have recognized among a hundred others. His dark eyes burned into hers, filled with admiration. "Andria. I'm devastated that you have not seen fit to visit me at Lochlade since you returned. Surely you would be eager to see your childhood home again. It is waiting for you . . . as it always will. You know that."

She nodded curtly, a shiver of unease coursing through her as she thought of Lochlade. "Good afternoon, Cousin Beauclerk. Nothing at Lochlade tempts me to pay a visit at this time."

"La! Your contempt hurts me," Beau said.

The other men bowed their powdered and bewigged heads and gave her rouged smiles. Oliver Yarrow, dressed in a coat of blue satin and black knee breeches, drawled, "I say, Beau, her words don't inspire confidence. What have you done to make the fair lady reluctant to visit her childhood home?"

Beau lifted his thick eyebrows, a gesture of subtle mockery. His hands caressed the tankard of ale. "I haven't a clue, Oliver. Not a clue. All my life I worked only to please her. I have made vast improvements to the estate; it is now the most brightly shining gem in these parts and shall so remain while I am in the high seat."

Andria studied her cousin, who had courted her with an insidious tenacity before she married Rafe. Beau did not take defeat well, but he had not showed his jealousy in any other way except with a few verbal barbs. He looked healthy, glowing with vigor, his tall body powerful and attractive in every way. His long, wavy hair was an odd silver color streaked with gold. Lady Stowe said he'd gone gray before his time. His eyebrows were black in stark contrast, concealing a pair of mercurial eyes that she could not read. She couldn't quite pinpoint the right word for her unease as she looked into his hooded brown eyes.

He had a sharp, angular face and always dressed with the utmost style and care. Today he wore a topaz velvet coat encrusted with gold braids, a snowy lace cravat, and a pair of silk breeches. His boots gleamed as if the mud in the yard had not touched him. Mayhap the landlord had spread a red carpet for his wealthy guests. Anything to secure their patronage, she thought with uncharitable dislike.

Beau said, "Andria, surely you will pay me a visit soon. I expect you to. I would be crushed if you totally reject my invitation."

"Maybe, but my commission comes first," she said cuttingly. "I work for Lady Stowe now, and—"

"Ah," he cried with a languid wave of the lace handkerchief he'd taken into his hand. "Say no more. Rebecca will surely grant you a day to visit your erstwhile home. I shall ask her myself." He darted a quick look toward the door to the private parlor.

"Don't bother, Beauclerk. She'll abide by my wishes,

and I don't need a day of leisure in the near future. Work will help me to forget . . ."

"Dearest Andria, you know you're wounding me deeply with your indifference. I do not take rejection lightly. Just give me a small hint—"

With a sharp nod that would have cut off the most spirited conversation, she maneuvered her skirts and started to walk away. He flourished a bow that held a hint of derision, and she swept past the group. Their gazes followed her, thrusts of curiosity that touched her keenly before she walked behind the safety of a closed door. She'd always been sensitive to the moods in a room, and her encounter with Beau had left an imprint of dread on her mind.

She trembled, and her hands felt clammy. Seeing Beau brought back a raft of bitter memories, all of them so sharp and detailed, they could have happened yesterday. Would the torture never end? She feared it had been a mistake to travel north and confront her past. Just the thought of facing the places where Bridget had laughed and played made her sick.

But the memories would haunt her forever if she didn't face them.

"Come, dear, help me choose between this ruby silk and the garnet. Which one does the most justice to my skin?" Lady Stowe lifted her bird-quick blue eyes to Andria's face. "Oh, dear. You look all done in; I told you not to take a walk in this chilly weather. The norther is bound to bring on a chest cold."

Andria forced a smile to dispel the dread in her heart. "Nonsense, Lady Stowe. It was most exhilarating." With movements that were too quick and brittle, Andria sorted through the swatches spread on the table. "Most certainly the ruby silk, milady. It will bring out your brown hair and your flawless complexion."

"You have an unerring eye, as usual. No wonder you are such a splendid artist, my dear," the older lady said fondly, and held the silk swatch toward the candlelight.

"You flatter me." To avoid her employer's probing gaze, she concentrated on the various materials. "This dark green would look very well with your rust-colored velvet cloak."

They chatted about the choices, made decisions and plans. The seamstress curtsied before leaving the room with her samples of material in a basket.

"Most satisfactory. I'm glad we stopped here on the way home. I needed a distraction; there's nothing as uplifting as a new gown or two." Lady Stowe gave Andria a searching glance. "I wish you wouldn't call me 'milady.' Why, your title is higher than mine!"

"I don't want to be reminded of the title, and you are my employer for the time being. It's my way of showing my respect—and gratitude."

Lady Stowe sighed. "Nonsense. There's no need for that formality. I know you respect me, as I respect you. I couldn't bear to see you work from dawn 'til dusk painting fans in that millinery shop in London. Just like a drudge."

"I was happy there. Mrs. Hopkins was kind to me." Andria brushed pieces of dead leaves from her cloak. "As I buried myself in work, I could sometimes forget—"

The older woman fluttered her painted fan as if the room were too hot. "I know. Ever since that day when Rafe left, I haven't slept well. When I see him next, I shall give him a piece of my mind for abandoning you, for leaving you to face the struggles alone. How could he do it?"

"I don't know."

"I don't comprehend what happened." Lady Stowe's voice contorted with emotion, and she fished in her pocket for a handkerchief. "Rafe always was my favorite, but he sorely disappointed me. I cannot understand what got into him—just left without as much as an explanation."

"He was angry and . . . confused."

"Don't make excuses for him, Andria. If anyone has the right to hate him, you do."

Andria sighed and sank down on the chair the seamstress had vacated. "All emotions have been burned away—except fear. I'm afraid of the truth, of what I will find out."

Lady Stowe took Andria's hand and chafed it between hers. "Your poor fingers are frozen, my dear. I do so wish I could help you, and I will support you, but I don't know how you'll prove that Julian was killed or how you can find out any more clues about Bridget." She flapped her fan so that dust motes danced in the air. "I get palpitations just thinking about the implications."

"You think it's something I concocted in my fevered brain, don't you?"

Lady Stowe's gaze moved around, unable to fasten on any one thing, least of all Andria's face. "Honestly, I don't know what to believe. But I've always had faith in you; you are not prone to flights of fancy. Yet you have a tender heart."

"No longer, alas. I don't *dare* to have a heart, or a life, even."

"You can't bury yourself in work indefinitely."

"My art is my pride and my solace."

"I wish I could turn back the clock. You and Rafe were so happy. I never saw a happier couple, and so well suited." Lady Stowe's lips trembled, and she pressed her plump knuckles against her mouth. "I'm sorry. I shouldn't mention his name."

"I'd prefer if you didn't," Andria said with a bitter

twinge in her heart as she remembered the probing stares from the members of the local gentry in the taproom. "But don't take on so; I'm not a hothouse flower."

Lady Stowe shook her head. "If you were, you would have been crushed a long time ago. I don't think I would've survived the ordeal. You are a survivor with great inner strength."

Andria clenched her teeth together as the sorrow she'd confined to a very small place threatened to burst through. "Nothing, I repeat *nothing,* that I encounter—for the rest of my life—will be worse than the events of the last two years."

"Oh, dear."

They exchanged long glances, and Andria felt completely alone. However much she liked Lady Stowe, the older lady could never understand the depth of her pain. Only a person who had lived through similar circumstances could.

Rafael Howard, the Earl of Derwent, rode his horse Blacky beside the carriage struggling along the muddy, rutted road. *Soon there,* he thought, *but I don't remember Yorkshire at all.* It was like riding into a foreign land, yet the very air was familiar—the sharp tang of late autumn, rotting leaves, and dried heather. The carriage pulled up to a ridge, and Rafe waited until it started its descent down the steep incline of the fell. Another rider pulled up beside him.

"There goes the most precious part of my life, Rafe," Nick Thurston said, and pushed his three-cornered hat to the back of his head, sweeping aside a lock of dark hair.

"I take it you're speaking of Serena in the coach. You haven't taken your eyes off her during the entire trip north," Rafe said. He laughed, happy for his friend, who had recently married the lady of his heart.

"Serena Hilliard came into my life and turned it upside down, made me take stock of my reckless ways. I complained a lot at the time, but now I'm grateful. Without her I would probably still be a highwayman headed for disaster, and you, too." He gave Rafe a glance from narrowed blue eyes. "How come we never see what's truly important until it's almost too late?"

Rafe shrugged. "Human folly, I think. I'm sure I've made plenty of mistakes in my life. The problem is, I can't remember them. I have a feeling I wouldn't be traveling to Yorkshire if I truly remembered what happened here. Somehow I don't feel welcome. I have a distinct impression of trouble ahead."

"You do recall some things, don't you, old fellow?"

"Yes . . . the river for one. There was some sort of a struggle. I also recall the pain I felt, as if my heart was crushed."

"Which it was, if the Rowan servant spoke the truth. I would be beside myself to discover that my wife had discarded our child on the steps of an orphanage."

"True, but your Serena would never do something like that. She's honest and true, not underhanded, like my wife must've been." Rafe rubbed the bridge of his nose. "Who in her right mind could discard her child like an inconvenient piece of luggage? If I ever meet her again, I don't know if I can keep my temper in check. That child at the orphanage meant a lot to me. She was my lifeline to the past."

"Yes, her death was unfortunate. The children are susceptible to illnesses, alas. Sometimes there's no cure."

The wind swooped down into the dale and flew up the side of the fell to tear at their hats and cloaks. The horses stomped impatiently. Rafe turned to his friend.

"I'm grateful that you found the time to accompany me. I would be lost without you."

"I never go back on a promise." Nick grinned. "Besides, Serena and I decided we'll spend our honeymoon in the wilds of the north. The tempest of the wind and the wilderness of the moors quite suit our fancy. It all reminds me of our night raids as the Midnight Bandit, doesn't it, my friend?"

Rafe felt the tug of a smile at his mouth. He nodded. "We had lots of excitement, but I'm glad it's over." He watched the carriage entering the valley below. If he could ever find an ounce of marital happiness that Nick was experiencing with Serena, he would count himself lucky. He touched his heels to the flanks of his horse. "Let's get on with it. I need some answers."

"Are you worried about seeing your father again after all this time?" Nick asked as they rode after the coach, which had crossed an old stone bridge and entered the village.

"Yes . . . I suppose. I don't know what kind of relationship we had. Mayhap we were enemies, but I rather hope that we were friends. His reaction will tell me the truth."

"He should have received your letter by now. If anything, he must be happy that you're still alive. After all, your family must have thought you were dead these last two years."

Rafe slowed down and looked at the curving road ahead. It wound upward, digging a trench among the rocks as if determined to keep its hold on the mountain. "I remember this road." He stopped on the stone bridge and looked at the black glassy water below. "This place on the river holds some significance, but I don't know what."

Nick pulled his cloak more tightly around him. "It's damned cold, and that water looks colder still."

Rafe lifted his face to the cloudy sky, feeling the brisk air fill his lungs. It bore a vague memory of fear, of restlessness, an urgency that said something awful had happened in the past and that it was tied to the river.

As if in a dream, he gathered his thoughts and continued up the road. He saw more fells rolling away into the horizon. As if cupped in a hand, the village of Rowan's Gate spread out before him.

Dark clouds hung over the village, sending out a flurry of snow, sweeping the church with its square unforgiving Norman style tower in a sudden veil of white. Nick had explained about various architectural styles, but Rafe knew he would have to study history again, or maybe it would all come back one day.

"There it is. Do you recognize it, Rafe?"

Rafe shook his head. "No, that village is no more familiar than the ones we've passed on the way up." They rode on. "There is the sign: Rowan's Gate. It must be named after the Rowan family."

"Yes . . . of which you are a part. I can't see the estate from here, though. It could be located on the other side of that mountain ahead."

They rode on in silence, and the coach, slightly ahead of them, pulled under a gatehouse and into the yard of the local inn. The buildings in the village were all uniformly gray stone, as if hewn from the rocks on which they rested.

Rafe tensed as he noticed a group of people in the yard. Would they recognize him?

A crested carriage with four matched chestnut horses stood by the front door to the inn. A young woman wearing a fur-edged cloak and a wide-brimmed velvet hat adorned with a curling ostrich feather stood on the step, speaking with one of the gentlemen, a striking silver-haired man. Another woman, this one older and plump, kept tugging at the younger lady's arm.

Rafe pulled in the reins as his gaze riveted on the lovely young face under the wide hat brim. Pale blond curls wisped around a perfect oval of a rose-and-cream complexion. Something held his attention. It was not the wide-set, luminous blue eyes, with their curving eyelashes, but something inside her, a sensation of such a weight, which was fraught with so many questions, that he felt quite distraught. Her deep sadness touched him, dragged him down in such a way that he could barely breathe. He shook his head as if to break the spell, but he couldn't take his eyes off her.

Dazed, he drank in her loveliness, but finally tore away his gaze as her pain got too much to bear.

Looking around, he located Nick and the carriage at the other end of the yard. Nick haggled with the hostler, but Rafe did not want to join them there. Even as the woman drew back his attention, he slid out of the saddle. He hitched his horse to a post and walked slowly toward the group on the steps. Normally, he avoided crowds, but this time, something compelled him to move forward.

She finally looked straight at him. A mallet could not have hit him harder in the chest. His step faltered, and thoughts rushed through his mind, but they could not form a pattern he recognized. His heart missed a beat, and a spell of dizziness overcame him.

She gasped, and her hand, so small in the glove, flew to her mouth. Her face paled instantly, and her eyes widened and darkened in fear, as if she'd beheld a ghost.

He remembered seeing her for a fleeting moment in London when Nick and he had visited Serena at a millinery shop. Ah, that's why she looked familiar. His heart pounded dully, as if filled with sudden disappointment. She probably wasn't important to his past, after all, but oh, how lovely, her expression so sincere.

The men on the front steps glanced at him with great disdain. He didn't look like them, for he wore a plain black coat and buckskins under his cloak. Ever since he'd returned to England, he'd avoided the peacock extravagance of the gentlemen's fashions.

The man with the white hair swept off his tricorne and made an exaggerated leg. "Well, well, if it isn't Rafael Howard, the prodigal son returning. We thought you had turned up your toes in Flanders."

Rafe only stared at the mocking brown gaze. He didn't recognize any of the men gathered there. "I'm afraid I have not made your acquaintance."

"Come along, Andria," the plump woman said urgently. "Let's not tarry here."

The woman named Andria stood as if turned into stone, her eyes still huge and dilated, her face contorting as if staring into the depths of a nightmare. "You!" she cried, her hands seeking support against the wall. "How *dare* you come back here?"

The white-haired gentleman offered his arm, and she clung to it, swaying as if close to a swoon.

Rafe gave her a curt bow. "I'm sorry if I have shocked you by my appearance," he said, "but I cannot remember you. Any of you. Until we've had a formal introduction, I daresay we shall remain strangers."

"Ecod, he takes on airs and hides behind excuses," the woman's supporter said. "As always filled with an abundance of arrogance."

Mocking laughter jarred him. This was a nightmare, to stand surrounded by members of his own class that showed nothing but contempt. Could it be that he had no friends in this part of the world?

"Surely you remember me," another man drawled. He wore a purple coat, his face powdered white. His black hair grew in a prominent widow's peak, and his amber eyes glittered with malice. "I'm your old schoolmate, Cunningham."

Rafe could not find a thought in the chaos of his mind. A feeling of stark grimness settled in his stomach. "I'm afraid your name does not trigger my memory. It looks like we might not have been very close."

"Why is that?" Cunningham purred, his arms folded over his chest. He was much shorter but appeared to have the tenacity of a terrier.

Rafe gave each man a sharp glance. He said coldly, "As much as I struggle to find a small sense of warmth, of welcoming, I fail to detect any."

The white-haired man chuckled. "Do you expect us to welcome you with open arms, Lord Derwent? After what you did?"

Rafe tensed, sensing that their hostility was only a small part of the whole, the precipice to a bottomless abyss. If he looked down, he might truly lose his mind.

He clenched his fists at his side. "Gentlemen, I don't know what you're talking about, and I'm not sure I desire enlightenment in the matter—not from you, anyway."

The white-haired man's eyes mocked him. "Let me introduce myself. I'm Beauclerk Saxon, and this is your wife, Andria Saxon, Lady Derwent."

TWO

The world spun around Rafe, and he closed his eyes for a moment until the chaos stopped. He glanced at his "wife" and found that she'd rushed down the steps and was even now climbing into the waiting carriage.

He had no idea what to say, but his legs bore him to the coach just as the coachman was about to close the door. Rafe gripped it, struggled for a moment for control, then looked closely at the lovely woman before him.

To him, her face was like a composition of music, each feature in perfect harmony with the rest. Her wide-set eyes complemented a straight nose, and a slightly too wide mouth lent her face an air of charm. He felt powerfully attracted to her. She had a hint of a dimple in her right cheek, a sign of humor, but her eyes held the expression of a storm gathering force.

"If it is true what Saxon said—that you are my wife—I regret that I cannot remember anything about our union, madam."

Anger suffused her face with red. *"If it is true?* How dare you question me—or him? How dare you approach me after all this time, after all the pain and suffering you brought into my life? We thought you were dead, and you were alive all this time without approaching anyone. I see that as utter contempt on your part."

"I didn't know about you until now."

She buried her face in her hands and turned a rigid shoulder toward him. Guilt washed through him as he hoped to see a sign that her rejection was evaporating, but she remained motionless.

He swallowed hard and plunged into that nightmare of frantic searching for the missing memories. "I'm truly sorry. I have no idea what injustices I have served you, madam. If they could be undone—"

The plump woman leaned over his wife and started to pull at the door, but he would not release it, not until he had some indication that his wife's mood had improved.

The older woman's voice was filled with annoyance. "We can't begin to enumerate all the grievances, Rafael. It is not my place to speak of them, but I'll stand by Andria in this. You have hurt her deeply."

"Milady, may I ask who you are?"

The woman's eyes grew round with distress and surprise. "You don't know me, either? I'm your aunt Rebecca, Lady Stowe, your father's sister. I lament the day when he has to see what you've become. That is, if he recognizes you."

"And what have I become?" Rafe asked, his desolation complete.

Lady Stowe moved her mouth as if trying out her thoughts before speaking. "I admit you look almost the same, a mite older, perhaps, but you are naught but a shell."

"I am still *me*. If we were our thoughts and memories, we would be nothing but air," he said sharply.

"Air you are certainly not! You are an uncomfortable reminder of past horrors."

Rafe gestured in anger. "By God, woman, tell me what

sins I'm guilty of! You owe me that much for insulting me."

"Your arrival here is an insult," his "wife" said, her eyes swollen and red with tears. "You have no friends here, not since the day you deserted us all."

"You are in error, madam," he said, his voice growing thick with fury. "I would never shun my duty and desert—"

"That is exactly what you did." Her eyes narrowed. "No matter how hard you try to justify your behavior, I won't listen. Nothing you say will impress me."

Rafe clenched his jaw. He didn't have an explanation, and he didn't know what crimes he'd committed. He searched her flashing blue eyes but found no answer except loathing. Clearly, she believed he'd done something utterly vile in the past. The thought made him cold.

Then he remembered his daughter. This woman had abandoned her at the orphanage.

He slammed the door shut, and the lady who said she was his aunt pushed the window closed with a snap. Rafe glanced at his wife. She sat with her face still buried in her hands. The hat brim soon shielded her from view, and bewildered, he watched as the coach rumbled under the gatehouse and out on the road. A strange emptiness filled him, but also anger at the knowledge that she'd thrown away their daughter.

"Not what I would call a hearty welcome," Beauclerk Saxon drawled.

Rafe hadn't heard him move, but the man stood right beside him. "Mayhap you would care to fill in some of the holes in my memory," Rafe said, regretting the words just as soon as they were out of his mouth.

"Rather," Beauclerk said, "but it would take me days,

and I would have to fortify myself with some strong wine to get through it."

"I have all the time in the world," Rafe snapped, not liking the cold glint in the other man's eyes.

Beauclerk turned to the group. "We must arrange a gathering soon, teary-eyed females excluded, of course, to tell Rafe his life story. We all have a little snippet of something to impart. Don't we?"

Rafe scanned the men's faces, noting with distaste the rouged lips and the gaudy silk and satin coats. If he wasn't mistaken, they were wearing evening attire, which meant they hadn't been home to change their finery this morning. Their eyes held that fevered look of too much drink. Nightlong parties of debauchery did not appeal to Rafe, not after he'd attended a few at Lotus Blossom's in London. He'd learned that heavy self-indulgence of any kind only brought misery. He preferred a clear mind.

He wondered if he'd spent nights in the past making merry with this group of indolent gentlemen. One, a stranger with a pimply face and a narrow jaw, fluttered a handkerchief.

"You gave me the scar above my right eyebrow," he said to Rafe, his voice touched with asperity.

"Let me introduce ourselves," Beauclerk said. "As I said, I'm Lady Derwent's cousin, and I suspect I'll have to dry the lady's tears later." He lowered his voice a notch. "I'll insist that she chooses me to do it." He gently patted Rafe's shoulder. "Your arrival brought havoc to this sleepy hamlet. We had heard *rumors*— "

"I have no intention of stirring up trouble," Rafe said tersely, closing his eyes for a moment to gather his thoughts.

"Well, you already have." Beauclerk gestured toward the men on the steps. "Oliver Yarrow, the childhood friend whose eyebrow you nicked with a knife. Robert Cunningham—we call him Romeo. You were rivals a long time ago, over some kitchen maid or other."

Rafe looked at the remaining two: one, tall and thin, dressed in silver cloth; the other, cherub-faced, with long angel-blond hair. His heavenly blue eyes held a sliver of malice.

"Crispin Pyper, Lord Durand; and Malcolm Hayes, Lord Whitecomb. Crisp and Cupid, we call them. Despite Cupid's angelic looks, he's deadly with a knife. You don't want to get on his bad side, Rafe."

The men surrounded Rafe, and unease traveled up his spine. He found it difficult to breathe as they moved closer. A silent threat, an elusive desire for vengeance, thickened around him. He wished he knew if there was a reason for revenge against him. His thoughts congealed into an impenetrable haze, and his temples ached abominably.

"You stole my sweetheart while we were at Oxford, Rafe," Cupid said, his plump hands clenching.

"And you rode one of my best horses into the ground," said Crisp.

"You drew my blood in a duel," said Cunningham. "I almost died."

"Gentlemen, your memories don't sound pleasant," Rafe said. "Tell me something pleasant as a contrast."

"Oh, no, there are many more," Beauclerk said softly, close to his ear. "Memories that would curdle the contents of your stomach."

"Surely that's not all," Rafe said as they tightened the circle. He didn't relish the idea of fighting his way out, but he could feel the anger rushing through his veins. He touched the sword at his side.

To his relief, Nick and Serena arrived, their faces alight

with happiness. He took a deep breath. The tension lifted as the men greeted the lady with gallant bows. Nick pulled Rafe aside.

"What happened here? Did you get into an argument? I could feel the tension across the yard."

"Oh, nothing of importance. I only met my wife and my aunt, and these *gentlemen* have graciously informed me of past transgressions." With a curse on his tongue, Rafe turned toward Serena.

"Serena, let's seek shelter from the wind. I see no reason to tarry here," he said with a warning glance at the others. He didn't introduce her. Reluctantly, they stood aside to let her pass. She surveyed Beauclerk uneasily.

Rafe offered his arm to the dark-haired beauty. She smiled and placed her hand lightly on his arm.

"Yes, please lead me away from these probing glances." Serena said with an exasperated laugh. Her slanted cat eyes gleamed; they hadn't always, as Rafe recalled. They had been filled with deep sadness. But after Nick had helped her catch the man who murdered her father, she had opened up like a rose.

Marriage suited her, as it did Nick, who seemed to have grown in stature since the wedding. Love did that to a man if it was allowed to flourish. In comparison, Rafe felt like a barren desert.

"You really met your wife?" Nick asked incredulously as they entered the private parlor. He helped Serena take off her cloak, and she righted the lace shawl on her shoulders and the dark ringlets that caressed her slender neck.

She closed her hand around Rafe's. "We already knew you were married, and since you're from these parts, 'tis likely your wife might also hail from here."

"I thought she'd left for foreign parts with her lover," Rafe said, not quite trusting his voice. "For some reason,

I pictured her a raucous, vulgar creature, but she isn't. She's a vision of loveliness, with eyes that are bright and innocent."

"An angelic face can hide a rotten heart," Nick said. "What are you going to do? Surely you won't take up residence with her—unless she lives at Rowan Hall."

"I honestly don't know what to do. She loathed seeing me; that much was clear."

"Your father shall inform you of any recent events. He might be able to explain why your wife . . . er, finds your presence disturbing, and we might learn why your daughter ended up at Sir James's orphanage in London."

"Yes, but I have a feeling he won't give me a warmer welcome than I just received from my 'friends.' "

"We are here to find out," Serena said, and squeezed his hand. "Not to worry."

There was a knock on the door, and the old, potbellied landlord brought in a tray of food. He served a neck of mutton boiled with capers, wild duck, a loaf of coarse bread, and tartlets. Ale foamed in the tankards, and Serena sipped a mug of mulled wine.

"I'm Mr. Brown, and if you need anything else, let me know." He glanced out the window. "Terrible traveling weather," he said, his quick brown eyes filled with curiosity. "If you don't mind me asking, ye're from the south, then?" His gaze lingered on Rafe, then lowered. "I know you, milord."

"Yes, we're coming from London," Nick said. "Tell me, my good man, any news about Lord Rowan? We plan to end our journey at Rowan Hall."

"He is in residence, will be to the end of his days, I daresay. Not that he could travel in his condition, mind you."

Rafe stiffened. "Condition?"

"Suffered an apoplexy, he did, two weeks ago." Mr. Brown wiped his hands on his apron, and his face turned red with embarrassment. "Thought that's why ye're comin' home, milord. Didn't you know about Lord Rowan?"

"No."

"The poor auld lordship says nary a word. Just sits there, ye see. A bit paralyzed on one side. Aye, it is a dark time at Rowan Hall." He gave Rafe a guarded glance. "He'll be that pleased to see ye, milord—if he recognizes ye that is. He should, seein' as ye're his only son."

Rafe braced himself against the wave of disappointment that coursed through him. First the cold welcome on the front steps, now this piece of bad news. Mayhap it had been a mistake to return.

"Lord Rowan can't be that bad," Serena said, her voice entreating.

"His Lordship is right bad, but some recover from the illness, they say. I don't know," the landlord said. "Enjoy yer meal." He bowed as he left the room.

Rafe drank deeply from the tankard, but he couldn't touch the food. Nick and Serena spoke a silent language as they looked at each other, a language of love. Rafe could barely stand to be in the same room, not after the blows that had come his way. He pushed his chair back. "Don't mind me. I want to take a walk to gather my thoughts before we move on to Rowan Hall."

"That's understandable. Rafe, you're not alone in this," Nick said. "As you supported me in the past, I will support you now."

"You can count on me, too," Serena said, her slanted eyes narrowing with a warm smile.

Unable to trust his voice, Rafe only nodded. He swept

his wool cloak around him and clapped his hat onto his head. "One thing is sure: I shall get to the bottom of my past one way or the other."

Andria swallowed every sob trying to escape. She hated to show her emotions in public, but her encounter with Rafe had demolished her carefully erected wall against sorrow. With the wall down, her emotions oozed everywhere, threatening to drown her. How would she ever manage to push the horrors back where they belonged, in a dark and hidden corner of her memory?

As she closed her eyes, she could still clearly see the man whom she'd loved to distraction—once, but never again. Tall and proud, muscles honed to steel, his strong face so serious, every line taut, his deep, dark eyes searching, questioning. She remembered every feature: the elegant thin nose, the generous mouth, the hard jaw, every scar and dent. Pain had matured him. He'd lost weight, but that compelling power that had drawn her to him at the beginning lingered in the proud lines of his body. An unfamiliar stillness had replaced his former restlessness, and the haunted look in his eyes had replaced his scorn for the world. The war had clearly changed him a great deal.

She heaved a deep sigh. He still held the power to attract her. *Damn him!*

"I never thought I'd live to see this day, Rafe riding up to the Quail and Hare as if nothing had happened. As cool as you please; I don't understand that young man. Has he no heart?" Lady Stowe pressed a handkerchief to her red-rimmed eyes as the coach thundered along the road. Her bottom lip trembled, and a ragged sob rose from her throat. "To think that I once doted on him."

"I could have accepted his faults—in death," Andria whispered. "But he's alive. He has come to wreak havoc on my life. Again."

"I won't let him," Lady Stowe said fiercely. "If his father hadn't suffered an apoplexy, he would send Rafe away. They never got along. That young man has done too much damage to too many lives in these parts. If I don't do it first, someone else will kill him if he remains in Rowan's Gate."

Andria dried her eyes on the back of her hand. "That satisfaction is my right." Bitterness flowed through her blood, making her throat clog with fury. "Rafe deserves to die for the pain he caused."

"If he comes to pester you at Stowehurst, I shan't hesitate to use Miles's blunderbuss." Lady Stowe patted her eyes and put away her handkerchief. She straightened her back in determination. "We must travel to Rowan Hall and warn my brother of Rafe's imminent arrival. The shock of seeing Rafe might kill Augustus."

"I'm appalled that Rafe would have the nerve to visit his father after all that happened."

"A man without a heart does not hesitate to take what he wants. It's likely he's come to await his father's death. Rafe will be Lord Rowan and the master of Rowan Hall."

Andria pressed her fingertips to her temples, trying to prevent her growing headache. When she found her voice, she said, "It was a mistake to return here. I ought to go back to London."

Lady Stowe bristled. "And let that *demon* rule your life? No, Andria. Problems were never solved by your running away."

"You're right, however much I loathe to admit it. This time, I shall fight. Rafe shan't bring me down to the pits of bottomless despair again."

* * *

Leaving Serena and her maid at the inn, Rafe rode with Nick to the top of the fell that towered over Rowan Hall. The wind tore at their clothing, and hard snowflakes stung their faces before settling on the ground. Rafe barely felt the cold; his mind absorbed the view in front of him.

Far below, on a hill above the village of Rowan's Gate, sat Rowan Hall, a severe building of gray stone that blended in with the hard granite backdrop of the fell. Two short wings with turreted towers at the corners angled back, the crenelated roof giving the estate the forbidding air of a fortress. According to the landlord at the inn, the Hall had been built in the fourteenth century, the wings added on a hundred years ago. The grounds had the bleak look of winter, trees skeletal and black against the brown earth.

"The place doesn't invite guests, does it?" Nick said, his voice terse. "No use to linger here. Let's ride down."

"Yes, might as well get it over with. I don't look forward to seeing my father."

"It might cause him distress. I shall smooth the way before you actually meet. We don't want his death on our conscience." Nick rode ahead on the curving path, which was lined with rocks and heather.

Rafe pushed his hat more firmly on his head and followed. The horse stumbled once on some loose pebbles on the steep path, but half an hour later, they rode up the long drive that culminated in front of a pair of spectacularly carved doors. Bare shrubs and dead flowers lined the walls, and the sinewy, naked arms of a vine clung to the front with a fretwork of branches.

Rafe spotted a coach by the stables but didn't pay any attention. He handed Blacky's reins to a young groom, who gave him a furtive look and paled visibly. "Cor, 'tis true, then; 'tis *you,* milord."

Rafe smiled grimly. "Yes, I'm not a ghost, not yet, anyway. How did you know I was back?"

"Heard it from the . . . er, servants first, but Lady Stowe is a-visiting the master. She and that young lady—" He scratched his head in embarrassment.

Rafe's heart hardened. "Please take care of our horses."

Joining Nick on the front step, Rafe faced the heavy oak doors, wondering if he had the right to walk inside without knocking; he didn't feel at home. A stranger visiting the home of a possible enemy, he thought, and rubbed the back of his neck. He hesitated, then applied the iron knocker.

A footman, dressed in a simple brown homespun suit, opened the door. No glittering livery or powdered wigs here, Rafe thought, relieved.

Nick spoke. "We're here to see Lord Rowan." He handed the footman his card. A stoop-shouldered butler with wispy white hair tied back at the neck arrived to inspect the visitors. His watery blue eyes widened as he recognized Rafe. To Rafe's surprise, they lit up, and a smile crinkled the butler's face.

"Master Rafael! Then it is true that you're back. If I may be so bold, I have prayed for this day," the butler said.

Rafe fervently wished he knew the old retainer's name. He found it difficult to smile but felt grateful nevertheless.

The butler nodded once. "We heard you suffered a loss of memory. I'm Travers, and I held you in my arms when you were but an hour old."

"Glad to meet you, Travers," Rafe said, his throat filling with emotion.

Nick said, "I'm Mr. Thurston. We'd like to see Lord Rowan."

"Oh, dear, oh, dear, he is rather poorly, but recovering. You are not, however, the only visitors this morning. Lady Stowe and—"

A flurry of movement at the top of the stairs commanded everyone's attention.

"And Andria Saxon," Rafe's wife filled in, her voice as cold as ice. "Lord Rowan does not wish to see you, Rafe. Go away."

An icy pail of water could not have chilled him more, Rafe thought, but it made him all the more determined to see his father.

THREE

"Lord Rowan might not desire a confrontation with his son at this point, but I would like to see him," Nick said, already walking upstairs. "Milady, I won't say anything that will worsen his condition."

He gave Andria a grin that could have melted an iceberg, Rafe thought.

She pinched her lips together as if ready for battle but allowed Nick to follow her. Rafe found that he'd held his breath and that his heart hammered against his ribs like the hooves of a runaway horse.

"Milord?" Travers said, his eyes innocent and questioning.

"Show me around, please, Travers. Maybe the house will trigger some memories." He glanced around the hallway, with its tall, narrow windows by the door, its gloomy wood paneling and carved rafters. A coat of arms, two broadswords crossed on a striped red-and-black background, hung over the door.

He followed Travers through a series of rooms that did not trigger anything but a faint interest. Furniture shrouded in holland covers and paintings on the wall held few secrets. Most of the walls had been painted stark white, except the drawing room, which sported silver damask panels and gold molding.

The only chamber that had a lived-in look was the library at the back. Large French doors allowed a view of a terrace and a formal garden. Rows of poplars lined a sandy path that wound through the park.

Rafe touched the heavy brown velvet curtains, and a hazy memory teetered in his mind. He had stood here once and seen the same barren landscape. Pain filled his head, and he heaved a deep sigh.

"Is there anything the matter, milord?"

"No . . . but I do recall seeing this view before."

Travers chuckled. "Yes, you spent many an agonizing hour in this room as your father lambasted you for your childhood pranks. You rather set the household on its ear in the old days, milord."

Rafe smiled. "Did I? Perhaps those are memories best forgotten."

"Lord Rowan was a severe disciplinarian, milord, but sometimes you deserved it. Especially when you took one of the hunting guns out of the weapon chamber and went hunting for poachers."

"Poachers?"

"Yes, you'd heard a story about poachers at some other estate and was all set to hunt them down. That's what you told your father."

"You're laughing, Travers."

"Aye, after Lord Rowan applied the strap to your backside, you were rather eager for consolation, which I and Cook gave. She was a soft one." He shook his head. "Dead now—for many years. Mrs. Parker, whom you'll meet soon enough, replaced her."

An obscure longing for times gone by filled his heart.

"Cook fed you milk and—"

"Molasses cake," Rafe filled in. "I remember the taste of that cake. Smoky and spicy, somehow."

"Aye." Travers rubbed his gnarled hands together. "I'm that pleased that you're back, milord. I was worrying about the future of Rowan Hall."

"As far as we know, my father has not accepted me."

"But he will; you mark my words. You're his only son, his heir, and I know his temperament. He'll be relieved that you're back."

"Son and heir, on all accounts a callous and reckless one. My 'friends' don't paint a rosy picture of my past, nor does my wife. Rather the opposite. They would rather see me gone than my taking up occupancy at Rowan Hall."

The butler shook his head and straightened a tasseled pillow on a sofa. "I'm sure you had your reasons to act as you did. I'm certain you are the *only* one who knows the whole truth. All I can say is that I didn't blame you for being angry the day you found out."

A shudder of dread moved through Rafe. "What truth?"

The butler gave Rafe an intent stare. "You don't know?"

"No, damn it," Rafe shouted, instantly regretting raising his voice. "I know nothing."

The butler hastened to avert his gaze. " 'Tisn't my place to speak of it, and I don't know for sure—I can't speak of heresy, gossip—" he said, his voice trembling slightly.

"Please—" Rafe begged, thinking he might explode if he didn't discover the truth of his past.

They were interrupted as the door opened and Nick stepped inside. "I've spoken with your father. The old boy is rather tired, but he has agreed to see you."

Damn. Rafe swam in a sea of frustration. He longed to continue his conversation with the friendly butler, but

Nick's words threw everything into confusion. "Is he waiting for me now?"

"Yes . . . and so is the young lady and the dragon. If you don't mind your manners, she has promised to consume you with her breath of fire." Nick grinned, clearly not daunted by the ordeal of visiting Rowan Hall and its forbidding master.

"Please be kind to him," Travers called after them.

As if I would be anything else, Rafe thought. *Father is a stranger to me, his sins against me wiped away, if there were any, but mine still very much remembered in his mind, no doubt.* Eager, but at the same time reluctant, he took the stairs two at a time. How would his sire receive him?

The corridor upstairs led to many closed doors, but a lackey at the end showed him the way. A massive door concealed the master suite. He took a deep breath as he halted on the threshold.

His thoughts swirling, he was only vaguely aware of the room, the large windows letting in the gray daylight, the red velvet drapes, the four poster hung with the same material. An Oriental carpet quieted his footstep as he walked toward the figure seated in an invalid chair by the window.

If Lord Rowan ever had been a proud figure of a man, there was little left of that in the shrunken body and sharp-featured head. Long strands of gray hair framed the face, and the tassel of his nightcap, hanging over his shoulder, lent a slightly rakish air to the man.

Rafe's heart hammered uncomfortably. He threw a quick glance at Lady Stowe's red face, noting the distrust, the anger.

"Good morning, sir," he greeted stiffly.

The old man's head lifted, dark brown eyes vacant but soon filling with questions.

"W-who . . . You are—?" Lord Rowan quavered.

"Rafe." Emotion thickened Rafe's voice, and he didn't know what to say next.

"Your son," Lady Stowe said frostily. "Augustus, don't get worked up about Rafe. I'm certain he has come to make peace." She threw Rafe a glance of warning.

"Is there need for peace?" Rafe said under his breath.

"Every need," she said, whipping her fan in front of her face. "You did not part on the best of terms. In fact, you were forbidden to set foot in this house again. That fool Travers let you in, didn't he?"

Rafe did not answer. He searched for a sign of recognition in the old man's eyes. This shrunken shell was his father. His long, slim hands lay ineffectually in his lap, covered with a quilted robe. They trembled as they rose toward Rafe in a pleading gesture. Finally, recognition lit Rowan's eyes.

"Rafael? You have returned . . . ? For good?" At least the old man could speak fairly clearly.

Rafe sank to one knee and took the icy cold hands in his, wishing he could give his father some of his own strength. One of the old man's arms seemed useless, and one shoulder drooped more than the other. "Perhaps. I don't rightly know. My welcome has not been warm."

Lord Rowan glanced behind Rafe, eagerly seeking something. "Did you bring Andria and your daughter?"

Heat suffused Rafe's face, and he shifted his weight as if to relieve himself of discomfort.

"Andria is here, Augustus," Lady Stowe said. "She went outside to catch a breath of air, but she'll return shortly."

"Where is my grandchild?"

The question hung like a living threat in the room. Rafe realized he and the people at the orphanage might be the only persons who knew about Bridget's fate. She had died in his arms—an event more tragic than any horror he'd encountered in Flanders.

He exchanged a glance with Lady Stowe, whose eyes communicated questions. "She is not here at present," he said. "We don't want to tire you out."

Lord Rowan seemed content with that answer—for the time being. He folded his hands in his lap and stared out the window, his sight turned inward. Rafe longed for a chair, but there was none nearby.

"Rafe was a wild child," the marquess mused as if Rafe were not in the room. "Always in trouble, always so . . . rebellious." The old man frowned. "He gave me nightmares."

"Surely that's an exaggeration," Rafe said, his voice thick.

"He put his mother in the grave," Lord Rowan continued, his voice trembling. "Rafe worried her to death. I could never forgive him for that. I once loved Ianthe so much—long ago. She's beckoning me now."

Rafe looked for some sign of anger in his father's face but saw none. *Damn him,* Rafe thought. *I don't remember any of this.* His heart sat frozen in his chest. He could not imagine sending his mother to the grave, not in his darkest dreams. Had he been such a monster?

The old man gestured feebly. "See? There she is, by the window, holding out her hand toward me."

Rafe saw only gray daylight pouring through the window, and dusty curtains. Somewhere there ought to be a portrait of his mother, which might trigger some more memories.

"What was she like?" he asked.

"A temperamental sprite . . . a flower so full of grace and light, but I didn't really see that until 'twas too late," the marquess replied, more to himself than to Rafe. "She had the fire of the Welsh in her blood. Gave that to our son."

His words filled Rafe with dread. He turned to Lady Stowe. "When did she die?"

Every line of her face held disapproval. "She died a month after you abandoned your wife and daughter as if they were naught but unwanted puppies."

"I did not—" Rafe began heatedly, but stopped. Clearly, everyone believed he'd run away, and he could not prove they were wrong. He didn't much like the picture painted of himself. To hear of his mother's death should have been a blow, but he felt nothing. *Nothing.*

The old man rambled on about his dead wife, and Rafe pieced together a picture of their life, shared fragments of happiness and times of difficulty. Only disappointment remained, and he was at the root of it.

He watched his father and curbed an urge to ask for forgiveness; so far, he knew only bits and pieces of his sins. The frailty of his father demanded kindness and respect. He did not want to upset the old man by dredging up the past.

The many questions filled his head, threatening to suffocate him. He felt as if he were standing outside himself. He knew that a piece of him belonged here, in this house, with these people, but mostly he was a stranger standing outside, looking in at a situation of which he'd never been part. He rose, his body numbing as he stood straight as a soldier at his father's side.

Lady Stowe patted the marquess's knee. "Augustus, don't tire yourself. You'll see Ianthe in due course, but now you have to rest. You're recovering very well, considering—" She beckoned to someone behind Rafe.

A valet, or a male nurse, stepped up, a stocky middle-aged man with sharp features whom Rafe had never met before.

"This is Dennis Morley, your father's nurse, Rafe. He was hired to watch over Augustus day and night. Dr. Knightbridge thinks very highly of him."

Morley gave a stiff nod to Rafe, who acknowledged him. The man looked capable enough, if not a joy-filled soul.

"There's a local woman who comes and relieves him for a few hours every day." Lady Stowe sounded tired, and her face drooped as she watched the stalwart nurse carry Lord Rowan back to bed.

Rafe observed in silence. Would his father die without revealing more of the past? The thought chilled Rafe, for he feared he would be unable to piece the puzzle of his life together without his father.

He offered his arm as Lady Stowe headed for the door, but she refused his support. Her stiff back spoke of her disapproval.

Rafe stepped up to the bed and looked down at his father's gray face against the whiteness of the pillows. "Father, I will be back."

Recognition dawned in Lord Rowan's eyes, a faint spark of anger illuminating their depths. "Rafe, I have not forgiven you. I doubt I ever will. If I were strong enough, I would call you out." His voice began to slur. "That would be the only way to blot out the stain upon the Howard name."

Rafe clenched his jaw in frustration. "I would never fight you, sir." He stood motionless for a moment, staring at his father. When Rowan had closed his eyes and drifted off to sleep, Rafe left the room.

Feeling utterly exhausted, he sought a place to be by himself. He went into the next room, finding there a shrine to his mother. An open diary lay on the escritoire, the goose quill laid across the pages as if the writer had only just left and would soon return.

Gold brocade hangings and fine French furniture adorned this most feminine boudoir. A thick carpet and embroidered pillows gave the impression of sumptuous luxury. With an urgency he could not understand, he opened the doors to the clothespress. Dresses hung in a white-shrouded row, and shawls and flimsy scarves were suspended on a rack on the door. An elusive perfume wafted toward him, a spicy, almost unpleasant fragrance that hinted of secrets.

He shut the door angrily. When would the feeling of walking on eggshells go away? Anger churned in his stomach as he looked out the window. The park stretched all the way to the foot of the fell, which rose in daunting majesty over the estate. Snow swirled around its crown, concealing everything in a white haze. The snowy ceiling pressed down upon the park, giving everything an air of mystery.

His gaze was drawn to a lonely figure walking along the sandy path. Out of a white mist came a woman wrapped in a blue cloak. Her hoops swayed in rhythm with her walk. In a flash, he recognized his wife. Before someone claimed her attention, he would have a private word with her.

He ran down the stairs and intercepted her on the terrace. Snow whipped against his face, and wind tore at his coat, instantly making him cold. He hadn't had the time to put on his hat and fur-lined cloak. She stiffened, her blue eyes dilating with fear. Taking a step back, she shook her head. Her fear angered him as nothing else had so far.

"I would like a word with you."

"I have nothing to say to you."

"Yes, you do." He gripped her arm and, ignoring her struggle, led her through the first door. A solarium. The strong scent of orange blossom and earth filled the humid air. The snow on the glass roof gave the room a milky light. Tall trees gave the impression of spring, of new life.

"I expect you to tell me everything that happened since the moment I left the area. Everything."

Andria looked at Rafe as if he'd grown horns as he towered over her, his face stubborn and closed. His eyes blazed with suppressed anger, and his frustration surrounded her like an itchy cloak.

"If you can't remember, let's not dredge up the past. No one will benefit from stirring up the bitterness." She shivered, his presence making it difficult to think. His power touched her, drawing her with invisible strings. He had made her resistance crumble so many times before, and he would do it again unless she guarded herself completely.

"*I* will benefit. So many insults have been thrown at me since I returned. I have the right to hear about all the old hurts for which I am accused."

She grimaced. "Thinking only of yourself, as usual. I have no reason to believe you have changed at all even if you can't remember the old Rafe." She clenched the folds of her cloak to steady her rising emotions. "I don't owe you an explanation. I don't owe you anything. If you want to treat me in a gentlemanly fashion, leave me alone!"

She ran toward the door leading into the house, but he caught up with her and barred her progress. His broad back leaning against the door, he said, "What do I have to do to make you talk?"

"You cannot force me to speak of the past." Tears started to swell in her chest, and she swallowed hard to crush the urge to cry. His face took on that haunted look she'd noticed at their first meeting.

"If I can't make you talk, can I *beg* you?" he said in so quiet a voice, she could barely hear him.

The Rafe she knew had never begged; he had taken everything he wanted or charmed himself to favorable results. Her breath caught in her throat. The Rafe of old had possessed an abundance of charm, which had undermined her determination at the best of times, but his humility touched her where he'd never touched before.

She didn't know where to begin; every painful word would bring back the past, and with it, the unspeakable pain.

"First, I want to know why you left our daughter at Sir James's Orphanage in London."

The question caught her like a whiplash across her heart. She lowered her gaze. Here, all at once, was her darkest pain probed.

"Answer me."

She took a deep breath. "I did not."

"You left our daughter in the hands of strangers so that you could travel unhampered with your lover."

"That is not true!" she shouted, feeling cornered, suffocated by his accusations. "Where did you hear such nonsense?"

"A servant who once worked here recognized Bridget or I would not have been any wiser. But I do know, and I have to know the whole truth. You owe me that much. The ledgers say you—her mother—brought her to the orphanage."

She only looked at the floor as the world tilted around her. Her mind sifted through the old memories, but she found herself unable to speak. She squeezed her eyes shut as tears filled them.

"Bridget died, you know. In my arms." His voice broke, and he covered his eyes with one hand. "You don't care, do you?"

Frozen, she stared at his face, now twisted in grief. "Died?" Her darling Bridget dead? *Dear God.* She had hoped against hope that one day she would find Bridget safe and sound. The fragile world she'd carefully built around that hope crashed around her.

"Andria, tell me, damn you!"

"I don't know anything about the orphanage." A black fog encroached upon her vision.

"You didn't know Bridget had died?" He sounded incredulous.

She shook her head as her legs lost their power to hold her upright. Sinking to the floor, she moaned.

FOUR

Rafe stared at the woman, the stranger, albeit the mother of his child, who lay in a faint at his feet. A feeling, something strange and wonderful, stirred in his chest, but no memories followed.

He dropped to his knee beside her. The flagstones were icy, and he lifted her into his arms. He set her down on a wrought-iron bench, loosened the cloak at her neck, and pushed back the hood. Pale tendrils of hair curled over her forehead, and her mouth was half open, gasping for breath. Pity moved in his chest, and that strange feeling of tenderness, as he watched her defenseless face.

She had the sweetest mouth, vulnerable, yet with boldly passionate curves. He touched her cool cheek, finding it soft and inviting. Her eyelashes fluttered, and her eyelids moved as if a nightmare had gripped her. Finely curved eyebrows lent grace to her features. He noticed every detail as if time had stopped and nothing existed except the two of them, as if they were alone in the world. But as soon as she awakened, he knew that she would shy away from him and her eyes would blaze with loathing.

Her eyes snapped open, and she stared at him in confusion until her memories returned. The innocence left her incredibly blue eyes, and anger darkened their depths.

She pushed at him. "Get away from me."

He removed his hand from her face and stood.

"What happened?" she asked, straightening herself on the bench.

"You fell into a swoon." Somehow he could not take his eyes away from her, even though every part of him protested against her disapproval.

She placed the back of her hand against her forehead. Her skin took on a sheen of perspiration, and she looked positively green.

"How are you? Would fresh air help?" he asked, eager to assist her in any way he could.

"I'll be fine shortly," she murmured even as she swayed. She gripped the armrest of the bench and clung.

"You need to lie down to regain your equilibrium," he said.

"Is it true? Is my daughter dead?" she asked, her voice trembling. She gave him a pleading look. "Say it is naught but a cruel jest."

He shook his head and watched as her lips pinched together with determination. "You're lying, Rafe."

Anger churned within him, but he could not berate her. It was clear she suffered her loss keenly. Perhaps he'd been wrong thinking she'd abandoned the child in London. He struggled to find patience, not more anger. "I wish you would tell me the whole, madam."

"The servant who worked at the orphanage—can you tell me her name?"

Her evasions provoked his hackles, and he slowly lost control over his anger. He sat down next to her and shook her shoulders. "God help me, you are more slippery than an eel!"

Her chin rose. "Why should I tell you anything? You would not believe me; you would question me. I have no desire to spend any more time talking to you."

"I don't remember any of our past conversations," he said tersely. "Can't you find it in your heart to help me by explaining the whole?"

She tore herself away from his grip and stalked to the window. She swayed, and he suspected she would fall into another faint.

"I know you've sustained a shock, Andria, but can't you tell me—"

"No!" Her eyebrows pulled together in a fierce frown. "I owe you nothing."

His temper flared, and he longed to shake her until she revealed the secrets of the past, but the sound of footsteps on the terrace halted him.

Lady Stowe joined them, her face set in lines of concern. "There you are, Andria. I've been looking for you." She threw a glance of mistrust at Rafe. "I can tell he has upset you very much." She placed her arm around Andria's waist. "Come along."

They walked to the door as Rafe watched in helpless frustration. Lady Stowe glanced at him over her shoulder before leaving. "Don't you dare pester her again. If you do, I shall report you to the magistrates, and you shall be thrown out of Rowan's Gate."

"I have not committed any crimes, Lady Stowe," he said coldly.

"If you don't call ruining lives a crime, I don't know what you call it." With a swish of skirts, she led Andria outside.

Rafe felt like shouting, ranting and raving against the fate that had dealt him such a difficult hand. "I won't leave until I've found out the whole truth," he vowed, his jaws aching as he clenched them too hard.

He could almost hear Nick's voice, even though Nick

wasn't in the room. *Patience, old fellow. You cannot force anyone to speak unless they wish to confide.*

"Damn patience, damn everything," Rafe muttered, and marched into the mansion, slamming the door behind him.

Andria slowly regained her composure as they drove away from the Rowan estate. She dared not touch on the revelation that festered in her mind. Two long years she spent looking for Bridget. She'd visited every orphanage from Yorkshire to London, but without luck. Finally losing hope of ever finding Bridget, she had accepted Lady Stowe's offer of employment.

"Rafe looked like he'd seen a ghost when I came upon you in the solarium. I wish I could have kept him away from you. Were you arguing?"

"More than that." Andria lost her fight against sorrow. She pressed her face against the older woman's shoulder. "Bridget is dead. She died in Rafe's arms, at an orphanage in London. He claimed *I* had left her there and gone away with my lover."

Her voice rose in indignation. "My *lover.* As if I ever loved anyone besides Rafe. I know he didn't deserve it, but I never learned how to control the love in my heart."

"Dear heaven!" Lady Stowe's voice cracked as she patted Andria's begloved hand. "There, there. I know the truth that Bridget is dead is hard to bear, but isn't it better than not knowing what happened to her?"

Andria nodded and dried her eyes. "Yes, in my heart of hearts, I knew I would never see her again. I have to find out the name of the servant who informed Rafe of his identity—and of Bridget's. He flared up in anger before I had a chance to discover the truth."

Lady Stowe dabbed at her eyes with a handkerchief. "You ought to stay away from Rafe. He will only bring you more unhappiness. You don't need 'flares of anger' at this time in your life."

Andria looked out the window at the snow swirling over the bleak fells. She tried to gather her emotions and push them under her control, but the more she tried, the more unruly they grew, like mushrooms poking up everywhere. Tears fell unchecked down her face. "I feel someone else will die before this ordeal is over. We cannot hide behind lies forever, but the pain of revelation will surely kill someone."

A gray shadow of unease filled every corner of her being as she sensed something beyond her consciousness, an unseen threat, a hint of evil. She held her breath, but in a moment the sensation had dispersed, leaving only the bleakest sadness behind.

Beauclerk Saxon sat in the library at Lochlade. After two years, he still admired the polished mahogany desk and book-lined walls. Every detail spoke of wealth, of sumptuous indulgence. It hadn't arrived with him; it had always been here with the prosperous side of the Saxon family.

After a childhood lived in genteel poverty in the company of a tight-fisted father and a sullen and bitter mother, Beau liked the security of wealth, and he enjoyed the comforts.

Most of all, he loved the power that money brought. He wore his lustrous title, the Earl of Lochlade, with great pride. He deserved it more than anyone.

He adjusted the lace at his wrists and sighed. There was only one regret in his life: his inability to attach Andria Saxon. Lochlade was her home, had always been, and she should have been the countess that ruled over the house. It would've been so perfect, just as he pictured it from the beginning.

The lovely and alluring Andria had turned her back on him. The worst insult was that she'd refused to visit Lochlade since he became master—as if the estate were filled with foul-smelling pestilence.

"Damn that woman," he said through his teeth. "She throws her pride in my face at every opportunity."

He lifted the silver-backed mirror he always kept on his desk and studied his face. Lines of distinction, a fine head of hair, eyes of power, a firm jaw. What more did she want? The maids at Lochlade could attest that he was a skillful lover. He could satisfy the flighty Andria Saxon if she could but stay long enough in his arms.

One day he would quell her spirits, subdue her pride. Her haughty disdain corroded him more every day, and soon would come a time when he would not stand for her rejection.

She would become his. It was only a matter of time.

The untimely return of the prodigal son was unfortunate, but Andria would not have him back—not after what transpired in the past. She would never forgive Rafe. Beau tapped a polished fingernail against his teeth as he turned over several plans in his mind.

Rafe should have died. He should have met his Maker that day in Flanders, but by some strange miracle, he hadn't.

Beau slammed his fist onto the top of his desk, and the pain shooting up his arm fought and won over the anger churning inside. He let out an explosive breath and hung his head.

He had to choose the perfect time and place to put a

finishing touch on the plans that he set into motion years ago. This time he would make sure everything went according to his plans. Then Beau would gain back his life, which Rafe took away by marrying Andria, the most beautiful, the most desirable, woman in Yorkshire.

On a palette, Andria mixed pigments with oil and turpentine until she got the exact shade of gold she sought. She immersed her brush in the paint and lifted it to the portrait before her on the easel. She found it difficult to capture the sheen of Lady Stowe's gold velvet gown. Her thoughts lingered on her last meeting with Rafe, and however much she tried, she could not shake the image of his sad expression. He had cared for Bridget well; he always had. He'd adored Bridget from the moment she was born.

Andria wished she'd spoken with him in the solarium. She could have put aside her resentment and found some answers to her many questions, but she had rejected him. Her emotions had been too strong to overrule.

Working here at Stowehurst had only stirred up her dormant emotions and brought back the pain. She'd come to understand that only the truth would reintroduce serenity to her life.

"Dear Andria," Lady Stowe said, fidgeting as she sat on a velvet-shrouded dais in the drafty room. "I'm cold and stiff. I don't have the patience to sit in this position any longer." She let her hand holding the beautifully painted fan fall to her lap. "I didn't realize there was such torture involved in having one's portrait done."

Andria smiled. "Surely an hour a day is not too long. At least you don't have to hold your arms in the air."

Lady Stowe sighed. "I daresay I brought it upon myself."

"I'm not happy with the light," Andria said, and glanced out the tall windows of the salon that had been converted to a studio. "It's too dark, and I can't seem to find my bearings."

"What with everything going on, I'm surprised you can concentrate at all on your work. In your place I would be devastated."

Andria suspended her brush in a jar of turpentine. "I admit my mind is not wholly on my work."

"Rafe's reappearance in these parts has stirred up a past best forgotten." Lady Stowe climbed down from the dais, her wide hoops swaying. "Oh, but it's cold in here!" Adjusting a wool shawl over her shoulders, she came to inspect the latest details of the portrait.

"I wish you would contain your curiosity until the painting is finished," Andria said with a sigh.

Lady Stowe's eyebrows lifted. "Really?"

"I'm not very proud of my work today." Andria scraped the paint off the palette with a knife and scrubbed it clean with a rag.

"I find it very flattering. And with that window at my back revealing the majesty of Abbey Fell, it's beautiful and dignified." She heaved a sigh. "Not that a little painted lie would enhance my face and figure, but I want you to be ruthlessly honest. I want people to recognize me the moment they see this, not wonder why my nose is straight when it's really bulbous."

Andria laughed. "Surely I wouldn't call it bulbous, only slightly turned up."

"You could *never* call it aristocratic," Lady Stowe mused aloud.

"Sharp as a blade and hooked, you mean?"

"Oh . . . you know, the kind of nose that makes one

look *noble*. But I daresay, the dress enhances the dark luster of my hair."

"I'm glad that you're pleased." Andria covered the paint jars and set them into their wooden boxes. "There, all finished for today."

"Let's go downstairs for a cup of tea. I'm cold to the very bone. A nip of brandy in the tea shall work wonders. You shall have a double nip."

Arm in arm they went downstairs. Andria tried to forget her frustrations, but her mind would not settle into a calmer pattern. Everywhere she went, she kept seeing Rafe's face in front of her, and she was weakening as the memories of their happy past slowly came to life. It was only in the last months of their time together that their marriage had fallen apart, all due to suspicion and false blame.

"Look, there is Derek riding up. He'll be cold after that long ride from Seddon House. If you greet him, I'll see to tea," Lady Stowe said.

Andria met her old friend at the door. Derek was not yet over his pain at losing the fingers of his right hand. Andria had never believed his story about being ambushed by vagabonds. Derek was a terrible liar, the dear heart. She'd supported him all through the year, convincing him over and over that suicide was not a solution to his problems. Like her, he loved to paint.

He had an awe-inspiring talent. When his right hand had been rendered useless, he had fallen into the deepest despair until Andria suggested that he learn to use his left hand. After a long struggle, he heaved himself out of the dark pit and began to paint, not without great difficulty, but at least trying.

"Derek, what a great surprise," she said, and kissed him on both cheeks. His long, lean face held some color due to the brisk wind, but there were more strands of silver in his thick black hair.

He took her hand in his. As always, he kept a glove on his mangled hand and hid it behind his back. "I had to see you. I heard that Rafe is alive and that he has returned to Rowan's Gate. His return must have put a terrible strain on you."

"Yes, I'm still reeling, but I'm slowly finding my bearings. I won't allow him to ruin my life again."

"No, he made you miserable, and I'm here to see that he doesn't destroy your life again." He held her tightly against him for a moment. "It's my turn to pay you back for all the support you gave me when my life was black."

"You owe me nothing; you know that." She hugged him, smelling the fresh scent of winter air on his coat. "How is your new painting coming along?"

"The mountains?"

She nodded and watched as the footman helped Derek off with his cloak and hat.

"They are . . . not what I had hoped for, but—"

"At least you're trying, Derek. Your talents aren't lost because you lost the use of one hand."

"But it's like starting over. I know the techniques, but I can't make my left hand obey me. It never performs the vision in my head."

Andria admired his dark blue frock coat, adorned with black braid, and his yellow waistcoat. "You look handsome today, and there's healthy color in your cheeks. Let's not dwell on problems; let's speak of other things."

He nodded, his blue eyes searching hers for signs of falsity. Her smile felt contrived, but she did not want to spend the time in Derek's company lamenting her sorrows.

"You're beautiful as always, Andria, but so pale. I can

see your anguish even though you hide it admirably; there's no need to conceal it from me. I'm practically your brother, if not by name."

She took his hand and drew him up the stairs to one of the back parlors where Lady Stowe liked to serve informal teas. His hand was cold in hers. She thought of Rafe and remembered why he'd been so angry and jealous in the past; he'd been unable to tolerate her close friendship with Derek.

"To think that Rafe thought we were more than childhood friends," she muttered to herself.

"What did you say?" He withdrew his grip and opened the door to the parlor. With a gallant bow, he offered her to enter first.

"An old memory disturbed me, alas. But no matter. I'm eager to sample Cook's seedcake—if there's any left." Winking, she walked inside, her head held high.

Derek chuckled and closed the door on the drafts in the hallway. A warm fire sparkled in the grate, and Andria held her hands out toward the warmth. Her toes, encased in thin satin slippers, ached with cold.

Lady Stowe accepted Derek's murmured greeting and peck on the cheek. "You have stayed away for too long, Derek," she exclaimed. "Are you brooding in that gloomy old house of yours?"

"No longer brooding; only working," he said, and sat down in an armchair, placing one leg over the other. His polished top boot bobbed up and down as if some question nagged at him inside. He'd pushed his ruined hand into his pocket and gingerly adjusted the lace at his throat with the other.

"From what I've heard, you've withdrawn from most of your friends and from all social entertainment," Lady Stowe went on. "Why?"

"I'm doing other things, among them helping my mother, as she's growing older."

"You're a personable young man who should mingle with the eligible ladies of the area. Many would give their eyeteeth to marry you."

"I'm not interested in marriage, Rebecca. Not yet, anyway."

"Hmmph!" Lady Stowe poured the tea and passed around a plate of sliced seedcake. "You need fattening up, young man."

Derek laughed and waved his hand in dismissal. "I didn't come here to hear a lecture, only to engage in congenial conversation with two beautiful ladies."

Andria noticed the transformation of his face as he smiled, and she wished she could love him as a man, not just as a dear friend. "How are your mother and Lilith?"

"Mother is worrying about me too much, and Lilith— you know her—always teasing the young men of Yorkshire and wild about her horses."

"Your sister is a sprightly one," Lady Stowe said ominously, and stirred her tea.

Andrea warmed her still-cold hands on the cup. Steam wafted from the hot beverage and tickled her nose. "Lilith is the beauty in these parts. It's only natural she should have quite a court of young gentlemen, breaking hearts left and right."

"There was a time when you were the leading beauty in the dales, Andria," Lady Stowe said. "I remember it well. 'Tis a pity that—"

"Let's not speak of those days. I was young and very foolish," Andria said hurriedly. She gulped down some tea and burned her tongue. "Dash it all!" Some liquid splashed on her gown as she set the cup down, and she tried to mop it up with her napkin, but her hands trembled so much that she dropped it.

"You're understandably upset," Lady Stowe said. "I wish I could ease your pain." She found a handkerchief in her pocket and dabbed at the spreading stain on Andria's gown.

Andria closed her eyes and counted to ten. Such raw emotions welled out of her chest that she shivered. Every remark, every smile, seemed to hint back at the same thing: the horrendous mistake she'd made with Rafe.

"Sooner or later he'll come after you, Derek. I know he will," she said more to herself than to her company.

"I take it you're alluding to Rafe," Derek said with a sigh. "Yes, I suppose you're right. If he's the man I remember, I know he won't listen to any explanations; if only there was proof—"

"He does not remember you at all, Derek," Lady Stowe said, and shook out her handkerchief.

Andria heaved a sigh of relief. "Yes . . . you're right. His affliction is indeed a blessing in this case."

Derek rubbed his jaw as if deep in thought. "I don't understand what made him think that we were romantically involved."

Andria had no answer. She only wished the leaden weight would lift from her chest. A knock sounded at the door, and Witherspoon, the butler, entered with a card on his tray. He held it out to Lady Stowe. "Lord Derwent to see you, milady."

Lady Stowe clapped her hand to her ample bosom. "He's not welcome here!" she cried. "Send him away immediately."

Andria spied a shadow by the door. A man dressed in a charcoal gray coat and breeches filled the opening. His dark gaze roved across the room to settle on her. She gasped, her heartbeat pounding harder with every second.

"Too late for that, I'm afraid," Rafe said, and stepped into the room. His hat in hand, he gestured to Witherspoon to depart.

"Really! This is the outside of enough," Lady Stowe said, puffing herself up like an angry hen. "How dare you trespass in my home!"

"I know I would not be welcome, but you can't deny me my right to find out more about my past. He encompassed the room with a sweep of his arm. All of you can help me remember. I have not come here to cause trouble."

"Your presence is trouble enough," Lady Stowe said. She pointed toward the door. "Out!"

Rafe shrugged his shoulders and let his cloak fall into a chair. He sat down on the sofa beside her. "Show some manners, Aunt," he drawled.

Lady Stowe's face suffused with red, and she gave Andria a pleading glance. Andria had discovered that she didn't want to send Rafe away. If her problems were ever to be solved, she had to face them.

"I daresay he won't attack us, Rebecca," she said. "The faster we answer his questions, the sooner he will leave." She indicated Derek. "Rafe, I take it you don't remember our old friend Derek Guiscard. We were all childhood friends together."

Rafe wrinkled his brow, such a familiar and dear gesture that Andria felt like crying. Rafe was here, but at the same time, he was gone—forever. She clenched the teacup as if it could give her the support she needed.

Derek extended his left hand in a greeting. Rafe looked surprised but shook it as if they truly had been good friends. A cold shiver ran down Andria's spine as she recalled their last meeting.

Evidently Derek had been thinking along the same lines. He said, "Rafe, you would not shake my hand if you could recall our last meeting. You would rather draw your rapier and run me through."

Sudden stillness filled the room as if everyone held their tension-laden breath.

Rafe studied the younger man, but Andria saw no spark of recognition, no flare of anger. "Really?" Rafe said. "Please explain before I expire with curiosity. I'm grateful for your honesty."

"You accused me of bedding your wife," Derek said, an icy edge to his voice. "First of all, it is a damned lie; second, Andria would not consent to any underhanded dealings. That's why we are such good friends. I would trust her with my life, which you evidently failed to do."

Rafe rubbed his jaw, beard stubble scraping against his finger. Andria remembered that his beard grew rather quickly and would show dark at the end of the day. "I doubt I would have accused you without some fact behind it," he answered coolly.

"You were a hothead; always acted first and asked questions later," Derek said.

Rafe pondered those words, and faint color tinted his cheeks. "I have difficulty recognizing the man you paint, that everybody paints in these parts. As far as I know, I've never acted rashly, so all I can do is take your word for it."

"Are you implying that we're lying?" Andria said hoarsely.

Rafe shook his head. "No . . . but what am I to believe? I know what I'm like, but you say I'm totally different."

Gloom fell in the room, and Derek threw a questioning

glance at Andria, as if asking if this truly was Rafe and not a changeling that looked like Rafe.

Andria lowered her gaze to the carpet underfoot and studied the swirling flower pattern.

"Well, did you bed my wife, Guiscard?"

Derek jerked to his feet as if stung and dropped his napkin on the floor. "Of course not! I just told you—"

"I wanted to test you by shocking you." Rafe looked from one to the other. "Now, who will tell me the story of my life?"

FIVE

"Rafe, you're unacceptably arrogant to expect us to receive you into the bosom of the family after all you did," Lady Stowe said, standing up. "We owe you nothing after what you did—hurting dear Andria terribly and leaving her to face the consequences of your cowardice." She pointed at the door. "For the last time, leave, and don't come back here. I can't forbid you to visit your father, but he would be much better off without your presence."

Rafe stood, his blood freezing with the chill of her condemnation. "I can't force you to cooperate, but I'm not the person I was, nor do I intend to cause any harm." Despair swelled in his chest; everywhere he went, people treated him with contempt—even hatred. What kind of person had he been to elicit such a cold reception? What wrong had he done? He shrugged, his head aching as if he'd banged it repeatedly against a stone wall. "I'm only here for information, but I suppose my hopes to learn more are fruitless."

Lady Stowe stood with her hands on her hips, and without her on his side, he could get nowhere in this house. "They are," she said.

"Rebecca," Andria said, her eyes wide and filled with distress. Everyone looked at her, but she didn't complete her sentence. A stillness wrought with tension expanded in the room.

"Very well, I can't force you to speak," Rafe said to break the uncomfortable silence. He marched out of the room, his frustration growing with every step.

Downstairs, in the octagonal hallway with marble floor and busts of Stowe forefathers, he gathered his cloak, gloves, and hat. He heard the swish of skirts on the landing above, and he looked toward the top of the sturdy oak staircase. Andria looked down at him, uncertainty evident in every line of her body.

"I want to speak with you," she said, her voice breathless with some emotion he could not decipher. Fear?

He nodded curtly, not daring to hope he would find an ally in her, but his heart hammered wildly by a will of its own. He waited for her to descend the stairs, noting the graceful lines of her slim body and the sway of her hips.

She looked demure, untouchable, in a garnet red wool sack gown over panniers and a frill of lace at her neckline. Blond curls framed her neck in a beguiling manner and ran riot at her hairline. It would be so easy to fall in love all over again with this woman. He was already halfway there. The current of attraction ran strong between them. A sudden urge to capture her in his arms and trail kisses along the column of her neck overcame him.

He wanted to invade her mouth with his and explore her hidden places.

He straightened his back and ruthlessly curbed his emotions. "I'm grateful that you're willing to give me a moment of your time."

"Nothing has changed between us, but you have the right to know the truth about yourself," she said coldly. "At least I know the whole truth, since I was there, at the heart of the tragedy."

She gesticulated toward the back where the hallway widened into an alcove that had a wall of latticed windows. Outside, a brick terrace and steps led to a formal garden with paths marching in straight lines toward a privet hedge.

"Come this way, Rafe."

"Do you mind if I call you Andria?" he asked as he walked beside her.

She gave him a quick, appraising glance. "No, but remember that I call myself Andria Saxon now, not Lady Derwent."

He clenched his jaw as her rejection stabbed him in the tender area of his heart, which had grown heavier than ever since he had returned to Yorkshire.

She stood by the windows, looking out at the garden, which was sprinkled with snow. "We were married ten years ago. You were twenty-two, and I was eighteen. The ceremony and festivities took place at Lochlade, my father's estate. He died two years ago. Beauclerk was next in line, since Father's heir, my nephew Julian, died—about a year before you left. He was ten years old."

Her voice broke, and Rafe listened with growing horror to her tale of deaths.

"How did he die? Was he very young?"

"We raised Julian as our own after my brother and his wife died shortly after his birth in Italy. Julian was the most precious boy, and I loved him dearly." She placed her hand over her eyes, and Rafe longed to comfort her, but he knew she would shun his touch. "A strange lingering illness took him. No one could help him in the end."

"I'm sorry I don't remember him. Did . . . did I get along with the boy?" He tensed himself against further recriminations, but she only nodded.

"You loved him, and he loved you. He was everything to us until Bridget came along." Again, Andria's voice broke, and she halted her story.

Sorrow clenched Rafe's heart as he thought about the daughter he'd held in his arms as she was dying. "Bridget was a bright child," he said lamely, not remembering anything else.

"Yes, we were a very happy family, but it's clear to me now that we were doomed. Our actions marched us towards the ruin of our happiness at all costs. We didn't seem to have many friends, and I don't know why. Beau stood by me during the darkest time, and he tried to help me find out what happened to Bridget."

A flare of anger blossomed in Rafe's chest. "He has his own plans, I'm sure. Tell me, why did you leave Bridget? Or if what you say is true about her disappearance, why did you allow someone to abduct her and put her in the orphanage?"

Andria gave him a hard glance. Tears glittered in her eyelashes, but she held her sorrow in check admirably. Her shoulders squared, and her chin rose in determination. "I will get to that part in good time." She paced to the other side of the alcove, and Rafe had to follow her.

She continued: "As I said, we were happy, but you didn't get along with your father. He always accused you of recklessness and failure to shoulder responsibility. I'm afraid he was right, but you were the only son, and your nurse spoiled you shamelessly when we grew up. In fact, all the servants spoiled you. They could not withstand your charm," she added, her voice wry. "No one could. I adored you and didn't dare to admit to myself that your character had any flaws. Well, it did—it *does*. You grew increasingly jealous of every man in my vicinity, and there came a point when I felt like a prisoner in my own home.

You would throw out every gentleman who came to visit, and you ended up with enemies left and right. The culmination came when you accused me of crawling into Derek's bed. Derek, who had stood by us always. The best friend a person could ever have. You accused him of every foul deed. You refused to listen, interrupted me when I tried to explain. Then just left."

"I'm sorry."

"I've lived with the stigma of adulteress since that day you accused Derek and the accusation became public knowledge. Nevertheless, he has stood by me, and since we're innocent, we decided not to let the foul accusation ruin our friendship."

The discomfort of guilt filled him. "I applaud your courage."

"Don't take on that sarcastic tone with me, Rafe. I have no obligation to tell you about the past." She gave him that flinty, cold look. "If you rake me over the coals, as you did in the past, I shall never speak with you again! Is that clear?"

He nodded, feeling as if his stomach were about to turn inside out.

"It all started after Julian died. As I said, he succumbed to some mysterious illness that the doctor could not diagnose. He grew weaker and weaker until nothing but a shadow remained. I prayed day and night, but Julian slipped away even as I was praying at his bedside. You were kneeling on the floor beside me, crying."

"It would have been a most difficult time."

"You changed then, Rafe. You would not share your pain with me. You grew cold and detached and pushed me away, as you couldn't deal with your grief. Gone was our happiness that had shone so bright. From then on, it was only a matter of time before the negativity surrounding us eroded the rest of our lives. Bridget came along almost as a mistake, and I thought it would be a new, happy beginning for us. It was for a while. Then came the Derek incident, the confrontation, and you refused to listen to anything I said. Then you just left without a word to anyone. You didn't even have the decency to say good-bye to Bridget, and you never wrote." She whirled around, facing him.

He saw her fists balling and barely had time to protect himself as she started pounding his chest.

"I hate you, Rafe!" she shouted. "I hate you so much I would like to kill you. You ruined everything; you ruined my life."

Tears clogged his throat as he tried to digest all that she'd told him. He caught her wrists and held her tightly. Her chest rose and fell rapidly in the storm of her wrath, and her blue eyes spewed venom. They did not lie. He groaned as he searched her face, seeing nothing but her anger and her rejection. Something in him yearned fervently to end the pain, to put a stop to the gloom of the past. He didn't know how to do it, what to say. Would there be any right words?

She fought to get out of his grip, but he only hauled her closer until their arms and locked fists were pressed between them. His chest expanded as if he would burst. He cried out and gathered her into his arms, quieting her struggle by folding his arms tightly around her and holding her until she stopped fighting.

Her hair held the fresh scent of roses; her skin, the elusive, sweet odor of femininity. His senses reeled. Some part of him recognized her unique scent intimately, but she was a stranger in his arms.

Time ceased, and he found he could stand here forever with her slight form pressed to his. Part of him found deep solace in her presence. Her soul spoke soundlessly to his.

"I won't allow you to hurt me again," she said, her voice muffled against the lace at his neck. "Not ever."

He rested his chin on top of her silky hair and stroked her tense back. "I shall honor that. I have no intention of ruining your life again, and I'm so grateful that you have the strength to speak of the atrocities that befell us."

She lifted her face to his but didn't try to move away. "I saw you once in London, with a gentleman who sought an artist living at Mrs. Hopkins's."

"I remember seeing you rushing up the stairs, but I didn't know you. My friend Nick Thurston was looking for Serena Hilliard. They are married now. In fact, she is in Rowan's Gate, waiting at the inn."

Andria's eyes widened. "Really? I worried about her, wondered what became of her after she left Mrs. Hopkins's shop."

"You are invited to meet her anytime you like. Nick and Serena are my friends, evidently the only ones I have."

Andria pushed away from him gently, her anger clearly spent. "I would dearly like to see her again." She looked around the room as if dazed.

"I'm exhausted, but glad that we spoke of the pain at last," she said. She spread her hands and looked at them as if they could speak of the past as well. "I did everything in my power to find Bridget, every day fearing more that she'd met with a terrible fate. I worried most that someone had sold her to a house of ill repute. Some gentlemen prefer young children." Her voice rose on a note of disgust. "I admit I feel easier knowing she did not have to suffer that horrible fate."

"Mayhap we should have a memorial service for her

in the church? I buried her in London, but she could be moved to rest here."

Andria's gaze searched his face. "Who told you about Bridget's identity? Who was the servant?"

"A rather coarse woman named Sally Vane. She had worked at Rowan Hall, she said."

Andria's eyes widened in horror. "As far as I know, no such woman worked at either Rowan Hall or Lochlade in my time. Perhaps she was sent by someone to lead you to believe—" She could not finish the sentence. She clapped her hand to her mouth, and her eyes grew enormous.

He felt as if every muscle had stiffened, his blood congealing into ice. He gripped Andria's hands convulsively. "What if the child wasn't Bridget? I have no one else's word for it," he said with a strangled gasp. "What if Bridget is still alive?"

Andria's eyes grew even wider as she met his gaze. "Alive?" she whispered, wild hope flaring in her heart. It died as quickly, for she dared not believe in the possibility. "I had a locket with her likeness but lost it as I traveled looking for her. That was another blow."

"If your suspicions are right, who's to say Sally Vane is someone who ever set foot in Yorkshire?" He loosened his grip of her hands, and she moved away while searching his face for any sign of a cruel joke. It wouldn't be the first time she'd been taken in by him. He'd joked in the past, but never about such serious matters.

"We must investigate, but I'm certain she never worked in the area or I would have recognized the name. I know everyone to the lowest scullery maid in the dales."

"She could have changed her name," Rafe said, hoping against hope he'd stumbled on a clue that would bring their daughter back. "It's painful to think that I wouldn't recognize my own daughter."

Her face hardened. "You deserve the pain nevertheless." She looked toward the door as an urge to renew her search of Bridget came over her. The possibility that Bridget was still alive infused her blood with new energy.

"Are you going to act upon this?" she asked, noting the muscle working in his jaw. He looked as if he'd received a blow to his head.

"Yes . . . will you come with me? We ought to work together, not against each other."

A negative answer was on the tip of her tongue, but she never spoke the words. "Since this concerns our daughter, yes, we ought to work together, but don't believe for a moment that we'll find a way to mend the rift in our marriage. I want nothing from you, not ever. Our marriage is finished, and if we cannot get a legal annulment, we shall never live together again."

He flushed, and a dark flame lit in his eyes. He brushed his hand over his face as if to wipe away tired thoughts. Curiosity consumed her about the years he'd been gone. "Tell me what happened on the battlefield."

"All I know is what others told me. I was rather a reckless soldier, but I don't recall any of it. All I remember is what happened after the accident. You see, I was kicked in the head by a dying horse and lay unconscious for a week. He took her hand and lifted it to his thick hair. "Feel it?"

She examined his scalp with her fingertips and found a shallow indentation in the bone. "You could have died," she said, removing her hand as if touching him were like touching fire.

"It would have pleased you all, wouldn't it?" he said bitterly. When she didn't respond, he continued: "I feel as if I did die. I don't have an identity any longer, but after what I've heard about myself, it might be a good thing."

"You believe our condemnation of you?" she asked in surprise. The old Rafe would have scoffed at their opinions and only listened to himself.

He crossed his arms over his chest, looking uncomfortable. "I have no reason to distrust it since so many have shown their disapproval. If I had been well liked, I would have received a warmer welcome."

He continued: "I woke up from that blow with a horrendous headache that still bothers me at times. From that moment, I had to start over, learning how to dress, how to eat, how to read and write. Some part of me remembered that, and I learned quickly. Ever since, I've read on quiet evenings. History, poetry, literature. It's likely I'm learning more than I did at school in the past." His lips curved upward in the beguiling way she well remembered. "If what you said about me is true, it's likely I did not apply myself seriously to my schoolwork."

"I'd say you were more interested in horse racing and the pugilist society. Not to forget other types of gambling."

"I'm amazed you considered marrying me," he said, his voice laced with sarcasm.

Andria remembered how much she'd loved him. "You did have a wicked knack for turning the heads of young ladies. I was not the only one."

"I almost stayed on in Flanders with the local farmer that took care of me. I was left for dead on the battlefield. The locals looted the corpses and took me in when they discovered I was alive. The English battalions had moved on, and no one recognized me. The local clergy took pity on me when he discovered I was English, and he taught me the rudiments of knowledge as I recovered my strength."

"Everyone believed you were dead."

He nodded. "I was not strong enough to go after the army. Besides, I'd lost all desire for war. I came back to England, not knowing my identity, lacking all skills except cooking simple meals and what little learning I'd acquired."

"A peer of the realm would not go into battle, Rafe, but I'm not surprised to hear that you threw yourself into the midst of it."

"I guess it *was* a way to forget. Even now I'd prefer to be a soldier than an aide-de-camp." He sighed. " 'Tis likely I had a death wish. Technically, I *am* dead. I'll have to rectify the war records."

He braced one arm against the window frame. Snowflakes whirled outside, filling the world with white. His face took on a haunted expression as he stared at the whiteness, as if remembering something.

"My mind was blank, covered with white nothing, like the snow covers the ground. I might as well have been someone who fell out of the sky."

"You're piecing your life together bit by bit."

"My friend Nick took me to the best specialists in London, who pronounced there's nothing wrong with me. With any luck, my memory will return"—he turned to her—"and so will my arrogance."

She wrinkled her nose and realized he'd held her spellbound with his tale. He'd been speaking from a depth of despair, and she'd felt the weight of every word. She shook herself mentally as if to remove any thought of sympathy. He would not beguile her again.

"Where shall we start investigating Bridget's disappearance?"

He took a step toward her. "I want to mend what I broke in the past. Finding Bridget is only the beginning." He touched the tip of her chin, slowly dragging his finger up to her earlobe. Sparks ignited inside her and flashed between them. She jerked away as if burned.

"Don't! If we find Bridget, nothing else matters."

He held out his hand toward her. "Come, let's get started. No need to delay everything by talking."

She nodded curtly but avoided his hand.

SIX

Rafe stormed into the private parlor at the inn where Nick and Serena had enjoyed an early dinner. Remnants of chicken and slices of ham reminded Rafe how hungry he was. With a chunk of ham in one hand and a leg of chicken in the other, he said, "Andria says no one by the name of Sally Vane worked at Rowan Hall. She was the servant at Sir James's Orphanage who told me about my identity."

Nick leaned back in his chair and placed his arm over the back of Serena's chair. He lifted his tankard, a thoughtful expression on his face. "Sally Vane did not work at the orphanage for very long. Come to think of it, she left her employment shortly after she told you about your connection to Lord Rowan. Disappeared; never gave an explanation. If I recall, she only worked there a month or two."

"That's odd," Serena said, and put aside a scrap of fabric to which she'd attached a thin gold braid with needle and thread. "It sounds as if she had a mission involving Rafe, but how would she know his whereabouts?"

"That's a mystery," Nick said. "We might never discover the truth of that."

"I have a feeling she lied to me about Bridget, if not about my father," Rafe said.

Nick and Serena exchanged concerned glances, and Rafe sensed their closeness, which automatically shut him out.

"I fear you're filled with wishful thinking, old fellow."

"I brought someone to see you," Rafe said to break the spell. His friends had taken his side, acting protectively. What if they treated Andria with cool disdain? She would leave, and he would be alone on the cold trail of his daughter. The thought made him uneasy. "Be kind to her."

Andria entered in the company of Mr. Brown. They chatted, and she didn't at first notice the people in the room, but when she folded back her hood, her eyes widened in delight.

"Serena?"

"Andria?" Serena pushed her chair back and ran around the table to greet her friend with a hug. "I'm sorry I had no chance to visit you at Mrs. Hopkins's later, but I spent most of the autumn in Sussex."

"I'm delighted to see you, Serena. You look different; that haunted look in your eyes is gone."

"I am happy at last." She threw Nick a warm glance, and he laughed. He gallantly offered his chair to Andria, and as the ladies talked, Rafe asked his friend to step out to the taproom for another tankard of ale.

"Nick, are you certain you want to spend your honeymoon at this godforsaken place?" Rafe inquired as the landlord served them. "You could be snowbound for days on end."

"Not a bad prospect under the circumstances." Nick gave the closed door a loving glance as if he could see his wife through the solid wood.

Rafe sighed. "I don't know what to do now. My mind is reeling with possibilities. What if Bridget is alive and longing to be back home? What if someone has mistreated her? Or worse, killed her? Andria would be devastated."

"It's better to learn the truth than not knowing." Nick wiped the thin line of foam from his upper lip. "She disappeared from the Lochlade estate? If that is so, you should start your search there, then expand in ever-widening circles."

"Yes, that is my plan, but I would dearly lay my hands on that larcenous maid in London."

"Leave that to me, old fellow. I have vast contacts in the capital, and if she's still there, we'll find her."

Rafe set down his tankard on the table. "I hope Serena isn't disappointed with her honeymoon in these godforsaken parts."

Nick clamped his hand on Rafe's shoulder and winked. "She's enchanted, and we promised we would stand by you, and we never go back on a promise. This is only the beginning. We won't abandon you now, Rafe."

Rafe shook Nick's hand as relief washed through him. Tears burned at the back of his eyes, and he realized that exhaustion filled every corner of his body. "Without you, Nick, I would be nowhere."

Nick laughed. "You were a damned wily highwayman in our wild days. We helped each other in a bad time, and we're still helping each other. Nothing has changed as far as I'm concerned. I've gained a wife since then, but so have you." He grinned, jerking his head in the direction of the private parlor. "And a damn fine one, if I may say so. If you play your cards right, Rafe, you—"

"No! What Andria and I had once is over. She'd rather be dead than let me touch her."

Nick frowned. "Surely that is a rather drastic observation."

"*Her* observation, not mine. She's lovely and kind. If

I'm not careful, I might fall in love with her all over. Something about her draws me irresistibly, but as far as I know, there's nothing to build on. *I* left her for something I can't remember. She told me about it, but I can't feel the anger that I once must have felt."

Nick punched Rafe's arm lightly. "You've earned another chance, old fellow, by surviving that blow, which should have killed you. This time, make sure you don't make any mistakes and she's bound to fall into your arms."

Rafe snorted. "You were always an optimist."

"I learned early on to make the most of my life. Take every chance that came my way."

"Yes . . ." Rafe finished his ale and wiped his mouth. "I'll have to shape my life—start where it all began."

"Mayhap you can let Andria help you shape it."

Rafe stood. "I don't know. I dare not hope, only take each moment as it comes."

Nick placed his arm around Rafe's shoulders. "I shall send a message to London posthaste and have people search for Sally Vane."

"Thank you. You've taken a load off my shoulders."

The next morning, very early, before the sun emerged, Rafe rose at the inn and washed his face in cold water from a ewer on the washstand. The freezing touch dispelled his dream-hazed mind and crystallized his thoughts.

Today he would start the search at Lochlade, where Bridget had disappeared. But first he would ride over to Stowehurst and collect Andria. He hoped she hadn't changed her mind. Fear laced his thoughts at the possibility. He wasn't sure he could explore his past without someone at his side. Who knows what he would learn? More than likely, his ears would be filled with more negative judgment about himself.

As he dressed in buckskin breeches, wool waistcoat, and coat, he remembered Andria's support on the previous day. Her eyes had expressed compassion, and she had allowed him to speak. The thought of seeing her again made his heart beat faster. Mayhap he would feel whole once they had discovered the truth about Bridget and he'd found all the pieces of the puzzle that was his past. Mayhap the dreaded black haze in his memory would be dispelled once and for all.

He pulled on his boots and tied back his hair with a leather thong. For some reason, he wanted to look his best for Andria. *Fool,* he told himself. *She's not interested in you personally. In fact, she loathes you.* Even if he looked like Adonis, she would not be impressed. He tweaked the ends of his cravat and buttoned his waistcoat all the way up. Taking a deep breath, he tried to dispel the uneasy feeling in his chest. He swung his cloak over his shoulders and put his hat on his head.

A thin layer of snow covered the ground, but Blacky, his horse, had no difficulty following the road to Stowehurst. Frost glittered on the branches, and the world held a crystal stillness. Chirping, two chickadees fluttered from tree to tree in search of dry seeds and berries. An early winter had arrived in the dales.

Andria gave him a cool welcome, but she'd been waiting for him at the door, already dressed in heavy cloak and gloves. He helped her into the saddle of a spirited chestnut mare, touching her boot longer than necessary. "I hope you are ready for any unpleasantness we might encounter," he said.

She removed his hand. "I've already lived through the

deepest despair. Whatever we find can only make things better."

He gripped her hand and kissed her through the glove. "Believe me, I'm grateful for your support."

She pulled away as if burned by his touch. "We've already wasted too much time."

Rafe clenched his teeth, as her rejection burned deeply.

She continued: "There used to be a portrait of my father holding Bridget as an infant at Lochlade, but I don't know if it's still there. I haven't been able to make myself go back to look for it. Too much pain would be stirred up."

"We'll look for it, but let's not mention any of this to anyone until we know something more concrete."

He heaved himself into the saddle and curled his hands around the reins as if they could give him the support he needed. He'd never felt more alone, and as they rode through the bare wintry landscape, his world seemed to slowly come apart. He knew nothing anymore.

Lochlade sat in a hollow between Great Fell and Devil's Fell, a hollow that widened into a valley that wound among the hills toward the robin's-egg-blue horizon. Andria stopped on the ridge before their descent into the dale. Her heart beat hard with distress. She hadn't seen Lochlade since Beau took over the estate. So many bad memories mixed with such moments of bliss, times she would never forget as long as she lived.

On the lawns of Lochlade she'd taken her first steps with her mother, a bright and kind figure with a soft voice, holding her hand. She remembered her mother only in radiant yet soft shades, a distant shadow that sometimes seemed to speak in her heart—as she did now, giving encouragement. There was no echo of her father, and Andria thought it best that way.

The last person with whom Andria wanted to enter Lochlade was Rafe. A sigh trembled in her chest as she turned her head to look at him. His hard, closed expression held a tinge of despair, and she sensed his inner struggle. He looked so appealing, and she quickly quelled any softer feelings that tried to emerge.

"White marble is rather pretentious for a manor in the dales," he said.

"My great-grandfather imported it from Italy at great expense. He must have been a rather ostentatious character. My grandfather added on the columns and the cupola not too long ago. Like his father, he maintained grandiose schemes. Not all of them came to fruition, thank God. He had the succession houses built at the back and erected the east wing, which houses twenty guest rooms. I don't think all of them were used no matter how large a gathering. It's a drafty old pile, the upstairs corridors freezing in the winter."

"The park is beautiful," Rafe said as they rode on.

"In the summer there are swans and ducks in the pond, but as you can see, the water is frozen at this time of year."

"There's activity at the stables."

Andria shaded her eyes from the blinding glitter of the snow. She recognized Beau's tall figure and some of her father's old grooms. She wondered how they got along with their new master.

Rafe placed a hand on her arm, and she pulled in the reins. "What is it? Did you remember something?"

Rafe shook his head. "No, but a thought struck me. We can't ride into this territory and demand to find out what happened to our daughter. For one, Saxon's hackles will be up if we as much as breathe that he might be somehow involved in Bridget's disappearance. We have to show stealth, ask the servants, ask the farmers in the cottages. Second, Beau might send us away before we have found a clue."

"Nonsense!" Andria said, and flicked the reins. "He has invited me countless times to visit. I will tell him I've finally accepted his invitation, and that I'm trying, at the same time, to help you recover your memory by taking you around to familiar sights."

"I daresay he harbors only ill will toward me."

Andria gave him a quick look. "I daresay he does, but he won't throw you out, not while you're with me. Beau has always had a soft spot for me and is eager to do my bidding."

"Rather like a spider spinning a sticky web around you."

"That was uncalled for," Andria said. "You were always jealous of Beau, and evidently that has not changed."

"I can only go by the feelings from my last meeting with Saxon," he said, his voice cool.

"If anything, he has all the reason in the world to loathe you. You treated him with utter contempt in the past." Andria did not understand why she defended her cousin, but something about Rafe rubbed her raw, as if his very presence worked to destroy the wall of protection she'd built around herself.

She stole a glance at the lean, handsome face of her husband. She *shouldn't* look, but she could not prevent herself, as if just looking at him filled some deep need in her heart. She had loved him madly—once.

"Looks like Beau is just coming back from a ride," she said as they rode into the snow-covered yard. "How odd. He never rises before ten in the morning."

Beau noticed their presence at that moment. He stiffened noticeably, but immediately a smile curled his lips, and he hurried to help her out of the saddle.

"Dearest cousin," he said, and kissed her cheek. "My eyes have never encountered a brighter sight! I thought you'd forsaken me forever." He threw a hooded glance at Rafe, who did not move out of the saddle. "I see you brought the prodigal son."

Andria took in the splendor of Beau's attire, the gold velvet fur-lined cloak, the forest green embroidered wool coat, and that glorious white hair tied back with a velvet bow. Black velvet patches adorned various spots on his face. "You've just returned from a night of festivities, haven't you? And I thought you'd changed your habits."

Beau's deep brown eyes glittered with secrets, and his black eyebrows lowered in an air of conspiracy. "I'm rather a night animal. Too late in life to change that now."

"I'm surprised that the local gentry entertain much in the winter," Rafe said.

"Who said anything about locals? Mostly a dull lot. I seek my pleasures in . . . other places," Beau drawled, and slapped his gloves against his hand.

"Don't start an argument," Andria said, the old, familiar dread settling in her bones. "I abhor raised voices."

"I have no intention of quarreling, and if Derwent is with you, coz, he's welcome in my house—as long as he behaves himself."

Rafe smiled coldly. "I can control my urges," he said, and jumped down. His horse pranced around, but he caught the reins and calmed the animal.

Rafe had always had a good hand with animals, Andria thought. Obviously that had not changed. Rafe—always so graceful, so vital, so charming. She hadn't seen much of the charm, but the grace remained in his every move-ment despite the tribulations he'd endured.

"Rafe needs to see every place where he lived. Something from the past might bring back his memory."

Beau shot him a quick glance. "I doubt Rafe will find the memories from Lochlade very attractive. After all, you two were not happy for long here." He leaned very close to Andria, and she felt heat rising into her cheeks.

"Coz, I'm surprised he's with you today."

"No need to be surprised. He has to go into the past in detail, Beau. Let him find his own memories. And I'm not afraid of him."

"You are protecting him," Beau murmured. "Why? Hasn't he hurt you enough?"

Andria moved away as she smelled the wine on his breath. Beau's rather sordid life disturbed her, and she worried about the servants. Was he treating them well? And what about the estate? Did he care about Lochlade? She looked at the house, noting the details. There were no signs of decay—yet. She had once loved living here, and she worried about the estate as if it were an old friend.

"Don't concern yourself, Beau. I can take care of my-self."

"I can help you arrange for an annulment, Andria," Beau continued. "You deserve a lifetime of happiness with someone who truly cares for you."

She searched his face but could not read any hint of mockery. "I'll think about it, but I dislike the thought of being dragged through scandal. My family name would be soiled beyond repair."

"Happiness is worth a short-lived scandal, m'dear," he said.

Rafe came toward her, his face closed to any emotion. "Are you cold, Andria?"

"How remiss of me to make you stand out here in the cold," Beau said, gesticulating extravagantly. "Come inside. A fire burns in every room to chase the chill from our bones."

She had to accept his arm, but she could feel Rafe's gaze burning into her back as they walked toward the house. This visit would not have been easy had she been alone, but it was doubly difficult with Rafe in tow. She sensed his frustration, and it tempered her own worry about Bridget. They had to act fast, but where would they start?

"If you don't mind, Beau, I'd like to show Rafe from top to bottom of the house. It's the least we can do to help him."

"Of course. I am afraid, however, that he will find only disappointment at Lochlade. After all, his memories won't have changed."

Dread traveled through Andria. Beau was right. This was the house where she'd quarreled bitterly with Rafe. Worse, Julian and her father had died here, and Rafe had abandoned her as she stood in the window watching him ride away. Life made some odd turns.

"The truth is better than not knowing," she said.

Beau gave her a mocking glance. "Always so righteous. Sometimes you are rather a bore."

"Do not insult my wi—Andria," Rafe said with a flare of anger. "Unlike others, she has been helpful in my time of need. I don't take insults on her virtue lightly."

"She needs protection from you," Beau replied sharply. "I won't allow you to ruin her life a second time." He stood between Andria and Rafe, and all at once she had the impression she was but a pawn in a greater game. A strange memory stirred in her mind, but she couldn't capture it. It dissolved like a wisp of smoke.

"I have no intention of ruining her."

Beau straightened his back as if making a decision. "Andria, I hope you will stay for some time. I'll send someone to show you to your rooms, and after your tour of the house, I'll meet you in the red salon for a glass of wine before dinner."

Without waiting for an answer, he strode across the hallway and disappeared into a dim room.

"That's the library, the private den of all Lochlade masters," Andria said with a sigh, and peeled off her gloves. "You drank your share of brandy with my father in there."

A lackey she'd never seen before appeared to take their outer garments. "I'm Hector, and I've been instructed to show you upstairs, milady."

They followed him up the old, familiar staircase. Her great-grandfather stared down at her from the wall at the top of the stairs, and beside him hung a smaller portrait of Father, jowls and thick neck as she remembered them, his hair receding at the temples. His eyes seemed to follow her as she passed. If only he were here now to lend his support. Not that she had ever felt very close and supported by her father. He'd never had much time for her, not as he'd had for Bridget when she came along.

"A portrait of Father and infant Bridget used to hang here, but I see that Beau replaced it with one of himself," she said, disappointed. "Masters of Lochlade."

Rafe had stopped in front of the portraits. He paled as he studied her father's face. "I remember him. He's your sire, the previous master of Lochlade."

"You're right," Andria said as hope flared in her heart. "Mayhap you will remember a lot more as we walk through the house."

"I have some recollection that we rubbed along well, your father and I."

"You did. He disapproved of you many a time, but you'd gained his respect, and he wasn't an easy man to get along with."

The footman showed Rafe to a room at one end of the corridor. "It's freezing in here," Andria said as she entered the chamber.

"A maid will make up a fire, milady."

"Very well. Ask her to make up another fire in the next room for me."

"But milady, the master said that you're to stay near the master suite—"

"No matter what the master said, Hector, do as I bid."

The lackey left, and Rafe gave her a questioning glance. "What's wrong?"

"My old room adjoins the master suite. I have no desire to stay there again."

Rafe looked deeply into her eyes. "Come now, all our memories could not have been bad. We must have spent some blissful moments together in the master suite."

Heat rose in Andria's cheeks as she remembered their passionate nights. She had sorely missed them, but passion was not love. "I know of many wonderful times," she said honestly. "But they are moments that would be better forgotten."

Still, she could not deny that her body spoke of her longing to be touched and to be loved. She suspected that Rafe was equally touched by her presence.

SEVEN

Andria moved away from Rafe. His dark gaze, so deep and so thoughtful, disturbed her no end. She heard him sigh, a sound that spoke of loneliness and rejection.

"Perhaps 'twas a bad idea to come here," he said.

"Not at all. The answers are here if anywhere." Andria looked around the room, with its holland-covered furniture and its large four-poster bed. The chamber held an air of disuse, as if no one had occupied the bed or sat in the chairs for a long time. She lifted one of the covers, and the armchair, upholstered in fawn brown brocade, indeed looked new.

"Do you want to start our search now, Rafe? No need to spend any more time in this dismal bedchamber."

He nodded, his gaze searching her face. "What do *you* remember?" he asked.

Andria went to the door. "I thought my grandfather wasted funds when making this house into a palace with rooms where no one ever stays, or rarely stays. 'Tis no better than a hotel, in my opinion."

"It is a rather grandiose estate, but it is friendly, draws you into a vast embrace."

Andria smiled, her face stiff from smiling so seldom. "I'm glad you noticed. I give the dedicated servants credit for the welcome. They were always keen on trying to make this pile into a home."

They returned to the chilly corridor. "Where do we start, Andria?"

"How about the old schoolroom? Bridget spent many hours there. Mayhap we'll find a clue to her whereabouts." Even as she said those words, Andria did not believe they would find anything of value; she'd tried before. If there had been a trail, it would have long since disappeared. Her throat clogged with the familiar pain of loss, but her eyes remained dry. She had cried enough; she had no tears left.

They climbed the stairs to the top of the house, just below the attic and the servants' quarters. A wide door led to the schoolroom. The air was musty, and dust whirled on the floor in the draft from the landing.

"No one has bothered to clean in here for a long time," Andria said, and swallowed the lump in her throat. "I daresay Beau doesn't consider it important, as there are no children at Lochlade."

She crossed the room and looked out the window. As far as her eyes could see, a thin blanket of snow covered the ground. Touching the faded cover of the window seat, she said, "Bridget used to sit here and make up stories of what went on beyond the hills. She always asked me about the mysteries beyond the horizon. For a child of such tender years—she was only three then—she was bright and curious."

Andria knew that her heart was close to breaking yet again. "Listen to me; I'm talking about her as if she is indeed dead."

"Tell me more about her," he said, his voice strangely hoarse.

"She had a doll that her nanny made out of a knitted

stocking. She sewed a face and attached arms and hair of yarn. It was Bridget's favorite toy; she brought it with her wherever we went and even slept with it on her pillow. When she was alone, she spoke to it."

"Perchance she was lonely, didn't have many friends."

"She played with the children of the farmers at times, and we took her along every time we visited other families. She had wound all the servants around her little finger. They helped me search, you know, but there was no trace of her in the area. I'm hoping I overlooked something."

"She just disappeared, and no one saw anything?"

Andria swallowed, feeling the guilt of her failure to keep Bridget safe. She couldn't look at him. "That's right."

"Don't blame yourself, Andria. I suspect someone planned this to ruin you—or us. I believe that, especially after that servant Sally Vane was so eager to inform me of my identity."

"Ruin us? But you were gone at the time." She met his gaze squarely and found it difficult to say the next words. "Actually, some said that *you* had come back and taken her, but I know now it's not possible. You had sailed to Flanders by then."

"Unless I commissioned someone to act for me," Rafe said with heavy sarcasm.

She clenched her teeth together to prevent herself from speaking out in anger. "I refuse to believe you would stoop so low!"

He halted in mid-stride and gave her a long, haunting glance. "Thank you, Andria. You are brave for daring to trust me."

"You might have been arrogant and thoughtless, but you were never cruel, and you were always honest even if that honesty wounded me deeply on occasion. But no, you would not have kidnapped your own daughter. You would have confronted me and tried to *take* her, perhaps. You doted on Bridget and would never hurt her."

"I find the unattractive picture of myself hard to accept," he said, and lifted his arm with difficulty, as if it weighed a hundred pounds. He pushed back a strand of his hair that had worked loose from the leather thong at the back. He touched some dusty books in the built-in bookshelf. "She would have looked at the pictures." He let a fingertip glide over the spines as if trying to feel her.

Andria wiped her hand over her eyes to remove the disturbing view of Rafe by the books. She'd seen him in that position before. He'd been laughing and telling her about his own early years with a tutor.

"What's the matter?" he asked, very close to her now. She hadn't heard him move. Startled, she took a step back.

"Do I frighten you?"

She shook her head. "No . . . my memories frighten me. Memories of you."

He gently touched her face, exploring the contour of her chin, his eyes deep and caring. "Don't torture yourself. The past is gone; all we can do is look forward and make the best of it."

She could not answer, and she could not move away from his touch.

"You feel it, too, don't you? The attraction between us? It is like a burning current that draws me to you with a power that is irresistible."

"I know . . ." she whispered, "but I would be a fool to let it rule my life ever again."

"You're not the woman you were two, four, years ago. I'm sure you would always be in control of your destiny."

"Don't tempt me with your soft words. What do you want with me, anyway? You don't even remember what we had together."

"No, but I know we shared something special, something powerful and irresistible. Why else are we here together? Shouldn't you have turned away from me, like the others, after you told me the truth?"

She pondered his words in silence. God, he was right. When everyone else had rejected him, she'd given him another chance. "Call me a fool, but I felt you deserved to know the truth no matter what you'd done."

"Andria . . ." he said urgently. He tried to pull her into his arms, but she resisted the lure of feeling his heart beat against her cheek and the strong, familiar embrace that always had the power to make her happy. He'd had the power to make her forget the most difficult problems, some of which he had been the source of. In his arms, she had melted, and his touch had always had the power to make her flare into a torch of passion.

She warded him off. "Stay away from me, Rafe. I mean it. If you touch me again, I shall return to Stowehurst and never speak with you again."

He dropped his arms to his sides. "I'm sorry. I can't seem to help myself. Part of me longs very much for the tenderness of a woman."

"Find someone else," she said coldly.

They searched the empty cupboards and chests filled with scarred wooden toys and old blocks with painted numbers. Andria found a yellowed sheaf of charcoal sketches, some of them faces, some of them people working in a field. She laughed. "I made these! To think they have stayed up here all these years."

Rafe looked at each one carefully. "They are lovely.

It's clear you were a clever artist even then. I wish you would show me your paintings someday."

Flattered, she smiled. "There are some downstairs. I'll show you later."

They found nothing else in the room, and the nurse's bedchamber, adjoining the schoolroom, held nothing but a cot with a moth-eaten bedspread and dust balls on the floor. A childish drawing of a fat woman had been attached to the wall with a nail. "Wait! Bridget drew that of Nurse Franson."

Andria detached and held it reverently. "This might be the only drawing Bridget left behind."

"Don't speak of her as if she's dead."

"It is easier to not have any hopes. I don't know if I can go on hoping one day and having my hopes dashed the next."

"Yes . . . I understand. You must have suffered great pain as you searched for her. Is Nurse Franson still at the estate?"

"No, she died shortly after Bridget's fourth birthday, and we never hired another nurse."

For some reason, Andria could not take the drawing with her. It belonged here on the wall, as if safeguarding Bridget's bright spirit.

They continued their tour of the house in the guest rooms on the floor below. There was no hint of Bridget in any of the formal chambers, and Andria wondered if Rafe remembered any of these rooms. She grew hot as she recollected having made wild love on one of the beds, but he never gave the four-poster another look.

Every time he didn't remember some detail, she felt the pain of loss. Why torture herself like this? Let him explore on his own while she made a thorough search of the house. But he seemed to need her support, as if he, too, suffered. It would be painful to know he'd lived here and was unable to recall a single detail.

"I'm cold and thirsty. Let's go in search of a cup of tea. I'll introduce you to the servants."

Rafe rubbed the bridge of his nose. "I'm surprised that they don't know anything about Bridget's disappearance."

"It happened in the middle of the night," Andria said as she began the steep descent of the stairs. "I'd put her to bed myself, and she fell asleep instantly. The maid, Daisy, who slept in the adjoining chamber, heard nothing. Of course, it didn't help that she slept like the dead."

"Is she still at Lochlade?"

Andria nodded. "Yes, she's a parlor maid—unless Beau sent her packing. She had a good hand with children but lacked housekeeping skills."

They went through a narrow corridor on the ground floor and down some steps. The kitchen area had been built into the wing. The gray daylight flowed through large windows where china dishes dried on long wooden racks and towels had been hung to dry on a contraption hoisted to the ceiling. The servants working there looked startled at seeing gentry in the kitchen.

"We're not supposed to show our faces here," Andria said ruefully, "but if we don't, we won't have a moment to speak with the servants who have no duties upstairs."

"Lady Derwent!" the cook said, clapping floury hands to her bosom. "And milord hisself. Lawks-a-day, I thought I'd seen a ghost." Her plump cheeks reddened like winter apples.

"Mrs. Waters, I thought you'd already heard that His Lordship has returned. Gossip travels quickly in these parts."

"Aye, that it does, but I niver 'spected to see him in this house again."

Rafe folded his arms over his chest. "And why not?"

The cook's gray eyes shifted away. "Aye . . . that's a question, an' all," she hedged. She pounded the dough on the table in front of her. "Not my place to speak of it."

"Could you make us a pot of tea, please?" Andria asked.

"Th' kettle is always hot in this kitchen," Mrs. Waters said as she wiped the flour off her hands with a towel. She moved toward the hearth, and Andria followed.

"Tell me, Mrs. Waters, what do you remember of the day my daughter disappeared?"

"Went off in the middle of the night, din't she? I was fast asleep, and God knows I needed my rest for the next day, when life turned upside down."

"Was anyone acting in a strange way in the servants' hall?"

The cook shrugged her shoulders as she measured tea into a pot. "All of us cried, of course, and Daisy the most. She was right distraught, she was. Felt as if she were to blame."

"It's strange that she didn't hear anything. You would think that the intruder would have made a noise."

The cook nodded and adjusted her white cap. She placed cups and saucers on a tray. "Aye. I thought that maybe Lady Bridget got up during the night, and . . ."

"And someone took the chance to spirit her away." Andria's chest clenched as if held by a tightening rope. Who would have lurked in the night, ready to abduct her daughter?

Rafe stood by her side, and she longed to lean against him to find some strength. Dredging up the past only brought more sorrow.

"If that happened, it's likely someone had planned this

for some time and was only waiting for the right moment," he said. "Were there any new servants at that time?"

Mrs. Waters shook her head. "No, but mayhap one of the servants was paid . . ." Her voice faded. She put a plate of plum cake on the tray and started carrying it upstairs. Andria and Rafe followed.

A bright fire burned in the back parlor. Mrs. Waters put the tray down on a table by the fireplace. "The new master brought some of the servants from his old home. Some arrived before Mr. Saxon—Lord Lochlade—moved here."

Andria's neck prickled. "We need to talk to all of them."

Mrs. Waters sent a glance toward the ceiling. "Does the master know why you're here, then?"

Andria shook her head. "No. I don't see any need to worry him or make him displeased by questioning the servants. It would seem that we suspect him of foul deeds."

"*I* won't say a word, Your Ladyship." Mrs. Waters smiled. "We all miss you. Lochlade is not the same without you."

"Thank you, Mrs. Waters. Please send Daisy up now."

The cook left the room, closing the door softly behind her. Andria and Rafe exchanged worried glances.

"This is more painful than I thought," Andria said as she sat down and poured the tea. "I'm sure you don't recall Mrs. Waters's cake, but it used to be one of your favorites."

With a sigh, Rafe sat down and accepted the plate she gave him.

"You're very quiet, Rafe. Is something bothering you?"

"The fact that I can't remember is bothersome enough,

but I wish there was some more tangible clue to Bridget's disappearance."

Andria stirred her tea. She studied the portrait of a woman in an oval gilt frame over the mantelpiece. "Yes. I asked everyone the same questions right after Bridget vanished and got the same answers. No one really knows anything."

They drank their tea in silence while waiting for Daisy. Andria noted the changes Beau had brought to the room. He'd added a lion gold carpet and a harpsichord.

"Gold is Beau's favorite color," she said, speaking to herself.

"I think he likes gold in all shapes and forms," Rafe said coolly. He chewed on a piece of cake. "This is truly delicious, all moist and spicy." He stiffened, then dropped the cake onto the plate. "I remember something. It was summer, and we had a picnic by the river. I carried a basket, and Mrs. Waters had given us a whole plum cake for dessert."

"You ate half of it," Andria said with a laugh. Her smile faded as she studied his face.

"I remember that day clearly. We were very happy, laughed and teased a lot. I held you in my arms; we kissed." He paused and took a deep breath. "We did more than kiss. Your face was like a blushing rose, and just as guileless. We *loved* that day. You were moist and spicy like the cake, and so hot."

Uncomfortable, Andria looked away. She remembered the day clearly. "Yes. But it happened at the very beginning of our marriage, before our troubles began."

Uneasy silence rose between them, like a fog of unanswered questions.

"Where is Daisy?" Andria said at last as the silence

grew unbearable. "I'd better look for her." She rose, but Rafe took her hand as she passed his chair.

"Don't run away," he said. "There's so much between us. Good and bad, perhaps, but something that can't be swept away and ignored. I wish you would give us a chance to rediscover—"

"Stop this nonsense! You don't even know what you're saying, Rafe. *You* left me; *you* wanted our life together to end. You made that choice, not me."

"I must have been a complete fool," he muttered, his gaze filled with pain and questions. He got up and started pacing the room. "Damn it all! I wish I could remember, if only to get some answers to the questions in my heart. Even if I left you, things were never finished between us. I'm certain I carried you in my heart, perchance like a weight of unfinished business, but nevertheless, I think there was more, so much more."

Andria straightened her back and quelled any longing that tried to raise its head. "Believe me, it is all best forgotten."

"By Jupiter, woman, don't tell me what is best when I can't remember the most important things in my life."

"I won't discuss this again," Andria said frostily. "Let your memory return in its own good time. Until then, let the questions rest." She left the room, giving the door an extra-sharp tug.

Rafe felt like smashing his fist into the decorated side of the harpsichord, but why ruin the lovely instrument? He pounded the wall once, almost breaking his knuckles. Feeling caged in, he paced the small room. A white vista spread in every direction outside. He could jump out the window and run until he fell and the snow buried him. Frustration ate at him, every day taking a larger bite out of his patience.

"Damnation!" He finished his tea, but it didn't bring a soothing calm. On the contrary. He longed to throw the cup into the flames and see it shatter. He might have acted if the door hadn't burst open.

"Daisy left yesterday without saying a word to anyone except the scullery maid. No one knows where she went," Andria said, her face parchment pale.

"She knows something. She heard that I'd returned and left in a hurry," Rafe said, his frustration turning to excitement. "Someone in the village would know where she's gone. Her family would."

"Yes . . . let's ride down there before dinner."

"I don't know if I want to come back here for dinner," Rafe said darkly. "I daresay I'm not very welcome in this house."

"Matters not. For your sake, we shall tour every corner."

"We can come back another day."

Andria didn't answer, only hurried to the hallway, where she sent a footman for their outer garments. "Daisy is the fifth daughter of the Swans, a cottager just beyond the village."

Half an hour later they rode through Rowan's Gate. The sky had darkened, and snow had started falling. Andria evidently knew every part of the area, Rafe noticed. She chose a path through a thicket of rowans laden with frozen red berries and soon came upon a row of cottages surrounded by fallow vegetable gardens.

She slid out of the saddle at the last cottage. Rafe followed her up the narrow path and noticed the broken windows and sagging roof. The sound of crying children could be heard on the other side of the door as Andria knocked.

"Let's pray Daisy is here," she said, her eyes full of hope.

"Why would she suddenly speak now?" Rafe said, not wanting to ruin her hope, yet knowing she would be disappointed if this trail led nowhere.

A woman of middle years stepped outside, a wool shawl with many holes swept over her shoulders. Lank strands of hair drooped from the grimy mobcap on her head. She bobbed a curtsy, then closed the door carefully behind her.

"Can I help ye?" She peered first at Andria, then at Rafe. Her tired eyes widened in shock. "So, 'tis true, then, that yer still alive?"

Rafe nodded. "We've come to see your daughter, Daisy. Is she home?"

"Ack, she was home yesterday, but only for a moment. Said she'd found another employment but would not speak about it. Very close-mouthed she was."

Andria's voice wilted with disappointment. "Do you know where?"

The older woman shook her head. "Daisy is one for secrets, milady. I was that angry wi' her. My daughter is a gullible fool. No sayin' what trouble she's got herself in. She took her bundle of things and started walking. I don't know where." Mrs. Swan pinched her nose as if making an effort to hold back her tears. Her eyes grew moist and red-rimmed.

"I'm sorry you're worried about Daisy," Andria said. "You don't have a clue?"

"She walked east, towards the river." Mrs. Swan shook her head and pressed a corner of her apron against her mouth.

Andria patted her arm. "Go back inside, Mrs. Swan. No need to catch a chest cold."

"Why are ye lookin' for her? Was she in trouble, then, at the manor?"

Andria shook her head. "Not that I know. We wanted to ask her some questions about the night Lady Bridget disappeared."

"Ack, what a dark time that was! Makes me skin crawl just thinkin' about that night." She hurried back inside. "Good-bye, milady, milord."

Rafe said, "Let's ride after Daisy. There's a chance someone saw her." A chill traveled through his body. A gray cloud seemed to settle over the valley, a feeling of ill will so deep, yet so elusive, that he could not begin to understand it.

"I don't like this," Andria said. "Why would Daisy leave in such a hurry and not tell her mother about her new employment?"

Rafe helped his wife into the saddle and handed her the reins. She pulled the hood of her cloak forward to keep the snow from her face. "We'd better find her before we get lost in the snowstorm. If we don't hurry, 'twill be dark before we catch up with her."

If we ever do, Rafe thought. A cold wind snaked under his cloak and up his back. The cold wind of foreboding.

EIGHT

A lavender dusk had fallen by the time they reached the River Fynn. As cold and shiny as onyx, it flowed without any apparent movement toward the sea. Andria rode along a path lining the river, and Rafe followed. A lacy fretwork of ice patterned the shore, and dead grass crunched under the horses' hooves.

Rafe admired his wife's endurance and determination. She harbored a small flame of hope that their daughter was still alive, and she would not stop searching until she knew the truth.

Saplings and brush tugged at their cloaks, but the path widened as the river took a turn. Rafe rode up beside Andria.

" 'Twill be dark in ten minutes. We'd better find a hearth with a fire, and a dinner—somewhere. I really have no desire to return to Lochlade tonight."

Andria did not answer. Her horse slowed, then stood quietly. Rafe noticed a tension stiffening the woman, then the horse. Andria pointed to the shore of the river.

"Look, what is that?"

Rafe maneuvered his mount to the edge of the slope and saw a large bundle of rags—or clothes?—submerged halfway into the water. He noticed wet hair and a pale hand among the dead reeds. Damn!

"Don't look, Andria. I think someone has drowned." A dark chill filled his blood as he slid out of the saddle and jumped down to the shore. A woman, a young one at that. Her face looked innocent and lonely in death. He pulled her ashore. Her clothes weighed her down, and a bundle had been wedged between two rocks by the water. Mayhap her possessions would tell him who she was. He had an uncomfortable feeling that this was the missing Daisy.

"It's her," Andria said in a flat voice.

He hadn't heard her step down to the river, and he tried to shield her from the sad find, but she stared as if in a trance. "She was a kind girl, you know, always in a good mood and eager to help. I would dearly like to know what made her leave Lochlade without telling anyone."

Rafe struggled with the tight knot of the bundle. "It could be the most common thing that makes female servants leave their employment—unwanted pregnancy. Perhaps Saxon sent her away."

"We'll have to report this to the authorities."

"Yes, and the doctor will have to verify if my theory is true. I do hope I'm wrong." He unfolded the four corners of the fraying cloth that held Daisy's belongings. There were pitifully few: a bone comb, a pouch containing buttons and a cheap brooch, folded garments, and a doll. "She's a bit old to play with dolls," he said.

Andria gasped and ripped the sodden doll from his hand. "This is Bridget's doll! The one I told you about." She clutched it fiercely to her bosom, ignoring the water soaking through her cloak.

Rafe tried to take if from her, but she struggled. He didn't like the dazed look on her face, as if she were on the verge of fainting. She swayed, and he gathered her into his arms and held her tightly. "Don't take on so."

Her hood had fallen back, and he caressed her hair, feeling its silken smoothness. A deep feeling awakened in his chest, and a worry nagged at his mind, like some memory knocking. But he could not catch it, and it faded away. He could have cried as he stood on the threshold to *something,* something incredibly important. Damn his feeble mind!

He kissed the crown of her head, feeling the tremor going through her. He could feel the cold wetness of the doll through all the layers of his clothes. It seemed to give out a dire message: *Where I go, there's cold and death. Beware.*

Ridiculous! His loss of memory had made him fanciful. He could not let his impressions throw him into a wild chase that might lead him from Yorkshire to the ends of the earth.

"She's still alive," Andria whispered, her voice trembling.

"Please, don't get your hopes up," he said.

"Daisy Swan knew something. Why else did she carry Bridget's doll in her bundle? She was well aware that Bridget loved this toy."

"I'm sorry it's too late to question Daisy, but perhaps she stole the doll—a gift to her unborn child?"

"Your theory is too simple. Besides, Daisy was honest and hardworking." Andria sighed and moved away from him. She stared at the doll as if it could give her the answers she craved. "Why didn't she tell me she had this all the time I was searching for Bridget?"

He forced her to move up the slope. "Let's leave this dismal place. Who's the local justice of the peace? We'll have to report this find."

"Beau is."

Rafe gritted his teeth. "So it's back to Lochlade, then?

Seems that we're destined to stay the night there whether we want to or not."

Many candles shone in the windows at Lochlade as they rode up. The estate sat cupped in a snowy bowl where lights winked and played in a welcoming manner. Rafe realized he liked the house; it was the owner he'd rather avoid.

Andria shivered with cold as he lifted her down. She was still cradling the doll against her chest, and he wished he could soothe her pain, dispel her confusion with solid answers. Filled with frustration, he carried her to the door.

A fire welcomed them in the hallway, and he set her down on the hard settle in front of it.

"Dimsdale," she said to the tall, gray-haired man who greeted them, "please ask your master to join us."

The butler bowed, then disappeared into a salon from which sounds of laughter reached their ears.

Rafe got down on one knee and started pulling off Andria's boots. She protested feebly.

"Don't argue," Rafe said. "You need to warm your toes by the fire or they might fall off." He tried to smile to lighten the oppressive air, but she only stared vacantly at him. Losing patience, he took the doll from her stiff arms and placed it in front of the fire. She bent to retrieve it, but he barred her way. "Later. Let it dry."

He massaged her icy feet, and she leaned back, closing her eyes. For some reason, a deep tenderness settled in him, and he longed to kiss her—if only to dispel the drooping sadness on her face.

The tinkling of glasses and the sounds of male voices reached Rafe as a door opened and closed. He glanced over the back of the settle. Beau strode across the polished floor, his tall form dressed completely in gold cloth. The finest Mechlin lace frothed at his throat and wrists, and his hair gleamed like silver.

" 'Sfaith, what has happened?" he asked, and bent down to kiss Andria's cheek. Wine fumes wreathed in the air, and Rafe wished he had a glass to offer Andria. "Have you been involved in an accident? You're pale as a sheet, dearest."

Andria shook her head and pointed at the doll.

Beau turned slowly, and Rafe studied his face. Beau's black eyes narrowed imperceptibly, hiding the sudden glitter. Rafe read caution in Beau's smooth expression, but a moment later, he turned into a study of concern. "I say! Where did you find Bridget's doll?"

Before Andria could open her mouth, Rafe spoke. "Your erstwhile servant Daisy Swan is dead, drowned in the river. We found her not an hour ago."

Beau's mouth tightened. "Dead? Is this true?" he asked Andria. "I only heard today that she left without as much as a by-your-leave."

She nodded. "I recognized her immediately. She's close by the turn of the river at Great Fell."

Beau rubbed his face, and his rings gleamed—a message of great wealth. "I'll have to send my men out to fetch her. Dashed inconvenient. I had planned a dinner party in your honor, dear Andria."

"I don't know if I can eat at all tonight," she said, her head drooping.

"One of the maids shall tuck you in with a hot brick. You'll have to drink something warm. I don't want you to get ill." Beau placed his hand on her head, and Rafe felt an urge to push it away. He had no reason to be jealous. After all, his wife was his in name only. He swore under his breath and turned away as Beau slowly caressed her forehead.

"Lochlade, it's of utmost importance that we find out if Daisy was in the family way. If she was, it'll explain why she ran away." If that wasn't the reason, what was? Rafe wondered. He had a nagging suspicion that she might have known something about Bridget's disappearance.

"I'll have the doctor examine her," Beau said. "Some of the maids are very free and easy with their favors."

Rafe looked hard at the other man to detect any sign of guilt, but Beau only lifted his black eyebrows in a guileless manner, a silent challenge to dispute his reasoning. He moved briskly to the door. "I'll take care of the matter instantly. The girl deserves a decent funeral."

You had her killed, Rafe said silently. He had no real reason to believe Beau Saxon was involved, but his intuition, which had grown keen since he lost his memory, told him that Beau was a vastly different person than he portrayed.

Andria rose with difficulty, as if she'd grown old in one afternoon. "Help me upstairs, Rafe. I don't think I can bear to be alone."

He put her boots back on her feet, gave her the damp doll, and supported her slender form as they walked upstairs. But instead of turning into the east wing, she wanted to walk the length of the portrait gallery that spanned the length of the main building at the back.

"We forgot to visit the gallery, as we only explored the upper regions. I want to show you a portrait of us, unless Beau had it removed."

They passed long rows of ancestors, faces that Rafe had never seen or couldn't remember. At the very end, behind a velvet curtain, he came face-to-face with a portrait of Andria and himself. She sat on a chair dressed in pearl white satin, and he stood behind her, resplendent in midnight blue velvet and lace at his throat. The background was a park, and at their feet tumbled spaniel puppies.

"This was painted right after our wedding. We looked happy, didn't we?" she said in a mournful voice.

He nodded, unable to speak for the lump in his throat. It had happened in another time, perhaps in another world. However hard he tried, he could not fit in here, not unless Andria created a space for him.

She tugged at his sleeve. *"There* it is. In the corner." Her voice vibrated with tension.

He wasn't sure he could bear more, but he found himself at a portrait of the late Lord Lochlade and an infant. The child had eyes so alike his own, Andria's blond curly hair, and a round, stubborn chin. She clasped a striped kitten in her arms. "Bridget?" he croaked.

She nodded. "Painted in her first year. Father doted on her as he's never doted on anyone before or after. He was a rather hard, selfish man."

"She is not the child who died in my arms."

Andria gasped, clinging to him. "So it's true."

"The girl who died was dark and had a pointed chin. Bridget is a sparkling child, isn't she?" he said, choking. "Yours and mine." He noticed another portrait hanging beside that of Bridget. Shadows covered most of the small face, but he knew without asking Andria that this was Julian. The memory of the boy as he lay in his last sickness washed through Rafe.

"I know Julian. He's lived in my mind all this time but only now reached the surface. I know we were very close."

"Our world broke apart when he died. We weren't strong enough to deal with the loss." A sob muffled Andria's voice, and he caught her in his arms. "Rafe, *she might still be alive.*"

He squeezed his eyes shut, but tears burned behind the eyelids. He clutched her against his chest as if he would never let her go. In a haze of need, he tilted up her face and kissed her sweet mouth. It was soft, so sweet and yielding, and tasted of salty tears. He delved into her secrets, surprised that she'd let him. Her mouth tasted of honey, intoxicating him—only the beginning of a long exploration, if she'd let him. So hot and sweet and spicy at the same time. His heart pounded, and his loins tightened with arousal.

She slowly pulled away as his entire being caught the fire of need. God, he shouldn't have fallen for the temptation to kiss her. Now it would be impossible to forget her. He would taste that kiss over and over and caress her smooth skin in his dreams and her breasts through the material of her gown. He groaned with the need to know her more intimately.

"Don't," she whispered hoarsely.

"I lost everything," he said, "and I have little hope of gaining an ounce of it back. I didn't just lose you and the children. I lost my very life, since you were my everything. I sense that you must have been my everything—once."

"Rafe," she cried, and tore away from him. "Don't speak like that. You have no *idea* of the horrors we lived through, and I will never put myself in that situation again."

The sudden burning hope died in his heart, and he folded his arms over his chest. He could not look at her; he focused on Julian's serious face. The boy had been Andria's nephew, but Rafe had loved the boy as if he were his own.

"He was a quiet child, but clever," Andria said. "He pondered everything we said at great length, then supplied his own opinion. At an early age, he showed signs of skilled negotiation. You always said he would become a great politician."

Rafe laughed to hide his pain. "I did?"

Andria nodded and moved away abruptly. He followed her reluctantly as she hurried to the bedchamber she'd chosen earlier in the day.

A fire burned brightly in the grate, and a cup of hot tea stood on the nightstand. A maid had turned down the covers and placed a brick covered with flannel on the mattress. There was no sign of the servant.

"Do you want me to leave?" Rafe asked, uncomfortable in the intimate atmosphere of the room.

"You can help me untie my bodice at the back, and then I'd like you to leave," she said tonelessly. She discarded her cloak and kicked off her boots. He could not take his eyes off her form as she unbuttoned her wool jacket and removed it. The simple bodice of her wool gown had been laced tightly at the back, and he stared at her slender waist, wanting to cup it with his hands and draw her close against him. His loins ached with desire as he imagined the feel of her backside pressed against his hard arousal.

The gown was sodden from the knees down, and he wished she would let him undress her. He took a firm grip on his desires and slowly untied the knot at her waist. The warmth of her skin wafted out to enfold him, bearing with it her unique scent. His fingers grew clumsy as he loosened the crisscrossing ties. His breath caught in his throat, and his heartbeat escalated, driving all thought from his mind.

Her bodice spread apart, revealing the white lawn shift

underneath. He wanted to push his hands inside her bodice
and hold her breasts and hug her to him, to feel her
warmth and her softness. He *needed* to feel her against
him, like a starving man willing to eat moldy crusts of
bread just to stay alive. Loneliness, that familiar companion, came over him as he stared at her vulnerable back.

She moved forward and turned around, peeling off the
bodice, then crossing her arms protectively over her
breasts.

He could not move, his longing a harsh reminder of
the chasm between them.

"Are you waiting for something?" she asked uncer-
tainly. "Your room is next door."

For a moment he'd caught the glimpse of the swell of
her breasts under the thin shift, the nipples hard, so intimate, so alluring, so—unprotected.

"I'm waiting for you," he said, his mouth stiff around
the words.

"You're wasting your time." Her gaze slid away, and
she bit her lower lip as if searching for something else to
say. "We have been thrown together in our search for
Bridget, but that doesn't mean you can claim me." Her
eyes hardened with remembered anger. "After all, *you* left
me, not the other way around. Don't ever expect that I'd
be willing to take you back."

She went to the door and held it open for him. "Good
night, Rafe."

He gave her tantalizing form a last look of longing,
lingering in her beautiful but tragic eyes. He realized it
would mean a lot to him to see her laugh again. He might
not remember her, but part of him *knew* her deeply, and
he trusted that feeling.

"I'm not the same man as I was, Andria. That you must
understand. I also know that we shared something very

profound, and that no one can destroy." He lifted her soft hand to his lips. "I promise you one thing, I will somehow bring back the sparkle to your eyes before our dealings are over."

She shrugged. "That is a lofty goal, sir, but I won't ever let you past the wall of protection I've built around myself. I'm not that foolish." She pulled her hand away, her eyes hard, her mouth set in a firm line.

Rafe left the room, the disappointment deep in his heart. He sighed heavily to fortify himself. There were so many problems to solve; his attraction for his wife would have to be secondary.

He had his horse saddled and rode through the still, cold night to the inn where Nick and Serena were staying. They were sharing a supper of fragrant shepherd's pie and crusty bread as he joined them in the taproom. Warming himself by the fire, he swept off his cloak. Nick greeted him with a warm handshake and a slap on the shoulder.

"How are you progressing, Rafe? I was ready to send out a search party for you."

Serena moved, flanking Rafe on the other side. Her eyes were dark with worry. "I'm glad you're back safe and sound, and with no frostbite."

Rafe felt soothed by their concern. "You won't believe this, but I discovered that my daughter is not the little girl who died in my arms at the orphanage. For some reason, that servant Sally Vane told me a lie, and I want to learn who is trying to keep me from my family."

" 'Sfaith," Nick said. "What happened?"

Rafe told them about the events of the day and the discovery of the dead maid. "Andria showed me a painting of Bridget, and that's when I discovered the truth. However, there's no clue as to what happened to her, and with the maid dead—"

"Where is Andria now?"

Rafe described Lochlade and Beau Saxon's invitation. "I'll return to Lochlade and see if I can discover something else. Not that I have any desire to hobnob with Saxon or his cronies."

Nick rubbed his jaw. "You know, Serena and I ought to return to London immediately and see what we can learn there. Bridget might still be at Sir James's. I ought to see the portrait of the child before we leave."

Rafe nodded. "I believe that's a sound plan. There's not much you can do here now. I'll be fine, and I think Andria has enough compassion for my condition to allow my . . . presence until the mystery is cleared up."

He hesitated, hoping that was the truth. A new wave of disappointment washed through him. "One thing is clear: I won't leave until I have all the answers."

Serena gave him a hug. "The truth, even if it is painful, is better than not knowing. I shall pray for you, Rafe."

Rafe cherished the comfort of her embrace. "Pray for Andria. She needs encouragement as much as I do."

"I'll be back shortly with news; good news, I hope," Nick said. "We'll leave at daybreak, but let's go sneak into Lochlade to have a look at that portrait."

Rafe nodded grimly, and they set off toward the estate. It wasn't difficult to go in without raising suspicion, as Rafe was expected to be staying there.

But, to his consternation, the wedding portrait of him and Andria and those of Julian and Lord Lochlade with Bridget were gone.

"Beau must've seen us looking at the portraits earlier. He kept them in that dark corner, covered with velvet drapes," Rafe said. "Out of sight, out of mind."

Their attention was drawn to the window at the back of the gallery. The coals of a bonfire glowed hot at the edge of the spinney. "I think that's where we'll find the paintings," Rafe said. "We're too late."

They went outside, keeping to the shadows. At the site of the fire, they kicked around some smoking debris and found pieces of gilded frames and curled-up canvas.

"Why?" Rafe asked, filled with sudden rage.

"Your arrival in Rowan's Gate was a force that set new things into motion." Nick stared grimly at the flames. " 'Tis a rather large statement of Saxon's true feelings for you—and for Andria."

Not speaking anymore about it, they hastened back to the inn at Rowan's Gate.

Rafe said good-bye to his friends. Now he was truly on his own, but he knew he would have to face the past alone. No one could live it for him.

Andria felt restless after Rafe left her room. Part of her wanted to feel his strong arms around her, to feel safe in a man's embrace again, to feel the fire of her passion burn, but another part abhorred the fact that she was speaking to him at all.

She had not heard the door close to his room, which meant he was still abroad. Earlier, exhaustion had pulled at her, but now she couldn't find the rest she needed. Her thoughts revolved constantly around Bridget and what could've befallen her. She got out of the warm bed, pulled her dress back on, and rang for a maid to help her lace up her bodice. Perhaps she could join Beau and his dinner guests even if she wasn't dressed properly. Perhaps someone knew something about Bridget.

A very young maid curtsied just inside the door. Over her arms frothed pale blue silk trimmed with an abundance of white lace.

"Milady, Lord Lochlade sent up this gown hopin' you might enjoy wearin' it—if ye're wantin' to—if ye're feelin' better . . ." Her voice trailed off.

Andria took the gown from the maid and shook it out. A beautiful sack gown. She admired the expensive lace around the neckline and the sleeves and the fine silk ribbons threaded through it. She knew it would fit her perfectly. The silk shimmered in the light from the fire. Why did Beau keep gowns at Lochlade? It wasn't new, but no one had worn it before. He had no female relatives living with him. Curious, she decided to put it on.

With the maid's help, she got ready, her hair put up in ringlets and the luxurious gown spread over hoops. The blue color brought out the glow of her skin, and for the first time in years, she felt feminine and desirable.

She went downstairs, and the butler had a word with Beau in the dining room. Beau joined her immediately, his dark gaze glittering. He took in her appearance with one admiring glance.

"Andria, I'm so glad you're feeling better! You must come and sit by me, and I'll feed you morsels of delicacies."

"Beau, I didn't really come here to be entertained."

He slapped a hand to his heart. "You wound me deeply." He tucked her hand into his arm, and they moved toward the dining room. "Where's the prodigal son?"

"I don't know. I was resting in my room."

He patted her hand. "I'll take good care of you. The matter of Daisy Swan lies in the hands of the doctor now."

"We can only wait. Tell me, Beau, why do you keep elegant gowns here as if you're expecting female company—in my size?"

He shrugged. "Oh, that's nothing. I ordered a few of various sizes just in case some hapless lady would find herself stranded in the vicinity of Lochlade without anything to wear."

"Ever the gallant rescuer, eh?" she asked, smiling, and pulled her hand away from his grip. "It's just a little difficult to picture hapless ladies finding themselves without clothes on your doorstep."

"That conjures up delicious pictures in my mind," he murmured in her ear. "But mayhap I pride myself on being the perfect host." He gave her a wicked grin.

"You are a very good host," she admitted.

Disappointment shot through her for a moment, as she didn't see Rafe anywhere. Why did she feel like that? She greeted the guests in the dining room with a gracious smile, recognizing the foppish Mr. Yarrow and his plump wife, Lord Durand and Lady Hayes, and Mr. Cunningham, all dear friends of Beau. She had never socialized closely with any of the guests who resided in nearby estates, but she knew them all, and she remembered the unease she'd felt as Beau and his male companions had confronted her at the Quail and Hare.

"Andria Saxon," exclaimed Oliver Yarrow. "I had lost all hope of seeing your lovely form tonight."

She forced herself to smile. "I decided it would be rude to decline the invitation." Dimsdale pulled out a chair for her next to Beau's at the head of the table. Feeling uneasy as all eyes fastened on her, she took her seat.

Immediately, a bowl of fragrant salmon soup appeared before her, and hunger stirred in her stomach. She felt some of her strength return as she ate. The food smelled and looked delicious.

She was aware of Beau's dark eyes following her every movement. Why couldn't she like him better? He'd never been anything but polite and thoughtful in her company.

"Your kitchen staff is legendary," she said to him as she finished the soup.

"That's what I'd expect—only the finest cooks and the best ingredients. I have a reputation to uphold as the most influential peer in these parts."

If he could've patted himself on the back, he would have, she thought uncharitably.

"You hold a greater standard than my father did. He was more interested in hounds and the hunt."

Beau's face tightened, and she couldn't decipher his emotion. He set his wineglass down slowly and precisely. "I'm sorry to say that your father did not embrace the finer points of his heritage." His smile looked forced. "You, however, are everything that is elegant and good."

"That's kind of you, Beau," she said, and tasted the red wine by her plate. It went immediately to her head.

Ophelia Yarrow sat on her other side, and she watched as the older woman spooned the last of her soup gingerly into her mouth.

Ophelia's gaze darted anxiously from one face to the next as the men spoke of a past hunting meet. Evidently, the talk of killing animals made Ophelia nervous.

Andria leaned toward her. "Tell me, Mrs. Yarrow, have you been to Lochlade often since Beau took over?"

The older woman nodded and gave Andria an uneasy glance as if worried about starting a conversation. "Never during your father's time, Lady Derwent. I must say it's a lovely old place, and Beau has made a lot of improvements."

"Yes . . . I walked through the house earlier in the day. The only things that haven't changed in some way are the nursery, the gallery, and my old bedchamber. You know, the nursery looks the same as when I was a child." Her voice sounded unsteady to her own ears as she thought of Bridget. "I had a little daughter who—"

"We all heard about that . . . and the rumor is that you took her away," Ophelia said with a disapproving frown. She righted an ostrich feather clasped to her powdered curls and patted her mouth with a napkin. "It's common knowledge that you let her disappear."

Andria lost her breath at the sudden hostility. She wanted to lash out but held her tongue. Finding her breath once more, she asked, "I know suspicion runs high, but *who* claims that I am to blame for my daughter's disappearance?"

"As I said, 'tis common knowledge."

"Is that what *you* believe?" Andria probed sharply.

"No mother in her right mind would let a small child sleep unguarded at night. A lack of care it is, so I'm not surprised that she disappeared. You probably wanted her gone to put closure to the past. I'm sure she reminded you of Lord Derwent at every turn."

Ophelia's brown eyes flashed with dislike. She turned away abruptly, leaving Andria to ponder this blatant insult. Upset, she addressed Beau, knowing he must've overheard the conversation.

"You know as well as I do that Bridget was abducted," she said. "Why would anyone spread it about that I'm guilty of callously dispensing of my daughter?"

Beau gave her an encouraging smile. "You know how twisted gossip gets from the words of many mouths. *I* would certainly never think such a thing. I know how much you doted on Bridget."

His mouth twisted with distaste. "Ophelia speaks without thinking." He slipped a slice of venison onto Andria's plate as the footmen removed the soup bowls. "Taste this, my dear. I shot the stag myself only yesterday."

It crossed her mind that Beau had probably been out hunting when he should've helped her and Rafe search for Bridget. "Cousin, I miss Bridget terribly," she said, her throat tightening with rising sobs. "I'll find her even if the search will take me to every hamlet in England."

He leaned close to her and whispered in her ear. "I missed you while you were gone. I searched high and low for you, never dreaming that you would go to London working as a drudge in a millinery shop."

"I was looking for Bridget, a greater effort than most people made around here," she said with some asperity. Pushing the plate away, she waited until the next course was served, a saddle of lamb with jelly.

"I'll have you know that I made inquiries all around Yorkshire," he said, his voice a notch cooler. He took a gulp of wine. "There's no trace of the child. Perhaps the gypsies took her."

Andria felt the familiar agitation in her chest. She wished she'd stayed away from the dinner party, as it would only stir up old memories. "Speaking of children, you're the last of the Lochlade line, Beau."

"I hope to repair that soon," he said, his voice reclaiming the customary warmth. "I'm ready to set up my nursery. I'm now a man of substance and wholly respected as the new lord of Lochlade. The next step is a large family."

Andria had difficulty picturing Beau carrying a son on his shoulders, small, muddy shoes dirtying elegant and expensive coats. Beau was not the type to dandle infants on his knee, but maybe people changed—as Rafe seemed to have.

"But first I have to find a wife," he said smoothly.

A silken noose seemed to close around Andria, and she felt an inexplicable desire to flee. His dark eyes glittered suggestively.

"I'll tell you more about it later, dear coz."

To avoid further intimacies with Beau, she threw herself into a conversation with Lord Durand, at the other side of the table. All the time she kept an eye on the ormolu clock on the sideboard. Where had Rafe gone?

NINE

For the fourth time that day, Rafe rode slowly toward Lochlade, unaware of the brittle cold of the evening. All he could think of was Andria and their missing child. Was Bridget even now crying herself to sleep? The thought made his heart skip a beat, and he took a deep, shuddering breath. The thought of her suffering made him want to rave against the dark, starlit sky.

Riding over the hill, he saw the lights blazing in the windows at Lochlade in the valley. Under any other circumstances the light would've been welcoming, but he didn't look forward to stepping through the massive old portals once again. He wanted, however, to be there when Andria woke up in the morning so that they could continue their search.

He left Blacky at the stables and walked across the frost-hardened mud to the front entrance. Wisps of smoke from the dying bonfire floated past him.

Dimsdale let him in, and in the golden light in the hallway, Rafe could see Beauclerk leaning over Andria, who wore a beautiful blue silk gown. He was whispering in her ear, and she smiled. Rafe felt the talons of jealousy raking over his heart. Andria looked rested and alert, no trace of fatigue lingering on her countenance. She hadn't wasted any time joining the party, he thought.

As Beau lifted his head and looked straight at Rafe, something stirred to life inside Rafe. He recognized the old feeling of animosity. He didn't know why, but he knew beyond a shadow of a doubt that Beau was his nemesis. Whatever had happened in the past, Beau had been involved somehow. The bonfire was possibly another indication of that.

Beau's eyes narrowed as if he sensed the feelings and questions going through Rafe's mind at that moment. Hatred simmered between them.

"There he is," Beau said heartily, his hostility dispersing. "We thought you'd abandoned us again, Rafe."

Rafe caught himself before he would snap. "Not while there are answers to be found," he said smoothly. "Rest assured I'll find all of the answers. And fast."

Andria walked across the vast Oriental carpet. "Rafe, I know you're tired, but would you take me back to Stowehurst tonight?" Her eyes looked haunted, and the bile of jealousy he'd felt earlier evaporated.

He took her hand. "Gladly. Let's not waste any time."

Andria turned to Beau. "I'm sorry about my abrupt change of mind. Your dinner party was beautiful and the food excellent, but I'm exhausted."

Beau made an elegant leg. "Your wish is my command, Andria." He paused, smiling. "I know you'll come again. This is just the beginning."

As they rode across the dale in the silent night, Rafe said, "I thought you wanted to interview all of the servants at Lochlade."

"I wanted to, but . . . I found I didn't want to spend the night under that roof. Beau's guests could not see past my reputation, and I felt a vague threat." She pulled her cloak closer around her as if to protect herself from the memories of the evening.

"Beau seemed very disappointed at your decision," he said, his horse sidling closer to Andria's mount.

"Beau always has designs for others, but I'm no puppet whose strings can be pulled. He respects my wishes too much to insist that I follow his plans."

Rafe's thigh brushed up against hers for a moment, and he wondered if he should mention the bonfire and the destroyed portraits, but decided against it. She didn't need more disappointment. He wished he could halt their progress and take her into his arms. All he knew was that it would feel soothing and right. Her horse moved away from the intrusion of his larger stallion.

"Andria, please tell me, how was my former relationship with Beauclerk?" he asked cautiously. "Was there violence?"

"I doubt that very much. Beau doesn't have a quick temper; 'tis more slow burning."

"And more vicious," Rafe muttered to himself. Speaking out loud, he said, "I have a feeling he didn't take to me, as he won't take to me now." He knew the answer but wanted to hear her version.

Andria nodded, her gloved hands gripping the reins more firmly. "You didn't have much contact after our marriage, as Beau spent most of his time at his mother's estate at York, except for when Julian was sick. During that time you had to be away from Lockdale a lot since your grandmother was dying in Scotland. I don't know if you've heard that he offered for my hand in marriage twice when I was sixteen. I could not see myself married to him, and my father supported my decision. I've never felt more than brotherly affection for him."

"It must have bothered him no end. I fear he's a man of long memory, a man willing to hold a grudge."

"*You* would say that," she replied, her voice as cold as

the night air. "In the past you always talked about him with scorn and would not miss a chance to rub the fact in his face that you'd won my hand. He took it well, though. Never had a nasty word to say about you, though I suspect he did his best to stay out of our way. You were a hard, thoughtless man, Rafe. You didn't care whose feelings you hurt as long as you could gain your goals. Your selfish goals, that is. You had the power as the most influential man in the district, and you wanted the most desirable 'catch' in these parts—me."

Rafe flinched at her words. "But you still loved me? I know I must've loved you despite any ulterior motives."

"I . . . also saw another side of you, a side you rarely showed to anyone outside of the family. That was the loving, tender father and husband. That side, however, disappeared more every day toward the end, and I don't know rightly why. It was as if your mind was slowly poisoned against me, and you railed against everything and everybody."

Rafe struggled to recall any detail that would support her accusation, but his mind was as blank as a sheet of paper.

"Again I'm shown that I must've been a very arrogant man," he said quietly, a feeling of shame filling him. "Perhaps a man has to go through many hardships before he's humbled. I can't think of a more humbling experience than to find out that you have to start over, relearn the simplest things. But it also gave me the insight that in the eyes of God I was *someone* despite my loss of memory. Knowing that, I could more easily accept my situation, and my friend Nick has been a great support."

"You were never a God-fearing man, Rafe."

"God-fearing? Surely there's nothing to fear in God's

love, Andria. I felt that sustaining love during my worst times."

"You speak like a stranger." Her voice was filled with doubt. "I have suffered, and I can't see any kind of love in this world of darkness. The hardships have been almost more than I could bear."

"You say 'almost.' You're not broken yet, and new hope has sprouted. Tomorrow we continue our search for Bridget." Rafe wanted to impart some hope, whereas he had difficulty feeling any himself. "Damned if I give up," he said to himself. "We shall discover the truth, have no doubt about it."

At Stowehurst, lights shone invitingly in the windows. Rafe wanted desperately to be invited to spend the night, but Rebecca, Lady Stowe, had no intention of letting him inside her portals. Rafe took Andria's hand at the door, wanting to warm her cold fingers, but Lady Stowe pulled at her other hand.

"I don't like that you're traipsing around the country-side in the cold, dark night, my dear," Lady Stowe said to Andria. "And particularly not with the likes of *him*." She pointed an accusing finger at Rafe. "Remember this, you're not welcome here. How many times do I have to repeat myself?"

Rafe let go of Andria's hand reluctantly. He gave a small smile. "Lady Stowe, you're supposed to be my aunt, not my enemy."

"When you act as you did, don't expect any sympathy from me, Rafe." Her fine eyes were hard, her face pinched.

Without another word, Rafe turned on his heel and walked back to his horse. The door slammed behind him, and a feeling of utter loneliness came over him.

Getting into the saddle, he contemplated going back to

Lochlade to see if he could discover anything by eavesdropping at keyholes but decided he was too tired to proceed with any strategies. If Beau was hiding something, it would come out in due time, Rafe thought, and headed his stallion in the direction of the inn at Rowan's Gate. At least Mr. Brown, the innkeeper, was happy to take his money for a warm bed.

Hours later, he was tossing on the lumpy mattress above stairs at the inn. The room held little cheer, for the small fire in the grate had long gone out. Utter silence reigned in the house. Everyone had retired to their own beds. Rafe could only guess at the hour, since there was not enough light to illuminate the face of his watch. He knew that there would be no rest for him tonight, not with so many questions swirling in his mind.

He got up, stumbling across the floor in the weak light from the windows to a table where a bottle of claret waited for him. He poured a glass and gulped it down, hoping it would induce an hour or two of sleep. Rubbing his aching eyes, he went back to the bed and pulled the rough blanket over his body. Still clad in breeches and shirt, he felt the cold trying to rob him of the last vestiges of comfort.

Finally, he lost himself in uneasy dreams in which angry voices and twisted faces fought for his attention. He moaned, feeling the increasing cold gripping him. He fought to get back to a waking state, but invisible snares held him back in the twilight of changing nightmares.

A hard slam woke him at last, and he sat up, his whole body covered in cold sweat. He realized that the bang had come from a closing door at the inn, and he got up to look out the window. He saw nothing but the snow-covered fells and the winding black ribbon of the river. He turned around and became aware of the draft along the floor. His own door had been opened, even though he distinctly recalled closing it last night.

"Damnation," he swore under his breath, and lit the candle by the bedside. He pulled the loaded pistol he always carried from the chair where he'd placed it. No one had touched his weapon, but as he looked around the room, he saw a dirty bundle at the foot of the bed.

A shiver of foreboding went through him as he looked down at the bundle. A knife was sticking out of it, and as he studied the carved wooden handle, he recognized the serpent design. He'd carved it himself a long time ago.

Without touching the knife, he folded back the corners of the bundle and found a blood-soaked organ, a heart. His own heart seemed to stop for an interminable moment, and all he could think of was Andria. *Andria,* his mind cried in alarm, but the rational part of him recognized that the heart was too small to be human.

Trembling, he went to the door and peered out into the passage. No one stirred. For all he knew, he could be alone at the inn. A tunnel of cold air streamed from below, and he ran downstairs to look at the courtyard through the window. Nothing stirred. He returned to his room and closed the door, locking it.

Pulling the knife out of the fresh heart, he dried it on one corner of the bundle and threw the organ on the dying embers. Who had seen fit to send him the heart of some animal? Clearly, some kind of warning. Who had kept his knife all this time? And where had he lost it? The questions annoyed him more than the mysterious delivery.

He thought of waking the landlord, but to what use? He didn't want anyone to gossip about this grisly find, and the messenger was long gone.

He watched as the blood-soaked fabric of the bundle

caught fire, hissing. Was his enemy telling him that his heart would be cut out next?

Beau. Who else would take the pleasure of sending him such a gruesome threat?

Anger stirred within him, but no fear. If Beau or anyone else tried to as much as tweak a hair on Andria's head, Rafe didn't care if he went to hell for murder. The only thing that really mattered was to set things right with Andria, and Bridget, wherever she was.

A heavy feeling clenched his heart, and his eyes felt gritty from the lack of sleep. Where could he even begin to set things straight? Without a clear memory of all the things that had transpired in Rowan's Gate before he left, he could only fumble in the dark and hope to come across the pieces that would make his life fall into place.

He prayed that he would not be too late. As the first weak light of dawn fought for a toehold in the world, Rafe was saddling his horse in the bitter cold. The collar of his thick cloak turned up and the tricorne pulled low over his ears, he turned his mount toward Stowehurst.

The estate lay in deep slumber when he arrived. The only sign of life was the smoke curling from the chimney of the kitchen domains. He did not wish to be seen, so he circled through the copse to the opposite side of the mansion.

He found one of the back doors that lined the terrace unlocked and slunk inside. As the morning light grew in strength, he searched for Andria's room. After peering around two bedroom doors, he found her. Relief washed through him as he studied her delicate face, so still and beautiful in sleep.

Her hair curled in golden abandon over the lace-edged pillows, and her mouth held that curve of sensuality that had captivated him the first moment he'd met her outside the inn.

Unable to resist, he leaned over her, taking in the floral scent of soap in her hair and the much more intimate scent of her neck, that female something that made his heart beat faster. His deep-felt longings stirred, and he whispered her name silently.

She looked wholly vulnerable in sleep, and Rafe placed a tender kiss to her lips. *God, how he wanted her.* She stirred but did not awaken. Her mouth curved into a sweet smile, and her eyelashes fluttered.

He kissed her plump lips again, this time curving his hand around the back of her neck to support her head. Desire as thick and heavy as syrup flowed through his body.

This time her eyes flew open and widened in alarm when she recognized him. "What are you doing here?" she hissed. She tried to move to the opposite side of the bed, but he held her back.

"Shh, don't give me away. I don't want Aunt Rebecca breathing fire down my neck, but I could not wait to see you. There's no time to waste, Andria."

He captured her mouth once more, savoring the softness and the feminine allure of her presence. His blood pounded hotly through his veins as he retasted the sweetness of her, his tongue plunging wildly into her mouth.

To his surprise, she curled her arms around his shoulders. Maybe she was still only half awake and would regret her actions later. He didn't wait for that but gathered her into his arms, feeling the rounded charm of her breasts pressed intimately against his chest, her nipples erect and inviting.

He longed to tear the clothes from his body and hers and bury himself in her tight, wet sheath so deeply that there would be no denying their ultimate union. There was the obvious response in her every curve as she pressed herself against him.

Feeling her in every nerve of his body, he kissed her throat, her ears, and unlaced the top of her nightgown, trailing kisses along her breastbone, toward the enticing swell of her breasts.

As she clung to him, moaning softly as his hands roved over the full breasts, her belly, and the sweet hips of her slender body, he grew bolder. He tore the top of her nightgown and sucked on one hard nipple until she begged for release.

Her lips parted, swollen and ripe, her eyes dark and moist as she threw her head back and whispered his name. Aching with need, his hand moved along the crease of her closed thighs to rest at the apex of her femininity, on top of the fabric of her gown.

He pressed the heel of his hand against her softness, and she squeezed her thighs together as if unable to contain the pleasure of his touch.

She moaned languorously and opened her legs as if still in the throes of a passionate dream.

God, how he needed her. Meeting no resistance, he pulled up the hem of her gown and slid his hand along her silky flesh, caressing the impossibly soft skin of her inner thighs.

"No!" she whispered, but he could not stop. "No . . ." Her voice held little conviction. She panted softly against his neck as he moved higher, his hand ever more daring against her hot skin.

He slid a finger inside the soft folds of her secret place and felt the swollen wetness of her arousal. Wanting to please her deeply, he held back his own longing and kept caressing the slick area that appeared to give her the most delight.

He circled his fingertips around and around and followed the hot crease that invited him to bury his fingers deeply into her wetness. As he slid into her, she cried out with pleasure.

He held back, softly sliding his hand over her stomach and up to her breasts. He savored the full roundness anew, finding the nipples thrusting into his mouth as if seeking his touch. On fire, he kissed her, plundering the sweetness of her mouth until she was burning under him.

Again, his hand found its way down the infinitely soft trail to the center of her being. He slowly worked the damp crease and slid his fingers into her until she convulsed around him with an agonized cry against his mouth. She shuddered in his arms and fell limp against him, as if he'd pulled all strength from her body.

"There, my sweet, there," he crooned against her hair, even as his hard member throbbed painfully in search of release. He could not force himself on her if she didn't invite him. If only she would sweep aside the covers and open up to him, he would not wait a second to claim his place between her legs. He teased the tender feminine parts, and she climbed another peak quickly, her face flushed and her eyes glittering with passion in the weak light of the fire.

But she never touched him where he ached the most. She finally came to her senses and stared up at him with dark, shadowy eyes, now heavy from sexual release.

"Rafe . . . I . . ."

"Shh, my angel. I could not help myself, and I'm happy that we haven't forgotten the dance of love. It felt perfectly right to me, Andria, as if we've never been apart. I have not forgotten how to pleasure you."

Agitation shadowed her face. "I don't know how I allowed you to come to me in this fashion, but you took me completely by surprise." She tore herself free from his embrace and rolled out of bed on the opposite side.

Rafe gritted his teeth, for desire still pounded hard through his veins and filled his loins with fire. "I want you, Andria, as I've never wanted another woman." He smiled ruefully. "Not that I . . . remember, but my body does."

She bit her knuckles, evidently in a great turmoil about what had just happened. "Am I so wanton that your hands and your mouth would throw me into such a vortex of desire?" she said more to herself than to him. "A man who has done nothing but given me heartache."

"You were not fully awake. Besides, you're a sensuous woman, Andria. You need to be pleasured and fulfilled. 'Tis only natural."

"Only natural," she echoed, hardness creeping back into her features. She gave him a long, thoughtful stare. "This will never happen again, Rafe. I need your word on it."

Rafe felt the full brunt of his unquenched desire fight with the demands she was putting on him. "You cannot deny that you gave yourself willingly."

She pulled on a wrapper and held it tight over her chest. "Yes . . . yes, I did, but I was still half-asleep. You took advantage of my vulnerable state."

He smiled tightly, still fighting the heavy sweetness of his desire. "You woke up soon enough, Andria. As far as I can tell, your body was fully awake, eager with need."

Andria didn't reply, her eyes still accusing. He looked away.

"If we want to interview the servants at Lochlade, we'd better catch them before Saxon awakes. He would be suspicious of our motives," Rafe said briskly, rising from the edge of the mattress. It would be better to keep their investigation as quiet as possible.

He thought of the heart and the knife that had been delivered to his room and decided to keep that to himself. He could not accuse anyone at present, but he could not rule out Beau Saxon. More than likely, Andria would not be willing to believe that her cousin would stoop to such low threats.

At that moment he was keenly aware of the wall of questions that stood firm between Andria and himself. He watched as she dressed hurriedly, feeling that she was just as unreachable as the moon. *God, he wanted her.*

His fingers trembled with need as she asked him to tie the lacing at the back of her bodice. She held up her hair and tilted her head forward, and he could barely hold himself back from kissing the nape of her neck. He clenched his jaw and laced the bodice harder than he intended. Impossible woman!

"You are teasing me," he murmured. "Do you know how much your neck is calling to me?"

"Nonsense!" she snapped, letting down her hair and facing him with angry eyes. "You behaved abominably, and I'm only going with you because Bridget still ties us together. Don't read anything else into it."

"No, madam," he replied sarcastically. "From now on, I'll be a model of decorum."

TEN

Andria closed her eyes and felt his strong hands on her back as he laced her up. She relived those bright waves of ecstasy that his seduction had caused, and she blushed in shame. She had succumbed to his seduction, something she'd sworn she'd never do. She would have to honor her decision. Rafe was not going to occupy any part of her life as soon as they had discovered what happened to Bridget.

"Rafe, you've pulled the strings too tight," she cried as the bodice closed around her like armor. She turned her back toward him.

He heaved a deep sigh and loosened the strings. She glanced over her shoulder at him and noticed the neutral set of his features, but in his eyes she could read a storm of anger and pain, and hot desire—so hot, a wildness barely restrained.

She swallowed a lump of guilt in her throat. She didn't need this kind of tension on top of what she was already experiencing. "I hope we find a good lead today," she said quietly. "I slept terribly, dreaming about Bridget every moment."

He nodded. "I did, too. Nothing but nightmares."

She quickly fastened her hair into a simple chignon, flung a heavy cloak around her shoulders, and donned gloves and a hat that matched the dark blue of her habit.

The curling ostrich feather echoed the deep blue of her eyes, but at this moment she didn't care about such trifles. She needed answers.

Lochlade, like a large satisfied beast, seemed asleep in the morning light. They circumvented the park and the spinney at the back, approaching the kitchen entrance like beggars. At this early hour, Beau would still be abed, Andria mused. They left their horses by the gate leading to the snow-covered herb garden.

Mrs. Waters, the cook, greeted them warmly, her plump hands again covered with flour. The kitchen smelled of fresh bread and frying bacon.

"Mrs. Waters, we don't want to stir up a lot of questions," Andria explained. "We prefer to keep our inquiries discreet."

"That's understandable, milady. You can use my pantry for your investigation, and no one will be the wiser. I shall bring up a tray of breakfast for you, and you stay as long as you like."

Andria felt her mouth water in expectation and remembered how little she'd eaten at Beau's dinner table last night. "That would be lovely, Mrs. Waters."

Without a word, Rafe followed her up a narrow set of stairs to a small apartment above the kitchen. The front room was lined with glass jars of all sizes, and Andria recognized the jams and jellies that Mrs. Waters was famous for. A small desk filled with slips of paper, a straight-back chair, and a braided rug completed the decor.

"Please send up the maids who worked most closely with Daisy," Andria ordered.

Five minutes later, two young maids dressed in mob-caps and brown homespun dresses entered timidly. Mrs. Waters brought up the tray and served steaming cups of coffee for the visitors. Rafe stood silently behind Andria's chair, and she could feel his support.

"This is Mary and Dottie, the late Daisy's cousins, milady."

Andria gazed at the two fresh-faced girls, reading the apprehension in their eyes. They curtsied. "Don't be afraid. Lord Derwent and I are looking for some answers about our daughter, Lady Bridget, and as you might know, Daisy spent lots of time with Bridget. You must've learned that Daisy is no longer with us."

Their eyelashes fluttered, and their mouths drooped. "Yes, milady."

"Can you tell us anything about Daisy's last days? Or anything at all about Bridget?"

Mary bobbed another curtsy. "Daisy was that fond of the li'l girl, milady. Always said she couldna wait to have children of 'er own."

"Did Daisy speak to you before she left Lochlade?" Rafe asked, his voice soft so as not to frighten the girls.

They shook their heads in unison. "No, milord. She didna mention leavin'; she was just gone."

"What about the time of Bridget's disappearance. Did you see anything strange or out of the ordinary?"

Again they shook their heads. Mary spoke for both of them. "No, milady. We slept through the night, didn't we, Dottie?"

Dottie nodded. "But Daisy was gone that day for a few hours, milady. Said she'd gone 'ome to see 'er mum but 'twusn't 'er half-day off."

Andria and Rafe exchanged glances.

"Daisy never spoke of her visit to her mother?" Andria continued.

"No, milady," Dottie replied. "She didna talk much of 'er family, and she didna like to gossip."

"Is there anything you could tell me about Bridget?" Andria took a deep breath to still her racing heart.

"She wus as 'appy as a lark, milady. Didna know she wus leavin' us, I'm sure," Mary said. "The authorities asked us lots of questions after Lady Bridget disappeared, but we didna know anything."

Andria nodded. "Yes, I know that, but we're trying to discover now why Daisy left so abruptly and the reason she left. She may have known something she didn't speak about when Bridget disappeared."

Mary nodded. "Aye, milady." She and Dottie exchanged worried glances, and Mary took a deep breath. "We figured she 'ad a lover, secretlike. She wouldn't talk about 'im to an'one."

"She seemed 'appy," Dottie added. "Sang as she did 'er chores—until the end."

Rafe bent over Andria's ear. "We must return to cottage row to question Mrs. Swan."

"Yes," Andria said. She thanked the maids as a wave of frustration swept through her. Everyone had been questioned before, but maybe they had missed something.

Patiently, they met with every maid and groom in the house, but came no closer to solving the mystery of Daisy's death or Bridget's disappearance.

When the last footman had left, Andria finished the by-now-cold coffee and bit into a buttered slice of bread. "Let's see Mrs. Swan again. I want to know why Daisy visited her the day after Bridget disappeared."

They thanked Mrs. Waters and left by the back door. As they went to the gate to fetch their horses, they ran across Beau. Andria was surprised to see him this early in the morning, and she felt uneasy about sneaking around his house without his knowledge.

He wore a splendid riding coat of emerald green wool

that contrasted with his dramatic pale hair to perfection. He swept off his tricorne and bowed, not showing any surprise at all.

"Cousin, you were never an early riser," she greeted him.

"Nothing like a ride in the cold to wake you up," Beau said smoothly. "I saw your horses from the spinney and came to investigate."

Andria waved her fur-lined gloves. "I . . . forgot these last night," she said, and Mrs. Waters kindly offered us an informal breakfast. "You know I wouldn't turn down an invitation to have some of her fresh rolls with jam." Andria kept her voice light. "I've never tasted anything that comes that close to heavenly."

Beau's eyes were sharp. He showed no traces of having drunk too much at the dinner table last night. He paused before speaking, studying them with narrowed eyes.

"Her rolls are superb, but I'm not sure I would use the word heavenly. I'd reserve that for . . . tasting a woman's lips."

Andria blushed and turned her face away. She wondered why she'd chosen to lie to Beau; lying made her uncomfortable. It wasn't as if she suspected him of ill deeds. He hadn't been anywhere near Lochlade when Bridget disappeared.

"I presume you don't want to embarrass your cousin," Rafe said tersely.

"Far from it. Is she not a mature woman who knows very well of what I speak?"

"That's neither here nor there," Rafe replied. "She's a married lady."

Beau shrugged. "She doesn't seem to think that, Derwent." He turned to Andria. "I was disappointed when you left early last night. As it is, I haven't had the chance to really have an . . . intimate chat with you."

Andria gave him a smile that felt false. "There'll be plenty of opportunities for a chat, as I'm back in Rowan's Gate."

Beau lifted his eyebrows in inquiry. "For good, I hope?"

Andria could not answer. There had been no rest or respite since she returned home, only the opening of old wounds. Seeing Rafe again had caused nothing but new problems.

He helped her into the saddle, and her mare pranced around as if nervous in the company of Beau's immense stallion.

"Come to the front door next time, Andria. You can taste Mrs. Waters's rolls at my table and also ease my loneliness with your lovely presence." Beau bowed gallantly, and Andria threw a glance at Rafe, who wore a thunderous expression.

Rafe was pointedly excluded from the invitation.

Andria said good-bye to her cousin and, with Rafe at her heels, turned her mare down the lane toward the cottages on the outskirts of the estate.

Rafe finally broke the uneasy silence. "He wastes no time flirting with you. Andria, I know you'd like to pretend that you're free, but you're still my wife—"

"Enough!" Andria threw him an angry glance. "*You* left me. That took away any sense of obligation that I might feel toward you, Rafe. The bonds that were forged can be undone, and I will see to it that they are."

"You're speaking in haste, Andria. I didn't leave without a reason, and you know the truth of that. Don't play the wounded innocent with me."

She noticed that he seethed with anger. "It's too late

for a display of jealousy. You have no claim to me any longer."

"As long as you're my wife, I have a claim to you." Rafe's eyes were black with suppressed rage. "You're the Countess of Derwent, and I expect you to act in accordance with that."

"There. Now I recognize the old pompous, arrogant bastard that you are. You've only employed your new tactics of gentleness to lull me into compliance."

"Don't be childish," he snapped. "I have no reason to play games. I want to know what happened, and I want to discover who my enemy is."

Andria's breath caught in her throat. "Enemy? That's a very strong word, Rafe. Who would be your enemy in these parts?"

"The same person who stole my child," he said, regretting his outburst. He couldn't tell her about the gory "gift" he'd received in the night.

She nodded. "Yes, but you've known the people all of your life, and so have I."

"Some don't support the same code of ethics as you do, Andria."

She nodded. "There's something horrible going on."

They rode in silence along the rutted lane of frozen mud. Clumps of snow fell from the tree branches as they progressed. The sun was creeping over the fells, and the sky held that clear, crystal blue of winter.

Smoke rose from chimney stacks in the cottages, and they halted in front of the Swans' simple abode. Rafe waited in the saddle as Andria went to knock on the door.

Mrs. Swan appeared, her face pinched and pale. Her nose sounded clogged with tears.

"I'm sorry about your losing Daisy," Andria said softly,

placing her hand on the woman's thin arm. "Daisy was a good girl."

Mrs. Swan pulled a threadbare green shawl more closely around her shoulders. She sniffed, wiping her red nose on a cloth in her hand. "Why are ye 'ere?"

"We're trying to find out what really happened to Daisy, and we also believe that there's a connection between my daughter's disappearance and Daisy's death," Andria said. "I've been asking questions at Lochlade, and the servants claimed that Daisy disappeared for a few hours on the day Bridget was found missing. The maids said she'd gone home, and I wanted to verify that with you."

Mrs. Swan's brow furrowed in thought. "That was so long ago, Lady Derwent, but I doubt Daisy came 'ome. She 'ad a life of 'er own. She rarely came 'ere on account that she didn't get along well with her father."

"I see." Andria thought of that statement and wondered where Daisy spent her time off from work. "You don't know where she might've gone?" She took a deep breath and plunged in. "Some say she might've had a lover, Mrs. Swan."

Mrs. Swan's lips drooped downward. "That would be 'er business, milady. She wus old enough to be thinkin' of romance, wasn't she? But she didna tell me or an'one abouts 'ere about it."

Andria nodded. "I understand. Then it wasn't any of the local lads, or someone would've noticed."

"Aye, can't keep nubbut from the people 'round 'ere. Daisy knew a lot o' people, though. She was right friendly with Widow Bostow's son, ye know, over by the river, the widow wot lost everything. But 'e is a young'un, lots younger than our Daisy. I don't think she would've 'ad a romantic attachment to 'im."

Andria looked at the long-suffering face before her and the pinched lips. She pulled out a small purse and extracted some coins from it. "Here, Mrs. Swan, buy something for the children."

Mrs. Swan took the coins and quickly inserted them into her bodice. She bobbed a curtsy and went into the cottage, closing the door softly.

Andria looked at Rafe. "What do you make of that?"

"Daisy's past becomes more mysterious every day. But I suppose we should follow every lead. The young'un might know something about Daisy that we don't."

Rafe got down to give Andria a leg up into the saddle. She felt his touch on her skirts as surely as if a brand had burned her bare skin. Heat filled her belly with a longing that almost overwhelmed her. His touch had always had the power to ignite her blood with passion, and that hadn't changed even if everything else had. His hand lingered on her boot, and he looked up at her, his gaze holding her own as if reading the simple truth of her feelings.

He turned away, his jaw tense and his mouth hard. "Let's find the Widow Bostow. Do you know where she lives?"

Andria nodded. "Yes, down by the River Fynn, some ways out of the village. She used to have a lovely estate, inherited after her husband. Not that big, but charming. At some point she was well off, but I don't know what has happened to her, because she seems to barely eke out a living on the premises. The Bostow farm was always abundant. She has lost all sparkle, and all of her gowns are out of fashion, which is strange, as she always wore the most fashionable attire."

"Young or old?"

"Of middle years," Andria replied. "Her only son must be around sixteen now. He should be off to Eton or some other school, but he's still at home, which makes me believe she doesn't have the funds to send him away."

Rafe nodded. "Yes, that would cost a packet. What's the boy's name?"

"Robert. Not exactly the friendly type. He spends a lot of time to himself. It makes me wonder how he met Daisy and struck up a friendship with her."

"She would've passed along the river to head back home. They could've met just about anywhere around here."

"Yes, you're right," Andria replied, and urged her mare into a gallop. She wanted answers.

Fifteen minutes later, they rode along the stand of poplars lining the drive to the Bostow farm. The sun was beginning to melt the snow on the ground, and the bright sunshine brought a sense of invigoration. Andria felt a bit more optimistic. At least they were doing something to find the answers they needed.

She glanced over at Rafe riding next to her and noticed how naturally they flowed together. The old stride had not disappeared with the time they'd spent apart.

Rafe caught her glance, and he clearly sensed the direction of her thoughts. He smiled, and she could not stop herself from returning the smile. The man always had been devilishly handsome.

"You're got pink roses in your cheeks," he said, reaching over but not able to touch.

"There's nothing that I like as much as a ride in the crisp air of late fall. I just wish this was a ride of pleasure, not one of urgency and fear."

"You shall have your ride of pleasure soon," Rafe said, wishing he could wipe that look of anxiety from her eyes. "All your questions will be answered. We won't give up until we know the truth."

They pulled up outside the front entrance; snow still lay in shallow drifts. No one had seen fit to remove it, Rafe noted. And no one came out to take care of their horses. The place held an air of abandonment. He glanced at the narrow windows on the second floor but couldn't see any movement behind the curtains. The old gray stone house held the air of someone rejecting any kind of intrusion by strangers.

"I doubt we're welcome here," Andria said as she slid off her horse.

Rafe tied both mounts to the shrubs lining the drive and knocked on the door. The sound echoed within. He knocked again when nothing stirred. They had almost given up when the heavy oak door opened a crack. To Rafe's surprise, the widow herself stood on the threshold, and as his astonishment deepened, he realized he knew the woman well, or had known her.

She was tall and proud, her black hair swept back into a severe chignon and her black gown covered with a great many shawls in varying shades of gray. Her eyes held lively intelligence, and her face lit up as she recognized Rafe.

"Rafael Howard, what a great surprise!" She glanced at Andria. "And Lady Derwent. I'm so pleased to see you back together. It takes a load off my mind to know that you've made peace with the past."

Rafe and Andria exchanged uneasy glances.

"Mrs. Bostow—" Rafe began.

"Mrs. Bostow? When did we ever stand on ceremony? It's Phoebe to you, Rafe." She held out both hands to him, and he clasped them.

"It's been a long time, Phoebe." He kissed her cheek. "How are you?"

She didn't respond immediately. She took Andria's hand and pulled her inside. "We never had a chance to get well acquainted, Lady Derwent. But your husband was a great help to me in my time of need. Not that it worked out as planned, but I'll never forget his kindness."

Rafe had no idea what she was talking about, and Andria looked puzzled.

"I lost my memory in the battles," he explained as they walked through the gloomy hallway. Lighter squares on the paneled walls spoke of paintings missing. Probably sold to raise some funds, Rafe thought.

"Memory?" Phoebe's voice held a tinge of surprise. "You don't remember me, then?"

"Yes, I do. As soon as I saw you, I remembered you, but I don't recall the past or our business in the past."

Phoebe gave him a warm smile. "You were a true friend, Rafe. You helped me with the finances of the farm and to apply for extensions on the loans, but in the end, something went wrong, and I lost everything."

"Everything?" Rafe racked his brain to remember the details and was filled with an uneasy feeling.

"Well, I finally had to sell. Robert and I are allowed to stay here until the end of the year, as the new owner could not take over until then."

Rafe's unease intensified. "Who is the new owner?"

"Oh, he was very kind and helped me through all the legal matters. Oliver Yarrow. You know him, or used to know him when you could remember."

"No friend of mine," Rafe said, his suspicions rising.

"Used to be," Phoebe repeated. "He owns another estate. Birchdale, across the mountains. A very well set family."

She led them into a parlor where a meager fire burned in the grate. The old carved furniture stemmed from a long-gone time, and Rafe thought they would fetch a good sum on the market if she were to sell.

"You still own everything inside the house, don't you?" he asked, suddenly knowing the answer.

"No," she said, shaking her head. "Yarrow bought everything, and the funds barely covered the debts, but at least we are debt-free. Robert shall eventually find a placement in London, where we have connections, and I have an elderly relative who needs a companion." She smiled wryly, but the smile never reached her eyes. "We shan't starve."

Rafe watched Andria look around the room, and he knew what she was thinking. "How did it ever get like this, Phoebe? The farms were prospering—I do remember that—and I know you're an intelligent woman."

Phoebe's gaze darkened, and two spots of red rose in her cheeks. "I'd rather not talk about it. You don't remember, but my late husband had some . . . problems. It affected us financially in the end."

Andria looked at Rafe, and he noticed that she shared his uneasy feeling.

"Were Yarrow and your husband friends?"

Phoebe hastily shook her head. "Once. I'd rather not talk about it. Robert and I shall manage just fine." She plucked at the fringe of her shawl with long, pale fingers.

Andria spoke, placing a comforting hand on the older woman's arm. "I'm sorry about your hardships. We're here to ask if you know anything about Daisy Swan, one of the maids at Lochlade. She was found dead yesterday in the river, and her mother indicated that she might've made friends with Robert. As you probably know through rumors, my daughter disappeared two years ago, and we're trying to account for Daisy's absence from Lochlade on the day after Bridget was taken from her bedroom."

Phoebe put a hand to her mouth. "I don't know how

you've managed to get through this horrible ordeal, Lady Derwent."

"I called on strength I didn't even know I had. We're trying to find out exactly what happened that afternoon. Could we speak with Robert?"

"Robert comes and goes like a specter," Phoebe said with a sigh. "Most of the time I don't even know where he spends his days. The boy needs the guidance of a firm male."

She left them in the parlor to go in search of her son.

"There's something hidden, some deed that isn't right," Rafe said. "Something happened, and Phoebe was forced to sell the place. Yarrow doesn't strike me as a helpful or kind person."

"You're basing that on what?" Andria asked with some asperity.

Rafe said nothing, for he didn't have any concrete facts that would support his claim, only that uneasy feeling and the ill will that Yarrow had shown him at the inn when he first arrived. He knew that a lot went on in Rowan's Gate under the surface, but it was too early to come out with any kind of accusation.

They waited in silence, and Rafe admired the carved wooden mantelpiece that badly needed a cleaning. Some craftsman had put all of his skill and effort into creating it. The rest of the room looked shabby, with its peeling plaster ceilings and dirty windows.

After a few minutes of uneasy silence, the boy entered with his mother in tow. He looked at Rafe sullenly, his whole body tense and ungainly. He had his mother's dark looks and tall frame but none of her charm, as far as Rafe could determine.

"Robert," he said, and shook the boy's hand, a grip that

reminded him of a dead fish. "Did your mother tell you why we're here?"

He nodded. "Yes, but I cannot help you. I used to draw by the river, and Daisy and I struck up a friendship. She always walked home the same route on her days off."

"Didn't she tell you anything about her life?" Andria asked, and went closer to the boy, who stood uncertain in the middle of the room.

"She . . ." He hesitated. "She didn't much like working at Lochlade, but she said she wouldn't have to stay there for very long. She had powerful friends, she did."

"Male friends?" Rafe asked.

The boy looked away. "I know she had friends who . . . took her places. She was privy to many things, but she didn't tell me any details. I know that she had a great deal of money; she sometimes gave me some."

"Robert, do you know about any unusual goings-on in Rowan's Gate?" Rafe asked.

The boy's mouth fell open. "Unusual? What do you mean?"

"Secrets? Strangers lurking, that sort of thing. We're trying to discover what happened to our daughter, Bridget, who disappeared from Lochlade."

"I heard about that," Robert replied, "but I don't know any details, and as far as I know, there were no strangers around at the time. I do remember that Daisy was fond of the little girl; she spoke of that to me." Robert scratched his head. "Not that Daisy was exactly suitable for a nursemaid," he added lamely.

"Why?" Andria's face paled.

"Daisy carried on with friends, older friends," Robert said reluctantly. "I don't know any more than that. She didn't tell me anything, but I have eyes in my head."

"Who? Can you tell us any names?" Rafe wanted to shake the lad.

Robert glanced from one to the other and gave his mother a long, lingering look of fear. "They were concealed in cloaks. I don't know who they were."

"How did you see them?" Andria asked.

"Daisy met up with them by the river, and then they were gone, all of them. Daisy always came back with a packet of money, and she told me she was saving for the day when she could leave Lochlade and make a new life for herself elsewhere. Always wanted to go to London. We often spoke about that." He glanced at his mother once more. "And we'll be going there, whereas Daisy will forever remain here."

A shiver went through Rafe. He marveled at Robert, so gangly and youthful but so old of mind. Rafe knew the boy hadn't told everything, but he read the stubborn line of the youngster's jaw. If Robert was holding something back, they would never be any wiser.

"Do you recall the afternoon after my daughter disappeared?" Andria asked. "Did you see Daisy that day?"

Robert seemed to be thinking hard. He shook his head. "I don't recall if I did. I might've, but I doubt Daisy would've sought me out in view of what happened to your little girl."

Rafe felt he was speaking the truth. He took Andria's elbow. "I doubt that we'll find any more clues here," he said.

He bowed over Phoebe's hand and kissed it. "We'll be back under brighter circumstances," he said.

"You're always welcome here, Rafe; you know that. I treasure your friendship." Phoebe kissed Andria on her cheeks. "I expect to see you, too."

152   *Maria Greene*

They left the house. "Where do we go now?" Andria asked.

"I want to know the names of Daisy's powerful friends," Rafe said. "I think one of them killed her."

ELEVEN

"We've reached a wall," Andria said with a sigh as they rode away from Widow Bostow's farm. "I searched all the inns in every hamlet from here to Glasgow, and as I traveled to London, I asked for information at every inn along the way. No one knows anything about Bridget or claims to have seen her."

"Perhaps because she's still near here?" Rafe commented, his heart squeezing with worry. "She could be hidden right under our noses, but I think the person who knows the most was the servant in London who recognized me as Lord Derwent. Also, Bridget could've stayed concealed in a carriage wherever she went."

"Do you think there's a chance of finding that servant?" Andria could not conceal the hope in her voice.

"If Nick can't find her in London, no one can. He has vast contacts. He'll discover the truth even though the woman disappeared. The people at the orphanage may know what became of her."

"It's our best hope," Andria said, her voice quivering.

"I wish I could assure you of a happy outcome," he said, feeling totally helpless, which he did not like in the least. He had left Andria, destroying all of their lives.

"Andria . . ."

She turned in the saddle to look at him, her eyes huge with pain.

"I'm sorry," he said, and yearned to pull her into his arms to comfort himself, and her.

She didn't reply, and he knew his apology had come too late.

After an awkward silence, she said, "I have a portrait to complete. I'm returning to Stowehurst to think about all the information we gathered, however meager, and about the next step."

Unable to think of something that would keep her in his presence, Rafe watched as she took the left fork in the road by the river.

Andria missed Rafe's comforting presence as she stepped into the warm interior of Stowehurst. She realized he'd lent her more steady support now than he ever did in their earlier times.

She handed her cloak and hat to a footman and warmed her hands by the fire that blazed in the large marble foyer. Having thawed her fingers, she climbed the curving staircase to the salons upstairs.

She heard the sound of Rebecca's laugh from the Sea Grotto, a chamber that had gotten its name from the masses of emerald and blue draperies and the sea green carpet on the floor. Paintings of shell motifs and ships in full sail adorned the pale green walls.

Beau sat on one of the sofas, a sharp contrast to the blue and green in his flame-colored coat. To Andria's surprise, she saw Derek sitting next to Rebecca. Since his accident, Derek preferred to stay away from every kind of social situation.

"Andria," Beau said, and rose to kiss her hand. He drew

her down on the sofa beside him and piled pillows behind
her back as if showing his support. "You look pinched
and cold. I don't understand this traipsing around the
county with your useless husband in tow."

Andria held back an angry retort. "I will not deign to
answer that." She turned to her old friend, noting the
closed look on his face. "Derek, I'm glad to see you,"
she greeted pleasantly. "I daresay the cold is seeping into
your poor hand."

Derek nodded. "Somewhat, but I manage," he replied
evasively. "I was going to ask you out for a ride, but I
see that you've already taken fresh air this morning."

"A lot more than that," Andria said.

"I'd be horrified to hear that you're contemplating taking back up with that husband of yours," Beau drawled.

Rebecca, dressed in a mauve morning gown trimmed
with masses of lace around her ample shoulders, chimed
in: "Yes, that would be a disappointment for all of us who
care about you, Andria."

"I have no intention of accepting Rafe back into my
life," Andria said coolly. "I'm wholly capable of taking
care of myself."

"That you are, my dear," said Derek lightly. "You are
the strongest woman I know."

Andria gave him a grateful smile. "Thank you." She
slanted a glance at Beau and was startled by the venom
in his narrowed gaze as it rested on Derek. She took a
deep breath as the tension mounted in the room.

"I have no intention of seeking solace in someone else's
arms at this time," she added, as if to diffuse the sudden
ill will. "I'm not ready." If Beau had any thoughts of
wooing her, she had just nipped that in the bud.

"I came to invite you and Rebecca to a dinner party

on Saturday night. It would please me to have you grace my table."

"Thank you, Beau. We shall see. I'll send word." She addressed Rebecca. "I'll go back to work today."

"I'll join you in the studio in half an hour," Rebecca said, setting her teacup on the table.

Before Andria left, she turned to Beau. "Did you hear back from the doctor?"

He hesitated for a moment. "Yes . . . Daisy was not in the family way."

"So there's nothing to explain why she left and why she died," Andria said, disappointed.

"I suppose you're right, Andria."

She rose and left the room. She changed her riding outfit to a light gray wool dress with a lace collar and went to the studio, where the easel held the unfinished portrait of her employer. As she put on a smock over her dress, Derek joined her.

"I see that you're coming along fine with the painting. Rebecca must be pleased."

Andria nodded. "Painting was never a problem." She turned to her longtime friend. "Derek, do you know Robert Bostow, Squire Bostow's son?"

Derek looked into the distance, thinking. "Yes, somewhat. He's a young colt by now."

"Sixteen. He said that Daisy, the maid who was found drowned in the river yesterday, had many powerful friends. Do you have any idea who would befriend a simple maid, if not for . . . a particular sport that the gentlemen are fond of?"

"That's highly likely. I didn't know Daisy personally, but I know of several gentlemen in the area who would pay handsomely to have a young wench available during their nights of drinking. Male gatherings, you understand." Derek inserted his finger under his lace jabot as if finding it too tight.

"I understand," she said. She mixed some colors onto her palette. "I wonder if Daisy might've overheard some kind of information or witnessed something . . . or someone doing something they shouldn't be doing."

"There's always that," Derek said, his face closed. He looked pale and agonized. His hand must be bothering him more than he was willing to let on. It hung limply at his side. "As I said, I didn't know her."

"Do you know anyone who might've called on Daisy's services in the past?" Andria studied her friend closely, aware of the shuttered look coming back to his face. She'd seen that look many times when she'd tried to find out exactly what happened on the night when his hand had been destroyed.

"I can't help you, Andria. I didn't know the young maid at all, and I no longer take part in those particular gentlemen's games. Though when I was younger . . ." He let his voice drift off and moved closer to the portrait. "You have such a delicate brush stroke, my dear."

"You're changing the subject," Andria chided. "But I realize you'd like to have your painting abilities back fully, and you will."

He sighed deeply and went over to a table where some parchment fans she'd been decorating with birds and flowers lay spread to dry. "You're very clever, Andria."

"I don't think I would ever have to starve as long as I have my artistic skills, but it is somewhat tedious to paint the same motifs over and over."

He glanced at her over her shoulder, his eyes guarded. "Your husband is duty bound to provide for you. There's no reason for you to fend for yourself now that he's back. He has his mother's legacy, which is plentiful."

"I won't take any of his money," she said dismissively.

Derek looked outraged. "It's one thing to paint because you love it, but it's another to eke out a living when you could be richly provided for. You're stubborn and foolish." He took her shoulders and squeezed. "Don't let pride stand in the way of . . . relief or satisfaction."

She touched his cheek gently. "You were going to say love, weren't you?"

His gaze slid away. "You always did love that rogue, and it's beyond me why you would, as he obviously cared little for your best interests. He always came first, didn't he?"

The old wounds inside opened, and she moved away from her friend. "Derek, with Rafe I made a mistake, but I'm older and wiser now. He won't be able to take advantage of me again." A wave of shame rolled through her as she thought of her wanton surrender at dawn. How easily Rafe had always stoked her fires. A longing for his embrace suddenly overcame her, and she did her best to suppress it.

"Remember when we were children, Andria? We swore never to have any secrets from each other."

She looked at him. "Yes, I remember. Things have changed, though, with the complications of a grown-up life."

He nodded and studied his useless gloved hand. "Yes . . . things have certainly changed. I'm keeping secrets from you, and I know you're holding back the truth."

"But that won't ruin our friendship, Derek. Sometimes we're forced to keep secrets—"

"Especially if the truth could be hurtful to others," he filled in.

"Exactly." She knew he carried a burden that she could not explain. She wished she could help him in some way, but he'd been withdrawn since the accident. He clearly suffered under a dark cloud of sadness.

"I can't wait to see your latest paintings," she said to lighten the mood.

He shrugged his shoulders lightly. "Not very impressive, I'm afraid. That part of my life will never be the same." His tone deepened as if he were struggling with profound emotions. "My dreams will never manifest the way I envisioned, but there has to be another way to discover happiness."

Andria placed her hand on his arm in a gesture of comfort. "Sometimes hardships are gifts in disguise, but we have to uncover the gifts, and it's not always easy to see them."

Derek nodded, his face still shuttered. "I'll be taking my leave now so that you can go back to your work." He looked her hard in the eye. "Andria . . . if you ever need anything, I'll be there to help."

Andria lowered her gaze, knowing that he meant so much more than just material comfort. "It gives me a great deal of comfort to know that you're there," she said quietly.

He kissed her hand gently. He looked so sad, but he gave her a smile and left the room.

Andria pondered their conversation. She felt keenly the cloud of doom that lingered. She wanted to know what secrets were pressing him down so drastically. She felt an urge to run after him and hold him back, to ask him to stay with her, but it was too late. She could see his cloaked figure hurrying toward the stables.

There were too many questions and too many unresolved feelings. Confusion filled her at the thought of Rafe. How could she still feel so attracted to him after the way he'd treated her in the past? True, he had changed, but was the change only temporary?

She didn't have the strength to go on with useless speculations. Frustrated, she continued to mix paints for the portrait.

Four days later, Rafe looked morosely at the plate of ham and congealed eggs in front of him at one of the tables at the inn. Andria refused to see him, and all of his investigations at public places in a five-mile radius had uncovered nothing, just as Andria had claimed. Bridget's disappearance was still a complete mystery.

And he was no closer to discovering who had given him the grisly animal heart in the night. He felt the hard contours of the knife in its sheath stuck into the waistband of his breeches. If only it could speak of the past. If only he could remember where he'd lost it.

He had drunk the last dregs of his coffee when the door burst open and Nick Thurston stood on the threshold, bringing with him a breeze of crisp winter air and flurries on his shoulders. They immediately melted in the warm room.

Nick's gaze alighted on him. "Rafe, you old codger, what is going on? You look like you lost heavily at gambling." Nick embraced his friend and slapped his back. Nick's sword swung against his thigh.

"No, I didn't lose anything, but I didn't gain anything, either. I was sunk in dark thoughts."

"That kind of occupation won't bring any results." Nick pulled off his cloak and gloves. His dark hair was covered with melting snowflakes.

"That's for sure, but I haven't rallied my resources for some workable plans. Everything I've tried has led nowhere." His heart filled with hope. "Tell me you have some good news. Did you find out what happened to the servant?"

Nick shook his head. "It's most confounding. She came to the orphanage about the same time you and I connected, worked only in the kitchen, and disappeared directly after the girl you thought was your daughter died."

"That's odd."

"My theory is that she fed you the information that the little black-haired orphan was your offspring so as to lead you astray. But what would she gain by telling you about your name and title? Was she sent there to bring you back here to Rowan's Gate? That's my guess."

Rafe rubbed his jaw where his stubble bristled. "Who would want me back here?"

"Andria? No, she didn't know you were alive. Your father?"

Rafe shook his head. "Most unlikely. He didn't know, either, and he believes I'm to blame for everyone's hardships. And my aunt abhors me."

"Then there are those who don't like your presence here," Nick said, warming his backside in front of the fire.

Rafe nodded. "Beau Saxon, Derek Guiscard, some of Saxon's cronies, Robert "Romeo" Cunningham. I've heard that he had an eye for Andria. I know for a fact that Beau and Derek would gladly take my place beside Andria—as soon as they can get rid of me."

"They're that ruthless?"

"Yes . . . possibly. Saxon has never been anything but polite, but with a coldness that could freeze a penguin."

"Very cold indeed," Nick said with a tinge of sarcasm. "You can't let that fop offend you."

"He gets nowhere with me. I would like to know more about him, though—without asking him directly."

"Well, that can be easily remedied." Nick called out to the landlord, who entered with a platter of breakfast. The scent of fried ham filled the room. "My good man, bring some strong coffee as well."

Rafe told Nick about the grim threat someone had left on his bed on that night of the many nightmares.

"And you couldn't catch him?"

"He had time to escape before I got my wits about me. The incident has to be connected to Beau—a rather blatant threat."

"Your life is in danger."

"Why does he play games like these rather than going in for the kill?"

"Perhaps he gets perverse pleasure in playing a cat-and-mouse game with you."

Mr. Brown came in with a basket of fresh bread.

"There's a dinner party at Lochlade tonight," Rafe said as the landlord left to fetch the coffeepot. "I wasn't invited, but I heard from Travers, the Rowan butler, that most of the gentry got invitations. Andria is most likely going with Rebecca."

"We'll use the commotion at Lochlade to do some investigation of our own. Knowledge is power. If someone is trying to destroy you to win Andria, we'll have to have proof of who they are and why."

"I need some answers badly," Rafe said. "My patience is running very thin. Andria is out of my reach for as long as this unknown menace stands between us."

Nick gave Rafe a long stare. "You're falling in love with Andria all over, aren't you?"

"I think so, ever since the moment I laid eyes on her

outside this inn. She has always held my heart, I know that much. The frustration is eating me alive."

"By Jupiter, I wouldn't want to be in your shoes, Rafe. At least the lady of my heart loves me back."

"How is Serena? Was she upset that you were coming back here?"

"No, she has a most generous heart. She wants the mystery of your past solved as much as I do, and she promised to keep an investigation going in London. She's looking into domestic employment agencies now." He cut up the ham into strips and spread butter on a crusty roll. "However, I think the answers are all to be found here."

Rafe nodded. "I believe you're right."

Around midnight, they rode through the hills toward Lochlade. The snow had melted during the day, but the ground was hard with frost. A sliver of moon lit their way, and as they desired to remain unseen, they were glad for the weak light.

They wore dark coats and breeches and kept the cold wind out with heavy black cloaks. Many a time they had ridden into the night like this in pursuit of fat rewards from unwary travelers. That activity stopped just as soon as the orphanage had been paid off, but they both felt the familiar excitement.

"We could fetch a good sum on a night like this," Nick mused aloud.

"Yes, but we're on an altogether different mission."

"That we are, and it holds the promise to be just as exciting as any holdup, old fellow."

They slowly approached Lochlade through the trees growing dense behind the estate. Leaving their horses tied in a thicket, they hurried up behind the brightly lit mansion, across the lawn.

Through the huge windows of the dining room they could see the glitter of chandeliers and the movement of many people.

"They must be on their last course by now," Rafe whispered to Nick. "And hopefully very inebriated."

"That's to our advantage. Their lulled senses play in our favor."

They sneaked along the terrace in silence, Rafe leading the way toward the side where he knew the library was located after spying it from the hallway while visiting Lochlade with Andria.

"This is it," he whispered, and tried the door. It was locked.

"Damnation." Nick tried another door that led to some kind of salon next to the library. Also locked.

"We might have to force a window." Rafe thought about alternatives. "If we go inside in any other part of the mansion, we'll be discovered. There are footmen at every corner."

Nick nodded. "Let's try that small window at the end of the terrace. It leads to the library, too."

"Just big enough for one of us to crawl inside."

The window was locked, but Nick cracked one of the diamond-shaped panes and the glass fell with a tinkling sound. He inserted a finger to open the latch. The window slid open easily. Rafe crawled inside, then let Nick in through the door. He closed the small window carefully, pulling the velvet drape to conceal the broken pane.

Nick lit a candle in the heavy candelabra on the desk. The weak light illuminated the papers strewn across the surface. Evidently, Beau had been working on something before the party.

They went through the drawers, finding nothing but writing implements and old correspondence. As Nick carefully went over the papers on the desk, Rafe rifled through the correspondence, which mostly consisted of dull letters from Mrs. Saxon, and Beau's aunt, always signed Aunt Margaret. Nothing that could point to any wrongdoing by Beau.

"What exactly are we looking for?" Rafe commented as he eyed the contents of a business ledger.

"Evidence of lots of money changing hands, any kind of correspondence with threats."

"Extortion?"

"Possibly. Look here, Rafe." Nick pointed at a listing of numbers. "This is some sort of debt, broken down into sections. This woman, Mrs. Bostow, whoever she is, owes—or owed—a large debt to our friend Beau."

Rafe stiffened. "Mrs. Bostow?" He peered at the sheet in the weak light.

"She's been owing for a long time. It looks like Beau has had the whole benefit of her farms."

"The whole estate, most likely. But he's not the one who bought the estate from her. It was Oliver Yarrow, one of Beau's cronies."

"Hmm, and look at these. More debts." Nick's breath hissed through his nose. " 'Sfaith. Your father's name crops up here."

Rafe tore the sheet from Nick's hand. "Hell and damn, Father is deeply in debt to Lochlade." Rafe felt anger clutch his chest; it filled him with an urge to explode. "I'll have to get to the bottom of this. We're talking about my inheritance, my family name."

Nick gently took the paper from Rafe's stiff fingers. "Tomorrow will be a good time to have a serious chat with your father." He glanced toward the door, for they could hear voices in the corridor outside. "I deduce from this that Saxon has a finger in every pie around Rowan's Gate. He's worming his way into total power."

"All with money that rightfully belonged to Julian, Andria's nephew."

"It's probably all legal. I doubt that he would leave evidence of crimes so carelessly on his desk."

Rafe put a finger to his lips. "Shh, someone is coming in."

TWELVE

They barely had time to hide behind the heavy velvet drapes in the alcove that led to the French doors by the terrace. They glanced at each other in the gloom, tensing. Rafe seethed as he recognized Beau's smooth voice and Andria's melodious one. She was laughing, and Rafe realized she had drunk more wine than she should.

Part of him understood her need to drown her sorrows, but the other resented that he had traveled in the cold searching for clues to the mystery of Bridget's disappearance while she was eating delicacies and flirting with her host.

"The dinner was wonderful, Beau. Thank you for trying to put some joy back into my life," she said.

"You only have to ask for my assistance. You know that, my sweet."

Rafe could hear her move around the room, stopping at the desk. "You haven't finished your accounts. Father never had that much clerical work."

"Your father was more interested in the sporting life, wasn't he? I find that business keeps my mind nimble, and as Lord Lochlade, I have many ventures. My steward does some of the work, but I like to keep an eye on things."

It sounded as if Andria was sifting through the papers. "Beau, why is Lord Rowan mentioned in various places?"

"Come here, Andria," Beau commanded, a hard edge to his voice. "Leave my papers alone! You're too inquisitive for your own good."

Andria laughed again, and Rafe knotted his fists at his sides.

"I'm sorry. I daresay power becomes you, Beau," she said smoothly. "But you're all alone in this great rambling mansion."

Rafe heard the rustle of silk as she moved around the desk.

"I expected to read an engagement notice in the papers that many years," she continued.

Beau took some rapid steps toward her. "You are teasing me, aren't you, my sweet? We have talked about this before. You know how I've always felt for you. As long as I can remember, I've been madly in love with you."

"There's something odd about that, Beau," she said coolly. "Most gentlemen would find someone else to marry when they found there was no hope with their first amour, and I've always made it clear that I had no interest in you."

"I'm not like other gentlemen, and you should know that by now."

Rafe could hear Andria stepping back, her heels clicking on the wooden floor. Nick placed a restraining hand on his arm.

"Beau, why exactly *did* you ask me in here?" she asked. "Surely not to show me your accounts?"

Rafe heard a flurry of movement, and Andria let out a sound as if she were choking. Nick gripped Rafe's arm hard, forcing him to quell his urge to rush to her rescue.

Sounds of struggle came to their ears, then an angry retort. "Beau, keep your hands off!" she cried. "Stop this nonsense. How many times do I have to tell you that I have no interest in your amorous pursuits. We're cousins, joined by name only, nothing else. Give it up."

Heavy silence fell for a moment. "I never give up." Beau's voice was thick with emotion. "You belong here at Lochlade, my sweet. The nursery should be filled with our children. You know I could make you happy in the marital bed."

"You keep forgetting that I'm already married, but besides that fact, I will never return here," she said flatly. "Now, why did you ask me in here? Not to maul me surely."

Beau heaved a long-suffering sigh. "You always were a difficult and willful woman, Andria, but I like that spirit. So like your father, really. He took what he wanted and had to be admired for that."

Rafe heard Beau's firm step coming closer. He held his breath as Beau stopped by the desk.

"Andria, I unearthed some old letters from your father. I don't know how they ended up here, but it looks like someone sent them back."

"What are they?" Rafe could hear the curiosity in Andria's voice. "And where did you find them?"

"Behind some books here in the stacks."

Silence fell as Andria was going through the papers. "They are love letters, Beau, to some woman who's nameless. He calls her Bijou."

"Something delicate and highly priced. Do you have any idea who he courted? It certainly was not your mother."

Beau sounded tense, as if he were testing her. *He knew,* Rafe thought.

"Father was not exactly the doting husband," Andria said with a sad tinge in her voice. "It was no secret that my parents' marriage was arranged." Her voice rose a notch. "What do you think I'll gain from reading these love letters?"

"Mementos of your father, Andria. Nothing more."

"I don't need these kinds of mementos." She flung the letters onto the desk. "These are things I'd much rather forget."

Beau's voice hardened. "I'm glad to hear that you have no illusions about him. His blasted *affaires de coeur* were a byword in these parts."

"Be that as it may, 'tis the past. Father is gone now, and I'm certain that by his terrible death he atoned for some of his crimes."

Rafe tried to remember how the old Lord Lochlade had died, but nothing came to him. Something to ask Travers, the Rowan butler, about.

"I want to return to the party, Beau. I'm sure your friends are wondering what happened to you. 'Tis rude—"

"I make my own rules," Beau said darkly.

Without another word, they left the room.

Rafe and Nick went back inside the library as the corridor grew silent outside.

"I would not put any store in Saxon's courting of Andria. It's obvious he didn't get anywhere with her," Nick said, looking closely at Rafe.

"I admit she handled herself well." Rafe, still upset by the situation, went over to the desk and took the thin bundle of letters. He stuck them into his pocket. "There might be some good information here. Beau might think that Andria retrieved them."

"We can always put them back later." Nick looked toward the terrace. "Let's go."

"I can't wait until tomorrow to see my father," Rafe said grimly as they found their horses and rode away from Lochlade. "From now on, I'm staying at Rowan Hall even

if I wasn't invited. Father can't keep me away any longer."
He kicked his heels into the flanks of his stallion. "Nick,
you shall sleep in a comfortable feather bed at the Hall
tonight."

As they rode up to the stables at Rowan Hall, Rafe felt
a wave of longing for Andria. He wished he were going
home to her, into her bed, her warm limbs wrapping
around him in welcome. But the tall house looked dark
and unfriendly. There were no welcoming smiles inside,
only an ailing old man who harbored a lot of resentment.

"I'm going to wake him up," Rafe said through
clenched teeth.

"I take it you mean your sire," Nick said, falling into
step beside Rafe. "Is that wise?"

"Wise or not, that's what I'm going to do." Rafe knew
the kitchen door would be open, and it was. Bits and
pieces of his boyhood were coming back, mostly happy
memories of sunny weather and infinite play. But he
couldn't remember his father as any part of those times.

They walked through the quiet house. A tall clock sent
out its heavy *tick-tock* from a corner in the foyer. Rafe
took the curving staircase two steps at a time. He showed
Nick to an empty bedchamber. "This will suit you well.
I shall see you at breakfast tomorrow, and if Travers in-
quires about your business, tell him you're with me. He'll
give you anything you need."

"Thanks, old friend." Nick closed the door behind him,
and Rafe walked to his father's rooms. He felt his insides
knot with worry, but he set his jaw and proceeded through
the door.

The room smelled stuffy and unpleasant. The air was
heavy, as if touched by the illness of the man in the massive carved bed. Rafe saw the male nurse sitting by the

dying fire, his head lolling forward in sleep. He decided to wake him up.

Morley gave a start as Rafe touched his shoulder, his eyes narrowing with suspicion.

"I'm Lord Rowan's son, Rafael. Please go downstairs until I call you back here," he said. "I have to speak urgently with my father."

Morley stood reluctantly. "An upset could bring on another attack," he said.

"I'm not here to upset him," Rafe lied. "Go now, and in the future try to stay awake when you're watching over my father."

Morley studied his face for a long moment. "Never failed in my duties," he said resentfully.

As he left, Rafe went to the bed and looked down on the pale face of his father. A candle burned by the bed, casting heavy shadows across the sharp features. The cheeks were sunken, and gray bristly stubble covered his jaw.

Rafe gently shook Lord Rowan's shoulder. "Sir, wake up."

The old man opened his eyes, staring straight at Rafe.

"Wha—? What's going on?"

Rafe helped him to sit up in bed and noticed that the slackness of Rowan's arm and shoulder, which was the result of the apoplexy, had lessened considerably. There was an alertness in his gaze that hadn't been there before.

"It's me, Rafe."

Rowan's gaze hardened. "As far as I'm concerned, you have no business here."

Rafe noticed that his father had regained some of his strength. "I decide that," he said, and sat down on the bed after arranging some pillows behind his father's back.

"What do you want? It's in the middle of the night."

Rowan's voice was harsh. "If it's money—your mother supplied you richly. You were the apple of her eye."

"My money is of no concern, but I've found out that you may have to worry about your own financial situation. I'm here to discuss that."

"Financial situation?" Rowan looked away.

"I trust that you're fit enough to talk about the debts you've incurred. I'm talking about your debt to Lochlade."

Heavy silence fell, and Rowan chewed on his lower lip, his fingers working the embroidered edge of the sheet. He tore off his nightcap and brushed a trembling hand through his hair.

"How did you find out about that?"

"I know a lot of odd things, Father."

"Not much to do around here," the old man muttered. "A man has to find ways to amuse himself."

Rafe nodded. "That I can understand, but we're talking about deep debt. How could you fall into such a hole?"

"I was obsessed . . . obsessed with winning." He gave Rafe a pleading glance. "Never was much of a card player in the past, Rafe. You know that—if you can remember. But something came over me, and Beau egged me on. I gambled night after night with him and his cronies. The autumn was long and cold, and we had to create some excitement."

"I want to know the full extent of your debt to Lochlade. Don't hold back; I know it's bad."

"Too late now to do anything about it," Rowan mumbled. "He has me by the throat. Soon I'll be lord of the manor in name only if I can't pay the twenty thousand pounds I owe. I put up the estate as collateral."

"Twenty thousand!" Rafe tore to his feet and paced the

room. The looming hulks of massive pieces of furniture seemed to want to suffocate him.

"Father, I never took you for a fool. Lord Lochlade is not a friend of yours. It's not as if he would ask you to play for penny stakes."

"That's what made it interesting." Rowan sighed. "It was a race of minds, not some boring parlor game."

"You would just throw away the estate like that?" Filled with disgust, Rafe stared down at his father, his hands balled into fists.

"With no one left in the family—or so I thought until you appeared—I didn't care much who got Rowan Hall. I don't have lots of time left to me."

"That is a very poor excuse. I've never heard of anything so irresponsible. Are you mad? Is Lochlade mad?"

"There's a man who never has enough," Rowan said firmly. "His greed is a gaping hole."

"You didn't have to feed it," Rafe said, quelling his savage anger.

"Enough!" Rowan snapped. "You have no right to judge me. Your own actions do not bear close scrutiny very well."

Rafe had to agree with that, but he couldn't speak until he'd gotten a tight rein on his emotions.

"I can't see my way to raise twenty thousand pounds, Rafe."

"I'll have to pay the debt if I want to keep the estate in the family."

"Your mother's portion doesn't come to much more than that, and I can't bear the thought that you would spend all of your funds to raise money for me."

"I'm doing it for Rowan Hall," Rafe said coldly. "The estate is worth a lot more than that. Lochlade has his eye set on the estate, not the twenty thousand pounds." Rafe rubbed his jaw in thought. "I just don't understand how he could drive you to the upper limits of what you could afford—all for some nights of gambling."

"There's no secret what the family estate is worth, Rafe. The farms haven't been producing as well as in the past, and I'm too old to bring reform."

"I will shoulder any reforms needed." He looked at his father as determination rose like a steel rod in him. "From now on, I'm taking over the running of the estate. It's the only way to salvage what has been lost."

Rowan looked aside, chagrin written all over his face. "I don't like being old and crippled."

"Father, you're a stubborn old fool. You judged my actions harshly and left me a heap of trouble. It is the height of arrogance."

"Rafe—"

"You would gladly throw away what has belonged to the Rowans for centuries?" Rafe could not believe his father had sunk this low, but the feeling of powerlessness that came over him again irked him more. He didn't know his father now, and he suspected he'd never really been close to his sire.

"We're going over the accounts tomorrow, Father. We'll find a way to make the farms profitable again."

Lord Rowan peered closely at Rafe, who was standing in the shadows. *"We?* You're serious."

"Of course."

"In the past you wouldn't have cared, Rafe. You would've left me to the wolves."

Rafe pushed a hand through his hair. "I was that . . . cold?"

Rowan plucked at the sheet endlessly. "Maybe we both were. I was not a very good father, I'm afraid. But the apoplexy took all the venom out of me."

Rafe sat down on the edge of the bed and looked intently at his father. The candle on the bedstand flickered and caused shadows to dance over Rowan's sunken features.

"I don't remember, Father." Rafe fought a wave of sadness as the force of his loss overcame him. "Tell me something about the past."

"You might as well know that your mother and I didn't . . . get along for much of the time. I was a disappointed man, a hard man, and I'm afraid I took it out on you, Rafe. Since you have no siblings, you got the full brunt of my displeasure."

Rafe was glad he couldn't recall that.

"My anger was against your mother, not you, but I couldn't fight her; she was ruthless."

Rafe couldn't remember anything about his mother. As if he could read the thought, Rowan said, "Her portrait hangs in the gallery. You inherited your eyes and nose from her, y'know."

"Why the anger?"

"There were many reasons. We never really loved each other, and she had a lover, which I could not accept."

"And you, did you have lovers?"

Rowan looked away. "I might've had, on occasion, but no one who captured my heart." He took a deep breath. "I'm tired."

Rafe caught the thin, trembling hand on the coverlet. "Whatever happened in the past is over. I long to create bonds with my family again."

Rowan clutched at Rafe's arm with his other hand. "Thank you for giving me a chance to be a good father."

"And as long as I'm alive, Lochlade won't control the Rowan estate. How much time do we have to pay your debt?"

"Ten more days. Ten measly days." Rowan's voice trembled. "There's no way—"

"I'll take care of it. Trust me." Rafe bent down and gave Rowan an awkward hug. "You need your rest."

Feeling lighter of step, Rafe left. Something new had been forged between him and his father, and that gave him hope. He had roots again.

Tomorrow he'd confront Beau.

THIRTEEN

Rafe paced the house like a caged animal. His head crowded with thoughts, he listened at Nick's door to see if his friend was still awake. Utter silence. Nick would be tired after his long trip from London.

He went up to the portrait gallery and studied the face of his mother in the moonlight streaming through the tall windows. She'd been a beautiful woman but looked bitter; the artist had not been able to hide the downward slant of the mouth or the hardness of her eyes.

He touched the cold surface as if needing to reestablish some sort of contact, but he felt nothing. It grieved him that he couldn't remember if he'd had a good relationship with her or not.

He prowled the rooms, looking for anything familiar, and had a moment when he felt as if the veil would be lifted from his mind. Nothing frustrated him more than to sense revelations close by, only to have them dissolve like mist.

He *had to* talk to someone. Pulling on his cloak and gloves, he decided he'd search out Andria in her bedchamber at Stowehurst, whether she liked it or not. His excuse would be— Well, he didn't need an excuse, damn it. She was still his wife.

The ride over the fell to Stowehurst invigorated him.

Just the thought of seeing Andria again excited him. He admitted that he'd longed incessantly for her these last few days. His longing sat lodged in his heart like a painful wedge, and he didn't know how to get rid of it. He'd never felt more alone. His throat suddenly choked with tears as he thought of all the problems stacked against him. No one could really understand the desolation he felt. He vowed to himself that somehow he'd find a way to heal the past.

Andria was dreaming of the river, the deep, cold onyx holding her in a silky yet relentless grip. She fought to pull air into her lungs but felt herself drowning, the bottomless water pulling, sucking at her legs.

A soundless scream tore from her, and she sat upright in bed, pushing desperately at the covers twisted around her. Renewed fear gripped her as she saw movement in the shadows.

A man stood by her bed. Just as she was about to scream, a cool hand dropped over her mouth.

"It's me, Rafe. I need to talk to you. Don't be afraid."

She calmed down, but the memory of her dream still lingered. She felt an inexplicable urge to cry, to voice all her pain.

"I didn't invite you here," she said, groggy.

"That's clear to me, but I couldn't sleep, and I needed someone to talk to. You can at least offer to listen," he said with little concern for her disapproval.

He lit the candles by the bedside, and she could read the distress in his eyes. She held back the scathing retort on her tongue.

"How did you get in, Rafe? I thought Rebecca would see to it that all the doors were locked."

"Evidently she didn't. I got in through a side door, the same as last time."

They stared at each other for a long moment, tension rising with every breath.

"I told you—"

"I know what you told me, Andria, but I need you to listen."

Without another word, she got out of bed and draped herself in a voluminous wrapper. "What has happened? I'm not sure I have the strength to receive more bad news."

She moved into the shadows at the other side of the room, as far away from him as she could. His presence made her weak at the knees, as if her body had a mind of its own. Her body longed for his touch, and her mind fought the desire relentlessly.

"Father owes Beau a major fortune—gambling debts. He's in danger of losing Rowan Hall if he doesn't pay."

Dismayed, Andria pondered his words in silence. She heard Beau's name at every turn, entwined with most other names in the area. "Looks like Beau is a very busy man. He has deals with everybody, it seems."

"Mostly unsavory business," Rafe pointed out.

Andria sighed. "I'm sorry that your sire is involved with Beau in any way. Tell me, how did you find out?"

"Rowan himself admitted it."

"He is now speaking to you after all the animosity that lay between you?"

"We came to some sort of understanding tonight. I don't remember the past, and I certainly have no desire to carry some unknown grudge toward him. I'm taking over the running of the estate, and I'll see to it that the debt is paid in full. However, I'm loathe to give Beau a penny of my inheritance."

He sat down on a chintz-covered armchair, his head slumped between his bowed shoulders. She could not help but walk across the room and touch his hair lightly.

"I'm sorry that you have to carry this additional burden, Rafe."

With a pained growl in his throat, he wrapped his arms around her thighs and pressed his head against her belly. A surge of unbidden tenderness flowed through her, and she stroked his hair, remembering the springy, smooth texture as if she'd caressed him only yesterday.

But the chasm of time and heartache hung between them.

"I . . ." she began, pushing at his arms, but he only wrapped them more tightly around her.

"Don't," he said, his voice hoarse. "Just allow me some solace from the relentless pain."

She gave in, cradling his head against her. A surge of sweetness pooled in her stomach and drained into her legs, making her weak. Her heart seemed to tremble in her chest, and her breath was shallow.

"I'm distressed about your father, Rafe. I truly am."

"Thank you." He looked up at her face, his eyes wet with tears. "This is what I needed—you."

Andria closed her eyes to shut out his disturbing, penetrating gaze. "Nothing has changed between us, Rafe. You know that."

"Your touch is a sweet song to my senses."

She tried to pull away again, but he only held tighter. Standing up, he lifted her into the air, and she was only aware of his massive strength. That had not changed.

"I want you," he said roughly, and let her body glide down the length of him until she was standing in his tight embrace.

"This is madness," she whispered, but she was unable to pull herself away.

When his mouth came down on hers, sweeping away all caution, she wrapped her arms around him. He smelled of leather and wool—and that virile male scent that was his alone. It intoxicated her senses until she was swimming in desire. Her body shouted with it, and he heard it as he slowly dragged the palms of his hands over her breasts, down over her hips and thighs.

He groaned as he pulled his hand across the center of her excitement between her legs, and she sighed with pleasure against his mouth.

"Oh, Rafe . . ."

He growled deep in his throat, closed his hands over her buttocks, and pushed her up hard against his huge, rock-solid erection. She clung to his shoulders as he ground himself against her. Wetness drenched her feminine parts, and he carried her over to the bed, tossing her against the soft down pillows.

She moaned as he lifted the hem of her silky nightgown and pulled it up over her hips. His mouth came down on her breast, sucking through her nightgown a tender nipple that grew taut with desire under his hungry onslaught. He treated the other to the same seduction, and she felt heavy and swollen with longing.

His hand sought and found the wet, distended folds of her desire and slid one finger in an agonizingly slow manner along the slick surface.

"Rafe," she groaned against his face.

His fingers played expertly with her, making her desire mount with every caress until she couldn't bear it anymore.

She unfastened his waistband and skimmed her hand over his warm, taut belly until his swollen manhood sprang free, so needy for her touch. He seemed at the bursting point as he thrust himself against her hand, and she wrapped her fingers around the velvet length, stroking.

He pulled her wrapper and nightgown off her body, and as she could barely hold back her need any longer, he got up and threw his own clothes in a heap on the floor.

Warm, hairy masculine skin slid against her, and she wrapped her arms and legs around him to pull him closer. He fitted himself at the opening of her feminine secrets and plunged into the tight honeyed sweetness.

"Oh, my God . . . Andria . . ."

In her sorrow, she had forgotten how it used to be between them, but her body hadn't. He fit her perfectly and moved as if he knew exactly what brought her the most pleasure. She could not get enough of him, and her breath came in rasping gasps as he possessed her completely and profoundly.

She strived for that release that surged closer with every thrust. Suddenly her body tensed, and his wild plunging sent her over the glittering edge, where she drowned in wave after wave of ecstasy.

He followed her into the sea of bliss, his whole body growing tight in a wild spasm of release.

They clung limply to each other. Andria struggled to get back her reasoning mind, but it, too, had gone limp. She could only savor the sweet glow, and when his fingers moved over the hard nub at the entrance of her femininity, which had erupted in such pleasure earlier, she flew apart again as another wave caught her. He silenced her cry with his mouth, and their tongues lingered in a deep kiss.

"Oh, Rafe," she whispered as he lifted his head to look

down on her face. His eyes glowed with an unearthly fire, and his smile was decidedly wicked.

"Finally some light in this vale of sorrows," he said, his voice teasing. "You're the softest, the sweetest, the most tantalizing of creatures. And the most exasperating."

"I have no comments," she said sleepily, already drifting in and out of sleep. He pulled her up to his shoulder, and she snuggled closer. Tomorrow she would allow herself to think again, but not tonight.

They slept, but Andria awakened as the first hint of dawn lit the colorless winter sky. She stretched luxuriously, feeling the heat from Rafe's sleeping body. This was her weakness, her madness. She had always responded wildly to his body even as he was breaking her heart in the past.

She caught her bottom lip between her teeth, not wanting to remember the past. He was a new man, was he not? He seemed more caring and patient, full of respect and not so prone to wild fits of temper. A changed man, a loving man.

She wished she could believe that wholeheartedly.

Rafe stirred beside her, his face still soft with sleep and remembered pleasure. Not even opening his eyes, he pulled her closer, and his hand made that well-loved trip across her body and stirred all her longings anew. He spun magic on her, played the instrument of her femininity, and found his own delight all over again.

The sun stood high over the horizon when they awakened again. Lady Stowe was banging on the door.

"Andria!" she called out. "Are you still asleep? Is there something wrong?"

Andria sat upright in bed, her heart pounding. "No . . . I'm just sleeping late. I'll join you downstairs shortly."

"I'm worried about you."

"There's no need. Have your breakfast in peace."

The sound of Lady Stowe's steps died down, and Andria swung her legs over the side of the bed.

Rafe caught her before she could move away. He hugged her tightly. "Thank you. I needed your warmth so badly."

Uneasiness mingling with love, she didn't know what to say.

"Andria, you don't have to worry about my being seen. I'll let myself out. Thank you again for a wonderful night."

She had expected him to voice demands on her, but he said nothing, only watched her silently as she got dressed in a simple light blue gown of sprigged muslin over wide hoops and a lace-edged white kerchief crossed over her bosom. She stuffed her hair into a bun and covered it with a lacy cap.

Unable to meet his gaze, she fled from the room.

Rafe stretched out in her bed. Every inch of him felt satiated, and the night in Andria's arms had given him hope he hadn't had before. He got up, whistling a tune under his breath. As he pulled his wrinkled white shirt from the pile on the floor, there was a soft knock on the door.

Before he could move, the door opened, and a young maid carrying a coal scuttle stood on the threshold. Her eyes grew huge as she viewed his nakedness, and she clapped her sooty hand to her mouth, but not before she'd released a high-pitched scream.

Rafe hastily pulled on his shirt to cover himself, and she blushed to the roots of her hair. He winked and put a finger to his lips to silence her, but it was too late.

Witherspoon, the butler, appeared, two footmen in tow.

"What in the world is going on here?" he asked, staring down his nose at Rafe.

"Good morning, Witherspoon, and a glorious one it is. You don't have to worry about me. I'll just take my clothes and be on my way." Rafe gathered his breeches, coat, and hat.

"Lord Derwent, I daresay we didn't expect you here," Witherspoon said haughtily.

"I daresay you didn't, but here I am. No need to worry Lady Stowe; I'm not staying for breakfast, and I'm letting myself out."

Witherspoon shooed away the young maid and ordered the footmen to go back downstairs. "Very well, sir." His lips tight, he gave Rafe another look of disbelief and closed the door behind him.

Rebecca would presently know the truth. He might as well face her wrath just in case she decided to turn it against Andria if he wasn't available.

He dressed, trying the best he could to smooth out the wrinkled clothes. They definitely bore witness to his haste in sweeping Andria into his arms.

With a bounce to his step, he went downstairs, his nose leading him through many sumptuous salons to the breakfast parlor at the back. It was a cozy room decorated in yellow damask curtains and a flowered carpet.

Andria sat at the table, a plate of eggs and kippers before her. Lady Stowe wore a large purple gown and a frilly mobcap. Rafe was surprised to see another guest, Derek Guiscard, looking like a fashion plate in a moss green coat, yellow breeches, and a flawless neckcloth. He would not meet Rafe's gaze.

Andria gave him a startled and guilty glance as he stepped inside. "Rafe!"

"Good morning, madam wife, and Aunt Rebecca. Mr. Guiscard. A pleasant day, isn't it?"

His aunt's eyes shot daggers. "What are you doing here? I told you never to set foot in this house! I'll have you thrown out."

"Calm down, Rebecca. I think it's about time we bury the hatchet, don't you? Holding a grudge is a very tiring business."

She puffed out her considerable chest. "A grudge? This has nothing to do with a grudge. I don't *acknowledge* you any longer."

"Rebecca—" Andria pleaded.

"That's neither here nor there," Rafe said, scanning the silver-domed platters of food. He helped himself to a plate of eggs and ham, and a couple of crusty rolls, still hot from the oven. "It takes two to fight, and I have no desire to fight with you, Rebecca. After all, we're family."

Rebecca's face took on a deep red tint. "Of all the outrageous—"

As Rafe sat down, he asked, "What exactly have I done to you to make you that set against me?"

Rebecca's eyes darted from Rafe to Andria and back. "You haven't done anything to me personally, but you have hurt the people whom I hold dear."

Rafe tapped his fork against his plate. "Would you be able to let bygones be bygones if other people forgive me for my sins?"

She seemed to think it over as Rafe considered the situation.

Derek was giving Andria a pitying look across the table, and Rafe sensed their closeness. It made him uneasy, wondering if all the progress he'd made with Andria was only on the surface. The deep friendship she evidently felt for this man excluded him. The thought plunged him into sudden sadness, and he wondered how he'd ever believed he could cross all the barriers to heal the past.

"What do you say, Rebecca, a truce?" He ate some of the eggs, but he couldn't taste them. The old loneliness was coming back as he stared at the inner struggle displayed across his aunt's face.

"I wasn't that bad of a person, was I?" he asked. He turned to Derek. "What can you tell me about my past? You must've been there through it all."

"Andria's problems are mine," Derek said hesitantly. Two bright spots of red glowed on his cheekbones. The cup in his hand rattled against the saucer as he set it down. "She was devastated when you left, and then Bridget . . . I thought Andria would break, and I can't help but blame you, sir. However, I never held a personal grudge against you. We had very little contact."

Rafe sensed that he was serious, and the brown eyes held sincerity. "Thank you for that, Derek."

"However, someone ought to call you out for what you put Andria through," Derek said with a hard edge to his voice.

"No one has challenged me, and I'm working on setting things right."

"I don't know if you ever can gloss over what happened," Rebecca said coldly. "Bridget's disappearance is a direct result of your actions . . . your selfish actions."

Rafe took a deep draft of coffee. "I've been told I was an arrogant, thoughtless man in the past. Ruthless, too, fighting with everyone." He glanced at Andria, who was staring at her plate. "But since I can't remember any of that now, all I want is peace and friendship. Father— because he has no other choice—is willing to let the past go."

"Resentment is not something we can switch on and

off," Rebecca said. "It's difficult to forget the past, seeing the devastation you left behind." She touched Andria's arm. "A lesser woman would've killed you as soon as you showed yourself in these parts."

"Let's not talk about that," Andria pleaded, her face contorted with pain. "All our efforts should go toward finding Bridget—if she is to be found."

Rafe lived in the bleakness of those words, knowing there was a great chance that Bridget was gone forever. The thought plunged him into that chasm of pain he knew so well. He pushed away from the table.

Andria would be better off linked to a soft-spoken man like Derek. They shared so much, and friendship could lead to more, couldn't it? The thought filled him with jealousy, which he pushed back ruthlessly.

"I appreciate your allowing me to speak," Rafe said with a bow. "It's not my intention to get into conflict with any one of you, only to get to the truth about my life and possibly, if God's willing, change it." He leaned down and kissed Andria on the cheek. "I'll go see Nick and set up our next strategy for the search of Bridget."

"As in Old Nick?" Rebecca asked scathingly.

"*Rebecca*— " Andria began, her voice dwindling.

Rafe gave his aunt a hard look in response. "I can see that my hardheadedness came from the Rowan side of the family." He bowed stiffly to Derek Guiscard.

Andria half-rose out of her chair, but Rafe strode out of the room before she could speak. He couldn't take any more recriminations, especially not from her.

His emotions in a turmoil, he decided to confront Beau about his father's gambling debt. If there was a way to pay it without any money changing hands, Rafe would find it. Perhaps Beau wouldn't be adverse to another night of cards, but Rafe had lost his skills. He barely had the rudimentary knowledge gleaned from evenings of cards in London. Nick, however . . . He let his thoughts drift as he rode toward Lochlade.

All he wanted was to find a solution to the problems of the past. Deep inside he knew that Beau had all the answers, but how could he pry them out of the man?

Frustration filled Rafe, and his hands tightened around the reins. The cool, crisp air did little to dispel his agitation.

He rode over the fell and beheld Lochlade sitting like a precious jewel in the dale, the sunlight glittering in a myriad of windows. He wished he could remember his time here with Andria, but no more than fragments floated around in his mind.

He wiped a hand across his eyes and began the slow decent toward the estate. As the path wound through a stand of trees, he could see the River Fynn and its slow progress toward the sea. The water looked icy cold, and something gripped his inside with dread.

He knew something connected to the river, something important that he needed to grasp. Pulling in the reins, he stared at the slow-moving water, searching deeply for some image that would trigger his memory.

Nothing happened except that deep feeling of dread. Something wicked had happened here. He slowly rode down the bluff to the river's edge and looked all around him. The Great Fell in the distance looked familiar, and he'd ridden all the paths around Lochlade, but this spot held him enthralled. Something . . . *something,* but what?

A voice came from behind him. He'd been so deep in thought that he hadn't heard the rider approach.

"Too cold for a swim," Beau drawled as Rafe turned around.

The man was dressed in a blue coat with silver facings

and a heavy velvet cloak with an ermine lining. His dark eyes flashed with cynical amusement.

"Everything and everyone is very cold here," Rafe retorted.

A small smile lurked at the corner of Beau's mouth. "You could not expect any other treatment."

Rafe shrugged nonchalantly, struggling to keep his rising anger under control. " 'Tis the past."

"You find the river interesting?" His gaze slid from Rafe's face to rest on the water. A flash of something—anger?—flared and died in those brown eyes.

"The river holds answers for me; I know it does," Rafe replied coolly. "I also know you could enlighten me on a few important points, but I won't even bother to ask."

"I have nothing to hide from you, Rafe. You're a sad shadow of your former self."

"Your gibes don't affect me, Beau. I'm pleased that I didn't have to seek you out at Lochlade but that you came to me. I have discovered my father's involvement with you, and I want to clear his debt. Whatever vile force is driving you to fleece people, it'll never get you the control you seek."

"So he has recovered enough to speak with you?" Beau mused more to himself than addressing Rafe. "I'm surprised he would take you into his confidence."

"Why? He's my father. Just because your father treated you indifferently—" Rafe didn't know where that came from, but when he saw the anger rising on Beau's face, suffusing it with red, he realized he'd touched a sore spot.

"Don't take the word 'father' into your mouth! You know nothing about my relationship with my sire, and you yourself are the worst father—" Beau sputtered, his temper for once getting the better of him.

Rafe felt an icy bleakness settle in his chest. He wanted

to place his hands around Beau's neck and squeeze until there was no more evil, no more life, in that body.

"At least I've made peace with my father, and his debt is now mine. You'll not get a penny out of Rowan Hall, and that's final."

Beau's voice was icy soft. "You have nine days to wash yourself clean of your father's disgrace, and if you don't, Rowan Hall is mine. There's nothing you can do about it. A debt is a debt."

Fury clenched Rafe's gut. "You had this planned. You have plotted and schemed to ruin my father, just as you ruined Phoebe Bostow. She never had a chance against you." Rafe didn't know if he'd hit completely on the truth, but he might as well bring it up, since it seemed to fit with the theory he'd just thrown at Beau. And there had been those ledgers on the desk at Lochlade.

"You're a power-hungry and money-grubbing scoundrel," Rafe continued, his heart pounding. "You want to own the entire province. You want everyone to scrape and bow to you as the most influential man in the area."

"What's wrong with that?" Beau asked in a deadly soft voice, inching his horse closer to Rafe's.

"Only your morals. You don't care how you get your gains, you ruthless bastard!"

Beau was upon him before Rafe could finish the sentence, and they grappled while still on their horses. Rafe's strength was fueled by anger, and he wrestled with all his might, knowing that he still hadn't recovered his full strength after the blow to his head.

He gritted his teeth as Beau flung obscenities at him. Rafe got a stranglehold on Beau's throat and squeezed, noticing through the red haze of his anger that Beau's face was turning blue.

Beau delivered a desperate blow to Rafe's gut, and he

lost his choke hold. Doubling over in the saddle, he wanted to retch. Beau landed a double-fisted blow to his back, and Rafe fell out of the saddle, hitting the hard, rocky ground with a thud.

Beau was upon him in a flash, but Rafe rolled over at that same moment, placing a well-aimed knee to Beau's private parts.

Beau screamed and crumpled into a heap in a patch of frozen mud. The horses danced around them, hooves dangerously close to Rafe's head. Seeing those hooves brought terror to Rafe, and he struggled to his feet, shooing the horses into a stand of trees.

He pulled Beau up by the collar of that luxurious blue coat.

"I have longed to fight you ever since I clapped eyes on you," Rafe shouted in the other man's ear.

"Sore loser," Beau snarled. "You'll never have Andria's love again, and you'll never be the master of Lochlade again. Nor will you have an acre of land once I take Rowan Hall." Taunting satisfaction spread across Beau's face.

Rafe roared in anger and punched the other man's jaw. Beau tumbled again but gripped Rafe's ankle in the fall and toppled Rafe with a twist of his hands. They rolled around on the ground, fists flying.

Nick was riding hard along the river. He joined the scene and worked to separate the combatants.

" 'Sblood, get hold of yourselves!" he thundered, finally hauling them apart. "Schoolboys' brawls. Enough is enough!"

Rafe shook his head, clearing the red haze. Every part of him ached. He looked at Beau as the other man struggled to his feet.

Beau brushed off his muddied cloak and retrieved his

mangled tricorne hat. He glared down at Rafe. "You'll regret this more than you'll ever know," he hissed.

Rafe got to his feet, his whole body shaking. "Your threats are useless. You're staging your own downfall. If I don't kill you, someone else will."

"Bah! You cannot touch me, and when I get Rowan Hall, you'll be a broken man." Beau smiled coldly even as his lip was swollen and bleeding. One eye was closing and turning black, but the man seemed impervious to the pain. He gripped the reins of his horse and got into the saddle.

"Believe me, I shall annihilate you, Rafael Howard."

Rafe wanted to go after him and continue the fight. "Why the devil, *why?* What did I ever do to you? Or is it just that you couldn't have Andria?"

Beau's face twisted in contempt. "Andria has her own mind. You can't rule her any longer, and she'll soon be ready to come to me."

"By thunder, the man is crazed," Nick said under his breath, and clamped a hand on Rafe's shoulder to hold him back from pursuing another attack.

Rafe was breathing hard, but as he watched Beau ride away, his anger dwindled, and exhaustion settled in.

He hung his head. "By God, I thought I would kill him."

"You don't want to kill him, Rafe."

Rafe looked at Nick. "You don't know the whole. I'm glad you arrived when you did, though."

"I had the hell of a time parting you two. What happened?"

Rafe shrugged. "He rubbed me the wrong way, gloated over my father's debt. Besides, I accused him of trying to ruin everyone."

"You know, there's a lot of truth to that, as we suspected after we broke into Lochlade's library. I've been around this morning speaking to some of the people whose names I saw on Lochlade's desk. Seems that they have either sold or given acreage to cover debts to Lochlade. He has more than doubled the Lochlade lands, and I suspect that the acres have been acquired through careful planning and with legal authority. He has only dealt with people who most desperately lacked funds."

"Visions of grandeur," Rafe said. "Well, there's nothing new there. You only had to look at the way he dresses." He slapped Nick's shoulder. "Thank you for helping me. 'Tis priceless to me."

"Rafe, your bed was empty when I looked into your room early this morning. Insomnia?"

Rafe smiled. "Yes, but I did have a few hours of excellent rest at Stowehurst."

Nick lifted his eyebrows in appreciation. "With Andria?"

Rafe nodded, remembering the bliss, then the disappointment, for he knew he was no closer to winning her back. "A moment of ecstasy, which I cannot hope to regain unless her heart changes."

"If we can recover Bridget, I don't see how she can refuse your love, Rafe. She is your wife."

"Refuse *my* love?"

"Old fellow, 'tis very clear to me that you're as much in love with her as you ever were."

Rafe hung his head, and his horse moved restlessly under him. "I don't want to admit it, but yes, I love her beyond reason, but I broke the delicate thread of trust when I abandoned her."

Nick's face filled with resolution. "We'll find a way to tie it back together."

FOURTEEN

They rode along the riverbank, watching as rolls of lead gray clouds formed over the horizon.

"More snow, I'll wager," Nick said, a frown creasing his brow. "Winter has come early to these parts."

Rafe told Nick the details about Beau's deal with his father. "Is there any way we can stop Lochlade in his unbridled acquisitions of land?"

"Not that I can think of right now. Beau is too devious to do illegal business deals."

"You're right, Nick. The deals all have the air of respectability, even my father's gambling debt. He wouldn't be the first to have gambled away his estate."

"Nor the last. At least your father didn't put a bullet through his head, as some do in desperate situations."

"Yes."

"Men like Beau have no conscience," Nick said at last. "I'm appalled to hear about your father's debt."

"In a strange, twisted way, it brought him and me closer."

"I guess you should thank Beau for that," Nick said sarcastically.

"Hell and damn, I would like to meet that ruthless man at dawn with pistols," Rafe said heatedly. "But finding Bridget is more important than anything else right now."

"Besides, you can't confront Lochlade. He'll just point out that he's doing business fair and square. He has the upper hand at this point."

Rafe grimaced. "You're right." He turned his mount in the direction he'd come. "Let's visit some of the cottagers at Lochlade once again. Maybe someone knows something or has a relative who moved to London—general information."

"Can't hurt. We're not getting any more details out of the gentry," Nick replied, and put the heels to the flanks of his horse.

"Only problem is that the servants are a close-mouthed lot."

They rode through the woods toward the back of Lochlade. The sun shone from a pale blue sky, and snow glittered in thin patches along their path. Chickadees chirped in the trees, jumping from branch to branch as if curious to follow their progress.

They heard riders around a bend in the lane. To Rafe's surprise, he almost collided with Andria's mare. Behind her rode Derek Guiscard on a large dappled gray. Andria's eyes widened as she saw Rafe, and she gave him an embarrassed greeting. Nick swept off his tricorne and greeted the newcomers kindly.

Rafe knew that Andria was hiding her insecurity behind a cool exterior. He didn't blame her after everything that had gone on in the past.

Derek stared at him uneasily. Was he expecting a jealous scene, perhaps?

"Morning ride?" Rafe asked, making his voice neutral.

Andria shook her head. "Yes and no. I was too restless to work this morning, so we're continuing the investigation of Bridget's disappearance."

"So are we," Rafe said.

"If we could learn the whereabouts of the servant at the orphanage in London, we might have a real lead," Nick said. "It's a remote possibility one of the cottagers knows something. If anyone does, they would know. After all, they are on Lochlade land."

"What does that have to do with the servant?" Andria asked. "You suspect Beau hired the woman and sent her to London?"

"Anything is possible," Rafe said noncommittally, and gave Nick a glance of warning. "I won't throw around accusations until we know the whole truth."

"Very noble of you," Andria said with heavy sarcasm.

"The main thing is to discover Bridget," Derek said, as if seeking to smooth the waters.

They rode in a line along the narrow lane to the ramshackle group of cottages at the far end of the estate. The view was as bleak as Rafe felt inside, but he set his jaw and trudged on. Would they ever find the answers?

They asked the cottagers all kinds of things, hoping to joggle their minds for any kind of unusual information. Had they seen strangers in the area? Had someone new moved in to seek employment with the gentry? Had faraway friends or relatives visited?

The humble people were genuinely concerned for the little girl, whom everyone had met on occasion. One old woman, wearing a gray knitted shawl full of holes around her shoulders, particularly caught Rafe's interest.

"There was that young maid wot worked for Mr. Yarrow at Birchdale for only a month, two or three years ago. I cain't rightly remember, but there was some to-do up at the manor house, and then she disappeared. She had relatives outside Pemberton, she did. I worked there to help out in the kitchen during some big house party the Yarrows put on."

Nick described the maid as he remembered her from the orphanage. "Does that sound like the woman you saw at Birchdale?"

" 'Ceptin' the color of the hair. As far as I recall, she 'ad light hair, not dark."

Rafe and Andria exchanged glances. Perhaps this was a true lead. The hair color could be changed.

"She may 'ave 'ad a sister wot worked in Lunnon," the old woman concluded. "Look up Pemberton way."

"A two-hour ride over the fells," Derek said, and Rafe wished he had some memory of the outlying areas of Yorkshire.

"Let's go," Nick said, already turning his mount.

" 'Twill be a hard ride," Rafe said to Andria. "Nick and I should go alone." He gave Derek a pointed look.

"You can't forbid me to come," she said angrily. "I'm dressed warmly, and the thought of possibly finding some solid clues excites me no end. And Derek knows the way to Pemberton."

"Fortunately for us, 'tis a small hamlet," Derek said. "I'm sure all the inhabitants know each other."

Rafe nodded curtly, annoyed that Derek would join in, but he pushed away his dark feelings. Nothing could stand in the way of their search.

They rode hard. Andria's cheeks held a warm glow, and her eyes had taken on a deep sparkle. It was no mystery that she loved to ride, Rafe thought. His own hope was rising the closer they got to Pemberton. He enjoyed the grand sweeping vistas of the fells, feeling the crisp air across his face.

Andria watched him turn his face toward the breeze, his wavy long hair blowing free, his chiseled features so familiar and so beloved. She drew a sharp breath. Love. There was no room for that or any chance of bringing it back.

Still, her heart remembered the love. His imprint was on her heart forever. She closed her eyes for a moment and remembered how her body had responded to his love-making. It was as if no time had passed at all; she had welcomed him in the familiar dance as if nothing had happened between them. Even now, her body threatened to betray her as she felt a sweetness pouring through her and the longing to invite him to her bed again.

Stop it! she cried to herself. She watched his broad back as he rode ahead of the group. He fit right in with the wild and windswept moors, untamed but controlled, as if knowing he was master of the elements.

Derek rode up beside her. "It would be a miracle if we could discover someone who knows that mysterious servant we're looking for."

"She knew who Rafe is—or was told who he is. Someone wanted him to know," she said.

Derek adjusted his hat. "It could've been innocent. She went to London, worked at the orphanage, recognized Rafe, told him, and left."

"Yes . . . but why can't she be found?"

Derek pursed his lips. "Any number of reasons. She could've married and moved to the south counties or to Scotland."

"Yes, it makes sense, of course. But why would she want Rafe to believe that the wrong girl was his daughter? That is strange." She maneuvered her horse around a tree with low-hanging branches.

Derek nodded. "Yes, that's a puzzle."

"I want to believe that we'll find her." Andria shut out any possibility of disappointment.

"So do I." Derek took her hand and squeezed it just as

Rafe turned to look at them over his shoulder. There was no mistaking the flash of anger that he shot her.

When they arrived in the hamlet of Pemberton, Rafe clearly was in a foul mood. Andria looked around, wanting to admire the square medieval stone church that sat in the middle of the village, but she was caught up in her own whirlwind of emotions.

The riders gathered together and looked across the village green, where a few dry leaves danced in the wind.

Andria felt weary and cold, the tension of wanting so much to discover something positive about Bridget giving her a headache. She shivered and pulled her cloak more closely together.

"I know Parson Stone," Derek said. "Let's inquire at the vicarage."

They rode down the slope to the only lane through the village and found the vicarage right behind the church. Dormant rose vines curled around the fence and over an arch that led to the narrow walkway leading to the front door.

Derek got off his mount and went to knock on the door.

A round old woman in a black gown and a starched apron and mobcap opened the door. Her kindly blue eyes peered at the group, and Andria found herself saying a prayer for success. Her heart hammered painfully, and she suppressed an urge to cry.

"Good afternoon," Derek began, and asked for the vicar.

Parson Stone came out a few minutes later, cloaked and with hat in hand, as if he were about to leave. His white hair curled softly over his shoulders, and his gentle smile included them all.

He shook hands with Derek. "I'm delighted to see you, Mr. Guiscard. How's your mother?"

"Her health is failing, but she's in good spirits." Derek introduced everyone, and after mutual greetings, Rafe rode forward a few paces.

"Parson Stone, we're looking for a young servant from Pemberton who worked for Oliver Yarrow at Birchdale. Would you know the woman or the family? Her name could be Sally Vane."

Parson Stone tapped his chin with a bony fingertip. "Hmm, yes. Widow Vane had a daughter who went to work for gentry near Rowan's Gate. As far as I know, Sally Vane's still over the fell, never returned home."

"You don't know if she went to London?" Nick asked.

The old vicar glanced from one man to the other. "What is this about?"

"We're looking for my daughter, Lady Bridget," Rafe said. "She disappeared from Lochlade in Rowan's Gate two years ago."

"I remember that incident well. Everyone was talking about it," the vicar said.

"Sally Vane might know something important. All we want to do is talk with her," Andria said.

"Well, she isn't here, but you can find her mother in the cottage at the end of the road. Turn right from here."

Andria's mouth felt dry with worry, and she swallowed hard as they followed the vicar's directions.

Mrs. Vane was at home, hanging out yellowed sheets and worn towels. She was tall and thin, stooped at the shoulders. Her brown hair straggled from under a wrinkled mobcap. She bent over to grip another wet garment when she heard their approach. She dropped the linen, and bracing both hands on her back, she grimaced as she straightened up to look at them.

"Mrs. Vane?" Rafe greeted.

She murmured a greeting, her gaze darting from one to the other.

Rafe introduced himself and explained their mission and mentioned what the vicar had told them about Sally. "Have you heard from your daughter, Mrs. Vane?"

She shook her head, her face taking on a look of annoyance. "Sally allus wus the ind'pendent 'un."

Nick proceeded to give her a description of the servant in London, and Mrs. Vane nodded slowly.

"Aye, that's my Sally. She allus wanted bright hair, not the brown God gave 'er."

Andria found that she'd held her breath as she'd waited for the answer.

"Sally worked fer Mr. Yarrow for a time. She came back sayin' she didna care for 'is ways but that some'un had offered 'er employment in Lunnon. That excited, she wus! Went off two days later, never to be 'eard from agin. But I know she lives—know't in me bones. Sally could allus take care o' 'erself. No dimwit, her."

"Do you know who hired her?"

Mrs. Vane shook her head. "No . . . I'm not sure, but I know 'twus a gent. She 'as a right good friendship with gents. Niver at a loss for suitors. There wus that one with the silver 'air wot she liked. Only saw 'im in these parts once, though."

"Silver hair?" Rafe repeated softly.

Andria saw his jaw clench.

"Aye, noticed 'im 'cause of the 'air. Rightly odd color that is on a young man."

"Beau," Andria said, more to herself than to Derek beside her. "Beau knew Sally Vane."

Mrs. Vane continued: "And I'm proud to say she made good use of 'er connections."

"The man with the silver hair is Lord Lochlade." Rafe

voice trembled. "Do you know if she ever worked for him or did him any favors? Well paid, of course."

"Sally niver mentioned it. She did tell me once that 'e's a friend of Mr. Yarrow, nothin' else."

She let the words hang, and Andria had a feeling that they were not going to get anything else out of her.

"She never returned from London?" Nick asked.

"If ye want to find Sally, look in Lunnon." The woman cackled. "That'll take ye some time. Needle in a 'ays-tack."

Nick smiled grimly. "I'm very aware of that."

Mrs. Vane returned to her chore. "Good luck t'ye. An' if ye see 'er, tell 'er to come 'ome an' see 'er ole mother. I could use a few bob."

"That would probably be a good thing," Andria murmured under her breath, and watched as Rafe gave the woman a handful of coins.

Her uneasiness grew as they rode out of the village. Surely Beau would remember Sally. He might know what had become of her. The thought made her queasy. She sensed there were more currents under the surface, like the dark depths of the River Fynn. She felt the urge to immediately confront Beau, but weariness weighed down her limbs. And there would be no direct confrontation. She knew that Beau would never give her a straight answer.

They halted their mounts on the ascent of the fell and turned to look back.

"Now we know Sally Vane hails from here and that it's her real name, but we're no closer to finding her," Nick said with a sigh. "I would've found her in London if there was a trace."

"If only we could make Beau give us some information," Rafe said coldly. "It would be easier to wring water out of a rock."

"I'll talk to him," Andria said with some hesitation. "He's never denied me anything."

Rafe gave her a dark, inscrutable look, and his lips thinned. She knew he wanted to say what leaped to his mind, but he held back.

She glanced at Derek, but he avoided her. He looked very pale, and the sadness around him was palpable. Something ate at him, and it seemed that the trip had done nothing to cheer him up. The sensitive man was taking the mystery of Bridget hard, she thought.

She shivered. It was colder now, and her feet felt numb. "Are we riding back today?" she asked, not wanting to complain.

Rafe glanced to the darkening sky. "The snow is coming in." He gave Andria another inscrutable look. "We can still ride back. It won't be dark until four or later."

Nick looked at Andria, noting that she was trembling. He said, shaking his head, " 'Tis better to take rooms at the inn in the valley. Not very comfortable, of course, but we need shelter from the storm."

"Shelter from the storm?" Rafe commented. "It hasn't even begun. 'Twill get a lot worse before it gets better."

FIFTEEN

The Fiddler, the inn at the outskirts of Pemberton, did not have much to recommend itself, but the taproom was warm, and delicious smells of cooking stew and hot coffee attracted the weary group.

Andria went to the large fire in the fireplace and pulled off her gloves. She welcomed the warmth with closed eyes. Feeling disconnected, she heard Rafe discussing food and rooms with the landlord in the background. His voice stirred all kinds of warm sensations in her. It wasn't just the fire enclosing her in a circle of warmth; his presence gave her strength and comfort.

She heard Nick and Derek say something about caring for the horses. The door hinges squealed as they left. A blast of cold air swept across the floor, and blessed silence descended upon the room.

She started as Rafe's hands closed over her shoulders and he began to pull off her heavy cloak. "You don't need this. The fire will do a better job of warming you without the barrier of thick wool."

She glanced at him as he folded the cloak and placed it on a wooden bench near the fireplace.

"Are you tired, Andria?"

She didn't want to admit it, as she'd sworn she could easily accomplish the ride over the mountains. "I'm glad we came here. Beau will remember Sally Vane and help us discover what became of her."

Rafe didn't reply. She sensed that he didn't believe her. "I don't understand the hatred you hold toward Beau," she said coolly. "Even before you left me, you could not stand his sight. Evidently that hasn't changed."

"When I returned, I didn't remember him, but he hasn't done anything to endear himself to me since I got back," Rafe said tersely.

"Jealousy is a vile feeling. It corrodes everything." Andria regretted bringing it up, for she saw the stubborn look on Rafe's face.

"I said nothing about jealousy," he said, and kicked at a smoking log that had rolled off its brothers in the fireplace. "And I know what you're going to say next, Andria. 'You don't own me.' Spare me, please! You own a dog but not people. At least give me that much credit."

Anger burned bright in his eyes, but he pulled up a comfortable, if decrepit, armchair to the fire. "Here, make yourself comfortable."

Grateful for his offer, she sank down into its depths. To her surprise, Rafe began to massage her tense shoulders and neck muscles. His touch felt divine, and she leaned into it, marveling at the sensitive fingers finding every hard knot of anxiety. His hands knew how to make magic in so many ways, she thought.

"You've never been this accommodating, Rafe. Is this something you learned in Flanders?"

"Certainly not!" He wove his hands into her hair and massaged her scalp. "This is something I want to do for you, as I know these past weeks have been very hard on you."

"I have difficulty getting used to the gentleness, Rafe.

You would never have thought about my aching shoulders in the past."

"How would I act then?" He dragged his fingertips over her forehead, every movement bringing more release to her.

"You would've thought of dinner and the brandy bottle afterwards. A card game with your friends, unless you felt like tumbling me in the bed. But you never really *knew* me."

"I hope to make up for that," he said, heaving a deep sigh. His voice softened as he dragged a finger over her collarbone and the sensitive length of her throat. "I'd love to follow this line with kisses right now."

Her eyes flew open as he actually bent down and trailed a series of kisses on her throat. The tender caress sent shivers of pleasure through her body, and she felt a sudden urge to cry. Why had this come so late—too late? He touched her breasts, and they responded immediately, honey flowing through her veins. She could hear him breathe more rapidly.

"I've been thinking about you all day," he murmured. "If our business hadn't been so serious, I would've been tempted to bring you back to bed this morning."

"Our lovemaking shouldn't have happened," she said, trying to pull herself away from his touch.

"Our lovemaking was perfect, and don't deny it, Andria. We were like two violins harmonizing together in the sweetest of music."

"I didn't know you had a poetic strain, Rafe." She could not make herself move away from his magic touch.

"I didn't know I did, but you brought it out of me, darling." He kissed the back of her neck, and she could feel the pins falling out of her hair as he kept massaging her scalp. She knew her face was flushed from the heat of him and of the fire.

If anyone saw her with her hair down, they would draw their own conclusions, wouldn't they? Dreams of passion mingled with that delicious feeling of relaxation.

When he covered her mouth with his in a deep kiss, she could only respond, by now a helpless puddle of desire. She wound her arms around his neck as his tongue invaded her mouth with exquisite sweetness. She found herself trembling for more, wanting no more barriers between their bodies.

He groaned against her mouth and almost toppled over from his precarious knee stand by the chair. "I want you badly," he said roughly, his hand unerringly traveling to her breast under the kerchief and teasing the nipple into a hard nub of throbbing desire through the fabric of her gown. Where was her resistance?

"Someone will come in . . ." she said dreamily.

She did not protest as he lifted her into his arms and carried her upstairs to the first bedchamber on the right. "We'll make this bed ours," he said, and kicked the door shut behind him.

The room felt cool, but Andria was on fire. He laid her on the bed, then pulled off his boots, unfastened his breeches and dragged them off. His hard manhood rose huge and swollen with desire, and he stood by the bed, pressing himself against her welcoming hand. She enclosed the velvet shaft and started a slow, maddening stroke that had him groaning and breathing harder.

His face was contorted with pleasure, and she teased the throbbing head with her fingertips until he bit down hard on his bottom lip. She raised herself on her elbow and took him into her mouth—the slippery wetness making him wild. With a moan as if in the throes of deep pain, he pulled away from her and bent to lift up her skirts.

Starting above her garters, he trailed wet kisses all along the tender skin of her inside thighs until she writhed with lust. She dug her fingertips into his shoulders, feeling the hard muscles beneath. His tongue found her inner lips and the throbbing center of her arousal. He skillfully moved around it, tasting her and flicking his tongue over her until she could stand no more teasing.

"Oh . . . Rafe . . ."

He raised his head and looked deeply into her eyes. His hand freed one of her breasts from the deep neckline of her bodice and caressed it, sucking deeply on her nipple as his swollen manhood pushed at her throbbing femininity.

"Come to me," she whispered. "Fill me."

He chuckled at her eagerness and fit himself to the damp folds. With a groan, he sank into her sweetness, and she cried out with pleasure. He invaded her mouth with his, their tongues making a mad dance.

"God, I've longed for this all day," he said as he came up for air. "You're like . . . fever in my . . . blood."

He moved within her in the perfect rhythm that brought her ever higher. Slowly, he increased the speed of his movements, his breathing coming more labored as he was reaching his climax.

"I need you inside of me," she whispered. "I need you so badly . . . *Rafe* . . ." She cried out as she flew over the edge and came apart in the storm of ecstasy.

He grew tense and held her hard as he exploded with pleasure, his tongue still mating deeply with hers.

The symphony of their lovemaking slowed down to the soothing music of their combined breaths. They lay in each other's arms for a long time, perhaps throughout eternity, Andria thought.

"I've never wanted anyone as much as I wanted you today, my darling," Rafe said, his voice hoarse with emotion. "As you bent your head forward by the fire, the sight of your vulnerable neck sent me into a frenzy of desire."

"You know how to take advantage of me," she said sleepily, every inch of her body singing with contentment.

They rested in each other's arms, whispering endearments. Aeons later, Rafe stood, smoothing down her gowns and adjusting her bodice. He pulled on his breeches and boots. "You ought to sleep now, my sweet. I'll see to it that a fire is laid in the grate. You must be exhausted."

"I am," she said, struggling with the love that was ever growing for this man who had caused her so much pain in the past. She felt infused with love, and she never wanted the harsh reality to come back and ruin it. She closed her eyes, and Rafe placed a quilt over her.

He bent down and pressed a kiss to her cheek. "You're the most maddening creature alive, and I can't seem to stay away from you," he said. "You're in my blood always. You are my perfect half."

Andria could say the same about him, but she only snuggled more deeply into the pillows.

"Sleep, Andria."

Rafe closed the door to the bedchamber and leaned his back against it. He relived every moment of their lovemaking, feeling that she had forever changed his life. God, how he loved his wife! Could it be possible to love someone that much after this short a time? Maybe the time wasn't short. Part of him had always known her even if he couldn't remember. She had responded to his every touch as if he knew exactly what she liked.

He wished he was as surefooted when it came to her heart. She was fire in his blood, and he had to be careful how he treated her. This time she'd been willing to engage in a wild, erotic dance, but next time? Who knows? All he knew was that he didn't want to lose her ever again.

He went downstairs and found Nick and Derek eating pork chops and mashed potatoes by the fire. Wine glowed ruby red in glasses at their elbows. Pangs of hunger went through him as he inhaled the delicious aroma of the meat.

"I made sure Andria is settled upstairs," he said sheepishly. "She was exhausted, even though she was putting up a brave front."

Nick gave him a wink. "I'm sure you tucked her in just fine."

Rafe looked away. He waved to the landlord. "I could eat two dinners right now." A few minutes later he was tucking into his meal.

"I'm rather tired," Derek said. "I think I'll go upstairs after dinner and get some rest."

"We'll return to Rowan's Gate first thing in the morning," Nick said. He swallowed some wine. "Derek, if you don't mind me asking, you've known Lord Lochlade for a long time. What are his motives?"

Derek heaved a deep sigh. "I think you've figured out that it's his greed for power, seeing as he had little as a young man. They lived on his mother's modest estate. Beau's father didn't amount to much and had little, seeing as he was a younger brother. I think Beau both loved him and hated him. If I were you, I would not make Beau into an enemy."

"Too late for that," Nick said, glancing at Rafe.

Tense silence hung for a moment.

"Enemy? Can you explain that?" Rafe asked, sitting down at the table.

"He'll fight for his possessions. He won't let anyone stand in his way or threaten him, as he's won everything fair and square."

"So you know about his land acquisitions?" Nick asked, breaking off a piece of bread from the loaf on the table.

" 'Tis not a secret."

Another minute passed in silence.

"Is there anything you can tell us about Lochlade, any secret vices, any strange goings-on?" Rafe asked. "He seems obsessed."

Derek's gaze slid away. "The usual, I'm sure," he said with little conviction. "Gambling and drinking, but Beau is careful about his health. He wouldn't do things that would ruin his elegant physique; you've probably noticed that he's most conscious of his outward appearance."

"Of course," Rafe said.

Nick and Rafe exchanged glances. Something was missing, Rafe thought, and they would never get Derek to talk about it. Rafe could sense the man's fear even if he tried to hide it with an expression of nonchalance.

They finished their meals in silence, and Rafe concluded the excellent dinner with a slice of apple pie. It melted on his tongue. The simple meal had been better than anything he'd tasted since he came back.

Derek excused himself and went up to rest.

"We won't see him until tomorrow," Nick said, downing the last of the wine. "What do you say we pay Beau a visit tonight?"

"Just my thought," Rafe said. "We'll somehow make the man talk."

SIXTEEN

The wind whipped over the moors and whined down chimneys as they rode into Rowan's Gate. A loose shutter banged against a wall, and the metal sign over the inn flapped on its hinges.

The village looked bleak in the faint night light, and hard snowflakes danced in the gusts, stinging Rafe's face as he turned into the wind. He swore under his breath, keenly aware of the cold. But no storm could stop him from his mission.

Nick pressed his tricorne low over his face and fell into step with Rafe. They slowed their mounts to a walk.

"What time is it?" Nick asked.

Rafe pulled out his watch on its gold chain. "Around seven. Not too late to beard the beast in his den. He's probably sitting down to a sumptuous dinner."

"He's more vulnerable then, with a stomach full of food and a bottle of claret under his belt."

Rafe laughed coldly. "I'm not sure you can use the word 'vulnerable' in the same sentence as 'Beau Saxon.' "

"I've been thinking as we rode from Pemberton. Let's just tell Beau we *know* that he hired Sally Vane to work for me at the orphanage. We can pretend that we know his motive as well."

"The truth is," Rafe said, "that he must've discovered

that I didn't perish in Flanders and then set out to pull me back up here via that servant."

"Couldn't he just approach you himself in London? Why the sneaky, backhanded ways?"

"I wish I knew why," Rafe said with passion. "He's gone to great lengths to ruin me and my family."

"All for his quest to win Andria?" Nick shook his head. "Unbelievable."

"There has to be a deeper motive. He knows Andria only wants friendship—if that."

"Friendship?" Nick snorted. " 'Struth, who wants to be friends with a poisonous snake?"

"Andria has polite ways of addressing the issue," Rafe said, feeling impatient. "I just know we're in some kind of a race with Lochlade, and I want to get ahead of him. It's only that I don't rightly know what I'm racing against."

"All I know is that we have to outwit him. Brute force won't get us anywhere except into the nearest jail."

Rafe nodded and retrieved the corner of his cloak that the wind had torn loose. He wrapped it more tightly around himself. "I'm ready. We'll play the bluff and see what happens."

As they rode up the winding road to the top of the fell right above Lochlade, they stopped and looked down at the white landscape.

"The snow is coming down heavily now. We'd better take it slow down the path to protect the horses," Rafe said.

"Let's head off the path down there." Nick pointed at a stand of trees. "Less snow, and the vegetation will protect us from being seen."

Rafe nodded and set his mount to the steep descent. They arrived at the bottom without incident, and the trees offered great shelter from the wind. They stopped for a time and stared toward the large estate. Candles glowed in some of the windows, but the stillness was complete outside.

"Evidently he's dining alone tonight," Nick said.

"People don't want to travel on a nasty night like this," Rafe said, feeling a strange premonition of danger.

"I'm grateful that Andria is safe and sound in Pemberton."

Nick nodded, slowly urging his mount along the narrow path among the trees. As they neared the estate, he held up his hand in a warning. "Someone is coming," he whispered.

The faint sounds of hooves reached Rafe's ears, and they waited, concealed, as a group of riders came out of the spinney behind the estate. The men were heavily cloaked, all wearing dark colors that looked stark black against the snow.

They rode in silence, almost as if in a procession up the fell, but veered off halfway up and followed a path that cut around the fell. Rafe had noticed on a previous occasion that between Great Fell and Devil's Fell wound a narrow valley that was barely accessible on horseback.

"What are they doing? I wonder," he mused aloud as the last of the men had disappeared around the bend of the hill. He remembered that Robert Bostow had mentioned men in cloaks.

"That would be interesting to find out," Nick said grimly. "I have a feeling they are not out to do charity."

They followed the men at a safe distance. Snow was coming down in earnest now, veils of white moving across their path.

As they turned into the narrow valley, they saw the horsemen up ahead, a dark procession that led to the heart of the valley. The two fells rose high above them, forming an impenetrable wall.

Then, even as Rafe stared at the line of men, they disappeared from view.

"What the devil? 'Tis as if they were swallowed by the snow," he said. "There's something sinister going on."

"Only crazy men would be out on a night like this."

Rafe laughed. "I suppose we fall into that category, then, but we have a mission."

"The mission was to confront Beau about Sally Vane," Nick reminded him.

"The night is young, and this has ignited my curiosity."

"Mine, too. Let's go." Nick urged his horse forward, and they followed the path trampled by the other horses. They slowed down as they neared the spot where the men had disappeared.

"I surmise there's a cave of sorts at the bottom of the fell."

Nick nodded. "Has to be. This is getting stranger by the minute."

They rode until the path ended and found a natural dark opening in the shape of a tall Gothic window. The horses had trampled the area in front to mud and disappeared.

"We'd better leave the horses out here," Nick whispered. "We don't want to alert their mounts of our presence."

"That might be hard to avoid," Rafe said grimly, "but we'll take our chances."

They left their horses tied to a gorse bush and proceeded into the cave. They could smell the other horses nearby and heard them chomping on hay. One of them whickered a greeting, but the others ignored Rafe and Nick as the two men followed the weak light at the end of the tunnel.

" 'Sfaith, this is more and more puzzling. Can you smell that?" Nick murmured.

Rafe was fully aware of the scent of burning wood and the more subtle waves of incense. "It smells like the church on Sunday," he whispered back.

"Myrrh, and something else. I've smelled that cloying scent in the opium dens of London."

They exchanged grim looks in the gloom and advanced. The light was growing brighter. Leaning back against the wall, they peered around the corner.

Masses of golden candle flames flickered in the large cave. The candles were black. Sitting around a large oval stone table were five men dressed completely in black hooded cloaks and wearing black satin masks.

Rafe held his breath, feeling the brooding evil in the cave. The space was steeped in darkness except for the candles, and the darkness had a thick, menacing quality, as if it had been summoned into the cave many times. The rough walls were steeped in it.

"Black magic," Nick whispered as one of the men's voices rose in an incantation of gibberish. His voice keened higher and higher, vibrating against the walls.

Rafe took another look around the corner and noticed the altar that had been erected at the far end of the cave. He saw layers of cloths, some type of altar covering in a shiny black material. Lit candelabras sat at each end. On top of the altar lay a still figure, a limp hand hanging over the edge of the rock slab.

Rafe's breath caught in his throat. "God's bones, there's something or someone on the altar," he hissed at Nick.

Nick took a quick look, and his mouth set in a grim line. "An offering?"

"A human offering? There's blood all over the cloth. That's what makes it look shiny."

The words hung between them, too hideous to contemplate.

Rafe pulled Nick with him back toward the horses so that they could speak without being overheard. "Let's talk about this, Nick. I cannot stand by and let these men offer one of my fellow men to the Devil. That's what they're doing."

"Yes . . . sure looks like it." Nick rubbed the back of his neck as if that would ease his tension.

"You know Lochlade is part of this group, probably that tall leader at the head of the table."

Nick nodded. "I believe you're right. He is the kind who would not hesitate to ask the Dark One for support in his endeavors."

"So if we give ourselves away, we'll have lost the element of surprise where Beau's concerned."

Nick agreed with a grunt. "But let's wait and see what happens. If the blood's any indication, the person on the altar is already dead."

" 'Struth, you're right."

"Let's go back and watch some more and see what happens." Nick patted the side of his thigh. "I've got my sword, and I have pistols in the saddlebags."

"Won't have time to retrieve and prime them." Rafe followed Nick and touched the cool hilt of his own sword. If they could save a life, he wouldn't hesitate to fight the men.

"Never expected this turn of events," he muttered to himself. "Beau is even more sinister than we thought."

They watched as the men surrounded the altar where the two candelabras sent out ample light.

Murmured incantations rose toward the ceiling of the cave, where smoke hung in a gray haze. Suddenly, one of the men, probably the leader, raised a glittering, jewel-encrusted dagger into the air above the body on the altar.

The body did not move, nor did it make a sound. It lay shrouded in black.

Rafe's hand flew to the sword's hilt as the dagger flashed through the air and plunged into the body on the altar. Nick placed a restraining hand on his arm.

"Only part of the ceremony," he whispered. "The person is certainly dead. Look at all the blood on the floor."

They watched in horror as the man carved figures with his dagger on the body. He spoke in that strange tongue and then placed the dagger blade in a brazier glowing red on the altar. The air filled with the odor of burning flesh. The men moved around the altar in a slow procession, each making signs over the body.

Rafe turned away, dragging Nick with him. "Let's get out of here. We'll come back when they're gone."

"I would like to know the identity of the person on the altar," Nick said, breathing deeply as they stepped out of the cave. The air was crisp and fresh, a blessing after the thick odors of the cave.

In silence they gathered the reins of their horses and climbed into the saddles. "Let's wait in that thicket of trees again," Rafe suggested, chilled from the scene he'd witnessed.

Nick didn't respond, but Rafe knew he didn't have an objection. They had ridden together at night for so long, they could read each other's minds. They huddled among the trees and waited for the procession to return.

One hour later, the men came back, their cloaks still intact, their face masks still in place.

Nick and Rafe watched in fascination as the procession passed their hiding place. Rafe prayed that the horses wouldn't give them away, and they didn't.

Just as soon as the men were invisible, Rafe and Nick turned back to the cave. Now it was filled with darkness, and they were loathe to go inside. But as soon as they'd entered the cave, they found tinderboxes and fresh candles on a ledge right at the entrance.

"They have thought of everything," Rafe said as he lit one of the black tapers.

" 'Tis obviously not the first time they've met here."

They cautiously went into the main cave, holding the tapers aloft. Rafe moved across the room to the altar, his heart pounding with dread.

It was one thing to fight a man face-to-face, but it was wholly another to fight the Devil. *If Lochlade has sold his soul to the Devil, I'll have to fight the Master of Darkness,* Rafe thought.

"The body is still here, Nick."

"Yes . . . let's see who it is." Nick touched the body. "Getting cold. Must've been dead for a few hours." He looked across the altar to Rafe, and they both took a deep steadying breath.

Nick lifted a corner of the shroud and pulled it back from the face. He gasped, suddenly bracing himself against the stone slab altar.

Rafe looked down at the woman whose waxy face looked still in death. He remembered her from the orphanage in London.

" 'Tis Sally Vane," Nick said.

"They killed her because they knew we were on her trail," Rafe said. "She must've been somewhere close for them to get to her that fast."

"Let's take the body and hide it. We'll use it as evidence against Beau later, once we can prove that he's at the heart of this atrocity."

"We ought to contact the authorities now. We have her." Rafe pointed at the dead body.

"Yes, but Beau is the magistrate of this area. We'll have to bring outside help," Nick said. "The best thing is if we could catch the men in the middle of a ceremony, because we can't prove a thing without them in action. Since we didn't see their faces—"

"One of them must've been Beau."

"I'm sure he's involved, but we can't prove he or one of the others killed this woman. One of them will have to be made to confess."

Rafe nodded. "Let's take the body to Rowan Hall until we can bring her to Pemberton. There's an old crypt where the family is buried."

"Yes. I've been pondering who could help us to arrest Beau," Nick said grimly. "My old friend Captain Emerson—south county militia—might be able to."

"Beau is quite mad," Rafe said. "It's surprising how he's been able to influence the men around here."

"I'm sure it started out innocently enough. Drinking, gambling, a few pipes of opium, willing maids. Boredom spawns all kinds of vices," Nick said. "I've seen it before."

"But death?" Rafe made a noise of disgust.

" 'Tis the height of arrogance to think one can mete out life or death."

They rolled the body in the shroud and carried her outside. Nick settled her across the rump of his horse. He glanced over at Rafe in the gloom.

"I know what you're thinking, old fellow. If Sally Vane is dead, what could've happened to Bridget?"

"You're right," Rafe replied, feeling the full weight of sadness inside. "Andria will be desperate."

"Let's find some proof of Beau's perfidy before we tell Andria the truth. There's no need for her to know right now." Nick pressed his tricorne deep over his forehead. "Let's go."

"I'll have Travers keep an eye on the body at Rowan Hall in case the men start snooping around for it. He's completely reliable."

Nick looked at Rafe grimly. "They'll know we took the body."

"They'll have to prove it; which they won't," Rafe replied.

They rode in haste to Rowan Hall and with Travers's help hid the body in one of the empty slots in the crypt. The old butler was appalled but assured them he would keep the secret until the end.

"I'm loathe to go back to Pemberton tonight, but we must," Nick said as they rode away from the Hall.

"I don't like to keep Andria in the dark, and as you know, she comes and goes at Lochlade as she wishes, vulnerable to Beau's schemes."

"At least we can be sure Beau won't hurt her. He's stubborn and proud; he'll continue trying to win her heart."

"Just the thought of her going anywhere near him makes me sick," Rafe said.

SEVENTEEN

The inn at Pemberton was quiet and dark as they rode up. Rafe felt exhausted and drained by the emotional shock of finding Sally Vane's body. A dark sadness had settled in his heart, and he heaved a deep sigh, hoping for some relief. It didn't happen; every moment would have to be lived through, he thought.

"I'll seek my bed, my friend," Nick said morosely. "This has been an eventful day, to say the least. On a brighter note, we might be closer to solving the puzzle."

Rafe nodded as they led their mounts to the dark stables. "Yes, 'tis only a matter of time. Beau has more on his conscience than we ever expected."

There was no sign of any hostlers around the stables. In silence they settled their horses for the night.

Cold from the ride, they stood in front of the dying fire in the taproom. The room was pleasantly warm and still smelled of the pork and onion that had been served earlier.

"Our next step is important," Rafe said. "Beau will use his henchmen to keep an eye on us."

"I ought to go back to London tomorrow and solicit the help from Captain Emerson. With him at our side, we can gain the support of the local militia."

Rafe grinned. "A splendid idea—especially since you must miss Serena terribly."

Nick nodded, a smile brightening his face. "You're right, but I will see you through this, Rafe. To the end." He looked closely at his friend. "Admit it; you've got your own longings for your beloved. Imagine that, falling in love for the second time with the same woman. That's a miracle, or maybe it isn't. Somehow that's proof that it's the right thing."

Rafe felt unbidden heat rise to his face. "Yes, I believe that. I have fallen deeply in love with her. She's like a fine wine intoxicating my blood."

Even as he spoke, a deep desire came over him to see Andria. "She doesn't allow me into her heart yet, and her trust in me has to be rebuilt before I can hope to reclaim her."

"She may not *show* the depth of her feelings for you," Nick said shrewdly.

Rafe grimaced. "Why would she? She didn't lie when she said I left her without as much as a word of regret."

Nick rubbed his chin. "Hmm. What I know of you, Rafe, you're not the type to run away from problems."

"Perhaps I was then. I just don't know."

"The past doesn't count anymore. You're an honorable, reliable man. We'll discover the truth, and you'll be vindicated."

Rafe nodded. "That I believe. We can't change the past, but we can make sure that Beau won't hurt anyone else."

Nick slapped Rafe's shoulder. "Good night, old fellow."

"Good night." As Rafe stood alone, weariness settled in his body, and he slowly followed Nick upstairs.

The upper hallway brooded dark and silent. He decided to look in on Andria before he went to his own room. The door creaked slightly as he walked into her chamber, but she didn't stir. The dying fire threw a faint light into the room.

As if in the throes of a dream, she moved her head back and forth, her fair hair spread over the pillow. She moaned softly, a sound that turned into a sob. Her hand flew from under the coverlet as if trying to ward off some unseen threat.

Rafe caught her soft hand and gently soothed it between his two. "You have no idea how much I missed you," he whispered. "But I'm glad you didn't have to see what we found tonight."

The back of her hand reminded him of velvet, and her long, thin fingers looked lost in his much larger hand. He caressed them, one after the other, and she settled down.

"Your courage and your spirit constantly inspire me and give me a reason to continue in this abyss of darkness. I live for the hope that one day you'll return my love." He lowered his voice even more. "You're the dream that always supported me in my darkest hour—even if I didn't know it then. When I held you in my arms, I knew I'd come home, and I knew my deepest desperation as you rejected me."

He lowered his head, tears burning in his eyes. "I don't know if I can ever truly win you back, but I'll have to spend my days trying."

He carefully lifted her hand and kissed each fingertip. She stirred, but he didn't move, wishing her back to peaceful sleep.

"You're the sweetest, the most exciting, woman I've ever met. The most alluring, the most maddening, the most intelligent, the most compassionate." He leaned closer to her ear. "And the most lovable."

She moaned as if disturbed by another nightmare. Without hesitation, he took off all his clothes and slowly slipped under the covers so as not to awaken her. As if aware of him, she cuddled closer, and he cradled her head on his shoulder.

"And you do have the silkiest hair and the softest thighs," he added, tracing a fingertip along the delicate contour of her face.

"What I'm trying to say," he whispered, "is that I love you, I love you, I love you."

Feeling the contentment of those words, he drew a deep sigh and settled his head against hers. He knew he would sleep tonight.

Andria awakened as the sun slanted through the tiny window in the unfamiliar room. It took a moment to remember where she was, and then she felt the warm body next to hers. She turned her head quickly and saw Rafe's face next to hers.

At first she had an urge to push him out of her bed, but relented. She had nothing to gain by fighting with him.

Dark stubble shadowed his jaw, and she noticed the twin creases between his eyebrows, worry lines that did not smooth out in his sleep. By the droop of his lips, she sensed his sadness. It echoed within her, and she wished that today would give them some definite answers so that they could go on with their lives.

As if he felt her scrutiny, he opened his dark eyes and stared right into her soul. Her breath hitched in her throat, and she swallowed convulsively. She was about to open her mouth, but he placed his hand gently on her lips. For the longest moment they remained staring at each other. Heat rose in her cheeks.

His hand smelled faintly of soot, as if he'd worked on

the fire during the night. He pulled her closer, and she didn't reject him. She believed he would try to seduce her in the bright morning light, but he only touched her face, tracing a pattern with his fingertip. He caressed her head, pushing back the tangles of her hair.

"You were having nightmares," he said at last. "When I got into bed with you, you calmed down. You settled so naturally on my shoulder, as if you'd never been away from it."

She glanced away. "The body remembers, but we've discussed this ad nauseam. You don't have me."

He stiffened imperceptibly. "So you have told me on various occasions. I'm not hard of hearing." He flung aside the covers and got out of bed, his naked body hard and glorious in the morning light.

The sweetness of desire filled her, and she found that she wanted him to return to her bed, but he didn't. She could not find the words to ask him, and the pain of the past held her back. It would take a lot to eradicate that pain, and she would never want to feel it again.

He dressed hastily, his back turned toward her.

"I'll have someone up here to make the fire," he said as he addressed her from the door. "See you downstairs as soon as you can be ready. There's no reason to linger here at Pemberton."

"Yes, I need to go back to Stowehurst and think about our next move and change clothes. We have to discover what happened to Sally Vane."

He only nodded, not meeting her gaze.

Rafe longed to sweep her into his arms and kiss her, but he had to concentrate on the work at hand.

Downstairs, there was a note from Nick saying he was fulfilling his end of the plans. *Expect me back with Emerson before the week is up,* he finished. Four days, maybe five, Rafe thought. By then I'll have some answers, he thought.

He met Derek by the fire in the taproom. The other man had already eaten his breakfast, if the empty plate was any indication. The room smelled of fresh coffee and baking bread.

Derek looked drawn and pale, as if in pain. Rafe could not feel any animosity toward Andria's friend this morning.

"Did you have a bad night?" Rafe asked.

Derek nodded. "Yes . . . it was filled with nightmares, but I'll recover."

Rafe indicated Derek's twisted red hand with its puffy fingers. "That must give you untold pain at times. Why don't you have it amputated?"

" 'Tis a reminder . . ." His voice drifted off as if he'd just caught himself. "I might have it amputated eventually, but all surgery is a gamble at best."

"Yes."

Rafe ordered a plate of ham and eggs from the landlord, and a tankard of ale. He was ravenously hungry. As he stared into the leaping fire, he said cautiously, "You're a man who keeps much to himself, aren't you? None of the local men has offered you a lasting friendship?"

Derek shrugged noncommittally. "We don't share the same interests," he said.

Rafe smiled. "Not one artist among them, eh?"

Derek shook his head. "The locals are more the sporting type. I have some friends, but they don't reside in Rowan's Gate."

"Sometimes 'tis easier to get along with the females," Rafe said. "Andria makes friends easily."

"Yes, she's a very animated and friendly lady," Derek said tonelessly.

"Lord Lochlade seems to think so," Rafe said, nudging closer to the main interest of his conversation.

"Beau always admired Andria, but I think he admired Lochlade more."

Rafe decided to take the plunge. "What do you know about Lord Lochlade's past besides what you already told me?"

Derek gave him a sharp look, his mouth set in a thin line. "I don't discuss others behind their backs," he said.

Just as Rafe wanted to try some persuasion, the main door opened, and two gentlemen stepped inside. Rafe recognized Crisp, Lord Durand, and Malcolm, Lord Whitecomb. They looked like fashion plates in brightly hued brocade coats and Mechlin lace at their throats, hair powdered and tied back into queues. They lit up with practiced smiles as they saw Rafe and Derek.

"Ecod, Malcolm, the inn is already packed with guests," Crisp said. "What are you two doing in a remote spot like this?"

"I could ask the same of you," Rafe replied coolly, convinced that the men had arrived to spy. He imagined the two dressed in black cloaks and masks as part of the demonic group but had difficulty seeing them in anything less bright than pink. Not that everything didn't have a darker side.

"Derek, I didn't know you'd struck up a friendship with the outcast," Crisp continued, and flourished a snuff box in one hand. With flair he took a pinch and inhaled it in each nostril and delicately shook out the lace at his cuffs.

"What do you know of my friendships?" Derek replied. "You are not my confidant, nor do you have any part in my life. That was my choice even if we grew up in the same area of Yorkshire and attended the same schools."

Crisp lifted his shoulders in a shrug. His eyes gleamed

with malice. "Be that as it may. An outcast and a cripple may be a good combination—one that I personally stay away from."

"Then why are you bothering us?" Derek spat, rising, his chair falling back. "We didn't start this conversation."

Rafe noticed the clenched fist at Derek's side and the stormy expression on his face.

"A touch of boredom, mayhap," Crisp said, exchanging a glance with Malcolm. "In fact, I've been raring for a fight." He slowly peeled off his embroidered kid gloves. "Derek, you're the ugliest bastard on this side of the River Fynn."

A haze of red filled Rafe's mind, and he could barely control himself. As Derek lunged, Rafe caught his arm in an iron grip. "Don't!" he said between clenched teeth. "Don't play into his games. He'll only hurt you—for no reason."

"I shall pierce his traitorous black heart," Derek shouted.

"Come on, Derek," Crisp said silkily. "Let's step into the yard and have this out."

"Stop this nonsense," Rafe demanded.

Derek was beyond hearing, but Rafe held him back. It took all of his strength to push Derek aside and step in front of him.

Rafe challenged Crisp. "You would attack someone who doesn't have the full use of his hands? Cowardly bastard, come to me." Rafe pointed at his own chest. "I haven't forgotten my skills—still deadly with swords—and I would thoroughly enjoy taking you on. The both of you, if necessary."

Crisp paled with fury, and Malcolm laid a hand on his arm. "Surely there's something else we can choose as entertainment," he said to Crisp. "Too early in the morning for a fight."

Silence hung heavy as Crisp weighed the challenge in his mind. He took one look at Rafe's hand on the hilt of his sword and slowly backed off.

"Your hot temper is legendary," he said to Rafe. "One of these days 'twill be the death of you."

Rafe had no memory of having a hot temper. It had disappeared along with the rest of the past. Anger did seethe in his veins, but he was fully in control of his emotions. "As I said, I look forward to testing my skills against yours, Crisp. Anytime."

Tension simmered between them, and Rafe wondered why such animosity had grown against him.

Malcolm pulled Crisp toward a table at the other end of the room. "Let's just get something in our stomachs, Crisp. No need to mingle with these people of no account."

Rafe clenched his jaw, his hands itching to connect with the weakest part of the man's body, but he restrained himself.

As Crisp and Malcolm settled down, he turned toward Derek, who looked pale and drawn. Anguish glittered in his eyes.

"As I see it, there was no reason to take up his challenge," Rafe murmured.

"I know . . . but reason flew from my mind. All I could think of was getting even, but the outcome would've been a disaster for me." He held out his good hand toward Rafe. "Thank you."

Rafe looked into those anguished eyes and could not feel any of the old suspicion and jealousy. Derek was nothing if not a man of honesty and integrity. No wonder Andria liked him so much.

"Don't mention it. I can't abide bullies," he replied, and shook Derek's hand. "What I don't understand is why Crisp would operate on such a level of malice toward you."

The sound of footsteps on the stairs came to his ears, and the door opened. Andria, her pale face closed and features controlled, entered the taproom, but Rafe noticed the inner turmoil in her eyes.

Crisp and Malcolm flourished elegant bows.

"You look your beautiful self, Andria, but so sad," Crisp said. "Didn't exactly expect to meet you here." His dark eyes flashed with curiosity. "If you need a confidant, you know I'm always available." He indicated Rafe and Derek. "These two are not confidence inspiring, if you know what I mean."

"I'm sure *my wife* would look for support closer than to mere . . . acquaintances," Rafe said icily, his arms crossed over his chest.

"Acquaintances?" Crisp raised his eyebrows. "Surely she would call me a friend. We've known each other from the cradle."

"No need to talk about me as if I'm not here," Andria replied angrily. "I don't have problems finding a confidante should I need one."

"Prickly, prickly," Malcolm murmured.

She swept past the men, not even looking at Rafe.

A feeling of loneliness swept through him, but he steeled himself against the emotion. This was not the time to get emotional about Andria.

Feeling heavy and unrested, Andria sat down at one of the tables and called out to the landlord, who hurried from the kitchen to attend to her.

"Please bring me coffee and bread and butter," she said. The night's darkness still hung over her. Her sleep had been filled with nightmares except for one dream in which a loving presence had spoken the most soothing, loving words to her. She clung to that feeling even as a premonition of doom was trying to close in on her.

She glanced at Rafe's face, afraid of what she would read there, but he was only concentrating on Crisp, his face hard and angry. He had slept in her bed last night, and she had rested her head on his broad shoulder. A sensation of safety and caring had filled her, and his leaving this morning had left her with a restlessness she couldn't explain.

She only listened with half an ear to Crisp and Malcolm droning on about their invitation to some festive gathering at a distant estate. That Crisp could talk about such trivialities while Bridget was still missing hurt her. She had to remind herself that Bridget's disappearance meant little to people like Crisp. He concerned himself more with the fall of his cravat than with missing children.

Feeling a deep despair that she couldn't begin to express, she slathered butter on a piece of fragrant crusty bread and ate hungrily.

Rafe appeared at her side. "I pray you had a good night's sleep, Andria."

"I didn't have a desire to wake up," she replied, "but now I'm more determined than ever to get to the bottom of the mystery. I'll not rest until I discover what happened to Bridget."

Rafe nodded. "I agree." He took a deep breath. "You didn't say anything about the fact that I slept in your bed last night. Are you just going to avoid the subject of—us?"

"I have difficulty coming to grips with everything that is happening," she said cautiously. "But I have to admit that you've been a great comfort to me—even if you don't have any answers."

"I promise you, Andria, that as long as there's breath in my body, I'll work to make amends to you."

She lowered her gaze as a frisson of fear skittered along her spine. *As long as there's breath in my body.*

Such fear engulfed her, but what did it mean? It struck her that the thought of losing Rafe again made the pain deepen inside of her.

She realized how important it would be to solve the problems of the past if she were ever to move forward. "I have the strangest premonition of disaster," she said.

"This is not the place for you. I'll take you back to Stowehurst so that you can take a relaxing bath and speak with Rebecca," Rafe said, his eyes tired and dark. "There's nothing more we can do here in Pemberton."

She nodded. "Yes, I know, but how do we find Sally Vane?"

"Nick returned to London to do another investigation. Since she hasn't come back to these parts, 'tis most likely she's still in London." Rafe looked away, a deep crease appearing between his eyes, and she wondered if he was telling her the entire truth.

"I deserve to know everything," she said sharply. "If you're keeping something from me, I'll never be able to trust you again. I have difficulty doing that as it is." She looked into his eyes, wanting to drown in them, to fall in love again, but she fought the feeling with all her might. The hurt he'd inflicted on her in the past would never happen again.

EIGHTEEN

After leaving Andria at Stowehurst, where he still wasn't welcome, Rafe spent some time with his father. The Marquess of Rowan had improved even more since Rafe's last visit.

Rowan's warm welcome had done much to lighten Rafe's sadness. He felt his father's support and knew he had to do something to alleviate the pressure of the old man's monetary debt to Lochlade. But he didn't have any good ideas on how to clear the debt except for paying it, and that was only the last resort.

Travers assured him that the body of Sally Vane was still in the crypt, no one the wiser of its presence. "She'll have to be buried soon or her spirit might turn against us," he said glumly to Rafe as they stood in the foyer.

"Don't give it a second thought, Travers. She'll soon rest in sacred ground, her violators punished."

" 'Tis most unfortunate that she lost her life so young."

Rafe knew the old man was trying to gain an explanation, but Rafe felt that secrecy was the most prudent course.

As he put on his cloak and hat, he asked, "Travers, can you tell me how old Lord Lochlade died? I don't recall."

"Oh, yes, milord, he drowned. 'Tis said he was set upon by footpads who knifed him and stole his valuables before throwing the body into the river."

"Footpads? That's rare in these parts, isn't it?"

"Aye, but it happens. 'Twas not the first time by any means."

Rafe clapped his hand on the old retainer's thin shoulder. "Thank you, Travers, and thank you for your loyalty."

Travers smiled. "I carry many a secret from your childhood, milord."

"One day soon, we'll sit down and you'll tell me all about them."

"That'll be my pleasure, milord."

As Rafe rode through the village, trying to decide whether to beard Beau in his den or wait until Nick returned, he met Derek outside Rowan's Gate. Derek's mount moved skittishly across the path.

Darkness was creeping in, long blue shadows projecting from the buildings in the distance.

"Rafe, I don't know if I thanked you properly," Derek said as he pulled up next to Rafe's horse. He wound the reins around his good hand as if nervous. He looked pale in the diminishing light.

"I could not have acted any differently," Rafe said. "Those men are not worth your losing a single drop of blood."

"Rafe . . . if I were you, I'd stay away from Crisp and Malcolm in the future. They are full of ill will. I also advise you not to ride alone at dark. Some people don't like your presence in Rowan's Gate."

"That's obvious, and thank you for the warning. I realized today that I have more enemies than I thought."

"They don't care whose toes they step on to gain their goals," Derek replied,

Rafe looked thoughtfully at the other man. It was as if his eyes had been opened and he saw Derek for the person he was, not as his rival for Andria.

"You seem to know a lot of details about these people," he said.

Derek shrugged as if making little of it. "I've known these men since I was born. Let's just say they have more time on their hands than what's healthy."

"Always looking for that special excitement, eh?"

Derek nodded. "Boredom spawns trouble."

"I saw that in London. The gentlemen here are not different, except maybe you."

"I feel purpose in life even if it often is an uphill battle."

Rafe glanced at Derek's distorted hand. "Yes, I can understand that."

"I've done my fair share of gambling and wenching, but that ultimately bored me beyond belief."

The horses snorted and pawed the ground.

"Derek, as we're speaking frankly, was I in your opinion as insufferable a man as Andria paints me before the accident?"

Derek's mouth widened into a smile. "Possibly."

"Things have changed since then," Rafe said.

"For me they haven't, not where Andria is concerned. There was a time when I would've done anything to gain her love, but I finally gave up. I cherish her friendship, but I would never dream of competing with you. 'Twould be energy wasted."

"If you have anything that could help me understand my past better, I'd like to hear it. Truth—even if it's brutal—is superior to ignorance."

"Well, you know the negative aspects, but I'd say you had integrity and honor. I believe you were a fair man, and you still are, evidently." He paused as if searching for words. "You were incorruptible, which wasn't liked by some here. As we discussed, vices are cherished in these parts."

Rafe felt a wave of relief. "Thank you. What you just said means a lot to me." He dared to voice one of his fears. "I haven't asked anyone this, but do you estimate that I could've had something to do with Bridget's disappearance?"

"No, absolutely not. You were long gone when Bridget disappeared. No one ever saw you back here until now. You loved Bridget; you would never have torn her from her mother." He took a deep breath as if to say something but halted himself at the last moment.

Rafe's stomach muscles clenched as he sensed something deeper. "Do you know something . . . important, Derek?"

The other man shook his head reluctantly. "If I knew something, do you think I'd keep that from Andria?"

Rafe detected the faint hesitation in Derek's voice. He thought for a moment, knowing he couldn't pressure the other man. Derek would only speak if he wanted to. "I daresay you wouldn't keep anything that important from Andria."

Derek shifted in the saddle. "However, I believe there are . . . evil forces that have conspired to wreak havoc on the region."

"You're talking about people losing their estates?"

Derek nodded. "Yes." He snapped his mouth shut, and Rafe knew he wouldn't get any more information. He suspected that Derek wanted to mention the Devil worshipers but couldn't for some reason. Perhaps he worried he would endanger himself.

Derek looked in both directions of the path. "Where are you going, Rafe?"

"I was toying with the idea of challenging Beau to a

card game or something—to relieve my father of his debt to the man."

"I don't know anything about that debt, but I do know that Beau is a cheat. You'll never win at cards, only fall more deeply into debt."

"You sound as if you have personal experience."

Derek looked into the distance, his face closed. Dry leaves rattled along the lane in a gust of wind.

"I do. I have lost my fair share of money."

No more information was forthcoming, but Rafe felt the need to probe deeper. "I realize you have a long association with Beau and the other gentry around here, but it's hard for me to see that you would have any kind of involvement in the evil that is going on. People have been killed."

He debated whether he should tell Derek about Sally Vane but decided against it.

"Young women," he said instead. "Daisy Swan, for one. If you know something, it might prevent more killings. You've got to help us."

Derek made a choking sound and stared down at his hand. Rafe noticed the glance and felt that Derek was torn in his loyalties.

" 'Tis sad that she drowned," Derek said. He looked earnestly at Rafe and took a deep breath. "I have to warn you; we are in grave danger now that you protected me against Crisp and Malcolm. That you and I would form a friendship is unacceptable."

"To Beau?" Rafe asked, feeling an icy shiver along his spine.

Derek nodded, pressing his lips into a thin line. "And to others."

"We are playing with killers," Rafe said in a low voice. "Are you afraid?"

"No."

"No?" Rafe admired the other's man courage.

"They'll have to be stopped. I knew that a long time ago, but I did nothing," Derek whispered. *Nothing!*

"What do you know exactly?"

Derek pulled in the reins of his horse and moved even closer to Rafe. "Let's just say that I know more than enough to stand witness even if that means implicating myself."

Rafe felt cheered but at the same time afraid for the other man. "Though I've found out a lot about which you speak, I can't discuss it now. Needless to say, you need protection, my friend. You need to go into hiding until the time for confrontation comes."

Derek nodded. "You're right. I have to do this for the people of Rowan's Gate. The evil has to be stopped."

"I think the law will treat you with understanding if you step forward. Do you know how to protect yourself?"

"I've got friends. I'll leave now and send you word when I've reached my destination."

"Derek, I wish I could come with you just to see you safe." He reached out to shake Derek's hand.

"That won't be necessary. No one knows I'm here now. I'll depart in haste. You can spread around the word that I left to inspect some horses in Scotland." He shook Rafe's hand.

Rafe said wryly, "If I remember."

Derek chuckled. "I believe you'll have your memory back in due time."

Rafe watched as the other man galloped off into the distance. Darkness closed around him, and only the hoof-beats echoed in the otherwise silent night. Soon he felt as if he were the only person alive.

He wanted to spend the evening with Andria. Time

seemed to be crawling since Nick left. With Derek as a willing witness, they could make swift arrests of Beau and his cohorts just as soon as the militia was roused. Captain Emerson was just the man to push this through.

Rafe decided to see if Andria would accept his presence even if Rebecca didn't. He turned his horse in the opposite direction and took the path along the river.

As he moved through a thicket of trees, he heard movement. Someone was running, and horses were crashing through the undergrowth. Before he knew what had happened, he was set upon by three men. One of them took control of Blacky, and another grabbed him from behind and pulled him out of the saddle. He began fighting with the dark-clad assaulters, but to no avail.

Everything was happening so fast, he couldn't get control of the situation. A blow to his head sent him sprawling, and as pain exploded, he knew no more.

His mouth filled with icy water, and he panicked. A coffin of ice seemed to encase his body, and his limbs were so heavy he could barely move them. His chest was about to explode with pressure, and he realized he was under water. He kicked hard; didn't know in which direction the surface lay. The water dragged at his clothes, but he emerged and coughed violently.

As he got another painful breath, he began sinking anew.

He knew he would drown if he didn't get out of the water fast. His head pounded, his whole body ached, as he kicked upward again and broke the surface. Coughing, he kept his head above water and scanned the land. The river. He was in the river, and the bank loomed close above him.

Mustering the last of his strength, he swam forward and gripped the frostbitten tussocks growing along the water's edge. With inhuman effort he managed to haul himself partly out of the river, and his boot found a toe-hold on a rock.

With a groan of agony, he crawled up and onto the flat area above. A coughing fit overcame him, then receded. The cold made his teeth chatter, and the headache shot slivers of light across his vision. A numbing desire to sleep kept pulling him down toward oblivion, but he fought it by shaking his head.

He had to seek shelter or he would soon freeze to death. He could barely feel his hands or his feet, and his body felt stiff as a board.

To his surprise, a large shadow loomed above. A soft muzzle nudged him, snorting warm air across his face. His horse.

"Blacky? Is that you?" he moaned. "They didn't take you, did they?" In a flash Rafe realized they would've spread the rumor that he'd fallen off the horse and drowned when his body was found in the river. No gory wounds to account for.

He struggled into a sitting position and grabbed the stirrup. The horse whinnied and kept nuzzling his face. The warmth felt heavenly against his freezing skin. "We've got to get to the inn. It's the closest."

With utmost effort, and even though his head threatened to split, he got to his feet and grabbed the pommel. The effort made his circulation work better and brought some life to his sluggish limbs.

Blacky cooperated beautifully as he struggled into the saddle. Gripping the reins, he urged the horse toward the direction of the inn.

His cloak was missing, and he crossed his arms over

his shivering chest. He saw the welcoming lights in the windows as he rode through the gatehouse and into the yard.

"The landlord will have the fires going," he muttered to himself. The horse stopped by the front door as if he knew the seriousness of the situation, and Rafe slid out of the saddle. He staggered up the steps and banged on the door, which opened shortly thereafter.

"Lawks-a-mercy!" Mr. Brown cried. "Come in, come in." He helped Rafe into the warm taproom and settled him in front of the fire. With many exclamations, he began taking off Rafe's coat and sodden shirt.

Rafe was grateful for the ministrations. The landlord rubbed life into his hands and feet, and the skin pricked as if stung by needles.

"Looks as if you had a meeting with the river," the landlord said, studying him under bushy eyebrows.

Rafe nodded, too tired to speak. "My . . . horse."

"I'll have him looked after right away, milord," the old man said. "What a night to be abroad, let alone taking a dip in the river."

Rafe hung his head, and suddenly bright pictures came to him. He saw Andria's beautiful golden hair spread on a white pillow cover and a man leaning on his elbows over her in the act of love. He recognized Derek's profile. The sounds of laughter and love talk filled his ears.

The memory overpowered him, and as the breath caught in his throat, he felt what he must've felt then, an overwhelming urge to confront them, but the pain had made him flee from the scene. The anger and the pain mingled freshly in his chest, and an avalanche of memories came back.

His days playing with Bridget—so familiar, yet much older than the infant in the portrait that Beau had burned.

Blond, sprightly, like her mother, so full of life. Julian. The time he'd spent with the boy teaching him to ride.

His family, the center of his universe, his love.

The landlord was speaking to him, and the odor of onions and leeks filled his nose. Soup.

In a daze, he looked up as the man handed him a wooden bowl; steam curled over its surface. His hands still aching from the return of sensation, he took the bowl and held it to his nose. Tears coursed down his cheeks and into the steaming soup.

He relived every moment of pain freshly, as he must've felt it then, but at the same time, the pain cleansed out a diffuse burden he'd carried for so long.

Newly born—that's how he felt.

The landlord must've noticed his distress. The man put a blanket over his shoulders and left him to himself. Rafe remembered Bridget's beautiful smile, the puppies she'd had, and Julian's dogs. Whatever had become of the pets? Rafe would have to ask Andria about that.

Andria. Beautiful and radiant in a wedding dress, rosebuds and pearls in her hair. Andria under him, her hair a wild tangle on the pillow.

Pain shot through him as he remembered. Derek and she *had* lain together despite their vehement denials of the fact. A sense of desolation filled him as he thought of the budding friendship he'd felt toward Derek. The man was a cheat and liar! His wife, so innocent in her tragic despair, was another one.

He had to confront them with the truth, but tonight he was too tired. With a weary hand, he lifted the spoon to his mouth and tasted the soup. It was delicious and warmed his insides. If he got some strength back, he could confront Andria—and also the men who had tried to take his life.

Anger gave him the fuel to spoon the rest of the soup into his mouth. He remembered the last words she'd said before he dropped her off at Stowehurst, "If you're keeping something from me, I'll never be able to trust you again."

Ha! She had trouble trusting him? What a fool he'd been to listen to her. All this time she'd played him for a cuckold.

He remembered Derek's sincerity. The man had clearly tried to make amends, but was this all part of the game they played?

He dragged a hand through his damp hair, feeling the lump right behind his ear. They had hit him good. The blow must've brought back his memory, because it surely hadn't come on its own. Always something to be grateful about, he thought, and rubbed his gritty eyes.

With a trembling hand, he set down the bowl on the floor beside him. His clothes were drying by the fire, but his breeches felt cold and clammy against his skin. He stood with his back toward the blaze, warming himself until the last vestiges of cold had gone. Determination settled in him as he got the full use of his limbs back. He would not be able to get any sleep unless he confronted Andria first.

The landlord came back from the kitchen with a tray of bread and more soup. "Thought ye might need something else to warm yer insides," he said, smiling cautiously.

Rafe schooled his features to appear calm. "Thank you, my good Mr. Brown. You've been the perfect host since I got back to these parts." Rafe adjusted the blanket around his shoulders and went to spread some butter on a slice of bread. "If you could bring me a dry suit of clothes, I'd be grateful."

The landlord's eyes widened in disbelief. "Ye're not going out agin, are ye?"

"I have to. I have some unfinished business to take care of."

"If I may be so bold, how did ye fall into the river?"

Rafe debated if he should tell the man the truth or not. He decided to walk the middle ground. "I had a bit of a toss-up with some vagrants, and I was overpowered."

The landlord nodded, his eyes narrowing. "I see." He hesitated as if wanting to say more. Rafe wondered how much the man knew about the diabolical practices going on in Rowan's Gate.

The landlord continued, "Well, 'tis a treacherous river, as you might understand. Many a soul 'ave lost their life in those deep currents, whether it be an accident or a crime."

"Yes . . . I know. I'll have to be more careful in the future."

"Should we report it to the law?"

Rafe shook his head. "No! They are long gone by now."

"Ye're probably right." The landlord left, and as Rafe pondered his next step in front of the fire, the man came back with a suit of homespun. Probably his Sunday finery, Rafe thought.

"I'll buy you a new suit of clothes to show my appreciation," Rafe said.

The landlord looked worried as he looked over the brown suit. "Not necessary, milord, but ye're a generous soul. These might be a bit short in the leg and sleeves."

"No matter, my good man. The suit will keep me warm."

Twenty minutes later, he was back on Blacky and riding through the village, this time staying away from the river path. Cold fury seethed in him, but it was controlled. Andria would have to tell him the truth even if he had to force it out of her.

Lights shone in some of the windows at Stowehurst. Rafe didn't care if he encountered Rebecca. She would have to let him talk to Andria.

Witherspoon opened the front door with a disapproving frown on his face. Rafe stormed past him before the old butler could react by closing the door in his face.

"Good evening, Witherspoon, and get out of my way." Taking the steps two at a time, Rafe ran up to the floor where Andria's bedroom was located. He tore open the door, but there was no sign of her.

He looked around for a moment, noticing the turned-down bed and her silky nightgown. A new wave of rage and disappointment overcame him.

He heard voices in the corridor outside. Rebecca would catch up with him in a second, and he had no desire to speak with her. The studio. He'd check the studio and then the salons.

Wearing a paint-spattered smock, Andria stood by her worktable cleaning brushes as he invaded the room. She started, her mouth falling open.

"Rafe!"

He rushed across the large room and gripped her by the shoulders. "You lied to me," he spit at her. "You thought your lies were safe, didn't you? That I would never find out, that I would never remember."

"Lies? I have no idea what you're talking about." Her eyes filled with anguish, and a crease formed between her eyes.

"You *did* go to bed with Derek. I remember it clearly. Do you hear me, *I remember.* If I had confronted you right then and there, I would've killed you both. And when I did confront you, you formed a solid wall of denial against me."

"That's preposterous," she shouted, tearing herself free from his convulsive grip. "As I said before, I never slept with Derek."

"You can deny it all you want. I *remember* every sharp detail."

In a haze, he could hear Witherspoon arguing with Rebecca as they sailed into the room.

"Go away, Rebecca," Rafe snarled. "Andria and I have important business to discuss."

The older woman carried an expression of outrage. *"You,* out of this house now!" She pointed toward the door.

Rafe crossed his arms over his chest. "You'll have to bodily throw me out, Aunt. I'm not leaving." He turned to Andria, whose pale countenance held deepening anguish.

He thundered, "I don't know what you're going to tell me, Andria, but I'll never know if you speak the truth or not."

"Then it matters not what I say," she replied icily. "Any kind of explanation would go to deaf ears." She pinched her lips shut, her stance mutinous.

"You must be taking me for a complete fool. What is this, revenge? And why would Derek try to win my friendship? So that you can play me for a double cuckold and laugh behind my back?" A black rage pounded inside him as he pictured her triumphant revenge.

He could feel Witherspoon's gnarled hand on his sleeve. "You'd better leave peacefully, milord, or I'll have to fetch the footmen to . . . assist you outside."

"You wanted me enmeshed, didn't you, Andria, so that you could cause me all the more pain." Rafe's voice broke, and his breath came in bellows. "Some kind of demented retaliation."

"He has completely lost his wits," Rebecca said disdainfully. "And look at his clothes. Dresses like a peasant now."

"Oh, shut up, Rebecca," he snapped. "Andria." He gave her a searching look. "Say something!"

"You've already tried and convicted me, Rafe. I have nothing more to say to you." She stood tall, her chin jutting in determination, her eyes hard and glittering.

He raged, throwing the nearest pillow across the room.

"Don't destroy my artistic background," Andria said without any hint of wanting to fight back. She picked up the pillow from the floor and put it back on the dais, where Rebecca always sat for her portrait. Two red spots glowed in her cheeks.

Rafe was filled with a paralyzing frustration. He wanted to lash out again, but two hefty footmen started pulling him toward the door. By their grim expressions, he knew he was overpowered. Witherspoon led the way, his face lined with haughty disdain.

Rafe fought off the footmen and straightened his coat. "I can walk on my own."

"There's no need to distress the ladies further," Witherspoon said, and Rafe glared at him. *Pompous ass.*

Thirty seconds later, he found himself outside in the cold again, feeling miserable. Still enraged, he returned to the inn. Just wait until he could get his hands on Derek. He would beat the truth out of him.

NINETEEN

Andria stared numbly at the closed door. She heard the raised voices and the scuffle as the footmen threw Rafe out. Anger seethed within her, but she was too stunned to erupt. At first, she had no idea what Rafe was talking about; then the truth flooded back.

Georgina. She remembered Derek's hopeless love for her cousin Georgina and the intense time they'd spent together two years ago. Georgina had then decided to leave Derek and marry a better "catch," Derek promptly forgotten. Love was not something her cousin based her life on. She liked position and money above all else, and now she was moving in the highest circles in London.

Andria was startled out of her thoughts as Rebecca spoke. "Rafe must've been three sheets to the wind or lost whatever sense he once possessed." The older woman was fanning herself rapidly, her mobcap askew and her face perspiring.

"I've never heard anyone rant and rave like that," she concluded, and sank down on a chair. "You must be beside yourself, and I'm rattled."

Andria tossed the rag aside and wiped off her hands on a clean one. She unbuttoned the voluminous smock covering her dress. "No, but what hurts the most is that he did not believe my innocence, nor Derek's. We spoke of this matter with Rafe right after he returned, and it was never an issue until now. He appeared to believe us."

"He said he'd regained his memory." Rebecca pressed her fingertips to her forehead and closed her eyes. "My head is spinning."

"A faulty memory at that. I know why he acted the way he did, but that doesn't excuse his lack of trust in me. I thought we had moved beyond the slights of the past."

"He evidently thought he saw you with Derek."

"He saw someone, but it wasn't me; it was Georgina. Remember when she visited me at Lochlade? What an upheaval that was, and Rafe left in the middle of that. It explains his leaving so abruptly." She thought for a moment. "I certainly didn't know that things had moved that fast with Derek and Georgina or that he'd be tempted to seduce her. He was brokenhearted when she left."

"Yes . . . he wore a perennial hangdog expression. Georgina was a fast one." Rebecca looked at Andria, her eyebrows raised. "Are you going to explain the whole to Rafe?"

"I would've explained, but now I have no interest after the way he treated me. If he had come here with respect, things would've been different, but I'm not willing to take his rage and his accusations. 'Tis the same old pattern."

Rebecca folded her fan with a snap. "I'm proud of you! Rafe showed us that the old nasty temper still lurks behind that calm surface he upholds these days."

Andria nodded, feeling a deep sadness. The old Rafe was coming back, and there was no way she could reconcile with that man. He had trampled her feelings one too many times, and his unpredictability would most likely sow more heartache.

He had never claimed that he would be staying in

Rowan's Gate when the mystery of Bridget's disappearance had been solved. He had never promised anything, and she'd given her body willingly—again. Would she ever learn?

"I'm going to bed," Rebecca said. "Stormy emotions spawn bad health." She held out her hand to Andria. "You can always count on me. I may not be handsome and virile, but I'm a better friend than he'll ever be."

Andria smiled through a film of tears. "That you are. I'm blessed with good friends." She took Rebecca's pudgy hand, and they walked out of the room.

"No matter what Rafe does in the future, you'll always have a place here with me, Andria."

Beau Saxon, Lord Lochlade, stood by the window in his library, looking out over the snow-covered gardens at the back of Lochlade. He tapped his fingertips on the windowsill, feeling the cold draft coming in under the window. A flood of triumph spread through him as he listened to the man standing by the door.

"Milord, we did everything you asked. The man is, even as we speak, sinking to the bottom of the river. We gave him a beating until he was unconscious, then threw him in. 'Twill look like he drowned, another victim claimed by the treacherous river. The banks are very icy this time of year."

Beau glanced at Dennis Morley, his trusted henchman. The man was willing to do just about anything for a price. His services did not come cheap, but he always did a good job. "And the other business?"

"I'm waiting for a report from my contact in London, milord. The last I heard, he had a good lead on the whereabouts of the little girl. No doubt she'll be arriving here shortly."

Beau rubbed his hands together and strode across the thick carpet to his desk. He gathered a bundle of bank notes and handed them to Morley. "Make sure no one sees the girl. Everything happens within absolute secrecy."

The man bowed. "Of course." His lank black hair fell around a round face, and calculation glittered in his blue eyes. "At least the mission with Lord Derwent has come to a satisfactory end—at the right time. It took us months of diligent work to locate him after Flanders."

"Tenacity is one of your strongest points, Morley. Now leave."

Morley bowed again and left, closing the door discreetly behind him.

All the details were falling into place. He had wanted to kill Rafe himself, but this had been a better solution. Beau touched his tender eye, which still throbbed from the fight.

Rafe had learned too much, and since Sally's body had disappeared, Beau knew he had to stop Rafe right away. He'd take care of the Londoner friend when he returned.

So close now. Rowan Hall was as good as his. After that, he would own all or part of the most lucrative estates in the area. He would be undisputed lord over the region.

All he had to do now was to present Andria with his heroic accomplishment—bringing back Bridget to the fold when all hope was gone. She would have to look at him in a more favorable light after that. And if she mourned Rafe Howard, well, he had plenty of handkerchiefs to share.

Then again, there was no reason for her to mourn Rafe. The man had been nothing but trouble in her life. *I did*

*her a great favor tonight, and it's about time she recog-
nizes my worth.* And she would. He had as much tenacity
as Morley. *Together she and I will create a dynasty,* he
thought.

Rafe slowly calmed down. The anguish quieted to
something akin to a nagging toothache. He had to think;
he had to go over these new details that were coming to
him. He glanced around the dark fells, noticing the stars
on the black canopy above. They had twinkled in much
the same manner every clear night, but he could see himself in this setting in the past, looking at the stars between
the fells.

This was home. He knew his roots even if some part
of his life was hazy. He recalled his struggles with his
father, knowing now that he would've been too full of
pride to mend the rift that had spread between them in
the past. It had taken dire injury to bring them back together.

In a sense, his loss of memory had been a blessing in
disguise. Without it, he would still be full of anger and
arrogance.

Glancing around the stand of trees along the path, he
realized that he was in continuous danger. If the men who
had attacked him found out that he was still alive, they
would make another attempt on his life.

A shiver of dread went through him. The river had almost taken him. It gave him a small sense of victory that
he'd bested the treacherous River Fynn.

He headed toward Rowan Hall. Keeping an eye out for
other travelers in the night, he veered off the path and
took the shortcut through the woods. Nothing moved in
the dark, not even the owls. It was as if the whole world

were waiting breathlessly for the sun to bring forth another day.

At the stables, he took care of Blacky and untied the bundle with his wet clothes that the landlord at the inn had sent with him. He felt around in the saddlebags to check if there was something of interest and came across the stack of love letters that he'd taken from Beau's desk at Lochlade. He'd forgotten all about them.

He glanced at them in the weak light of the moon. There might be something interesting here, he thought.

A warm meal, some mulled wine, and a hot fire would all contribute to his calming down even more. He was glad to be *home*.

With a new bounce in his step, he went through the kitchen entrance, startling the cook, who was busy preparing the breakfast trays for the morning. She dropped her jaw and pressed her hands to her heart.

"I'm sorry, Mrs. Parker." He walked up the few steps to the door that separated the kitchen from the rest of the house. "Would you send up some dinner and some mulled wine to the library, please?"

"Certainly, milord. Right away."

Travers met him in the hallway and stared at his peasant garb. "I say, milord, high fashion is not what it used to be."

"Never mind," Rafe said, and handed him the wet bundle of clothes. "Maybe you can do something with these. And have someone build up a really good fire in the library."

"Very good, milord."

"I'm home, Travers. It means a lot to me."

Travers's face split in a wide grin. "Welcome home, milord. I'm that pleased to have you back."

Rafe went to see if his father was still up but found

him asleep, the male nurse, Morley, snoozing in a chair by the fire. Probably wouldn't hear a thing if Father woke up, he thought. He contemplated waking the man, but there was no need. Father looked peaceful enough.

Rafe went to the library and sat in front of the fire, his stocking feet up on a small table. The heat toasted his toes as he untied the ribbon around the love letters.

He read the first one, finding that it included some very intimate details about the old Lord Lochlade's liaison with Beau's mother.

The wrongness of the whole situation bothered Rafe. Beau's father must've been alive at the time; it was likely that he knew about the love affair.

If Beau's mother had kept the letters, she evidently didn't worry about their being found someday, possibly by the wrong person. That spoke of a leaning toward arrogance or even cruelty if they were meant to be found.

Rafe leaned back in the armchair and closed his eyes. His memory was somewhat hazy on the subject, but he recalled a ball at Lochlade before he and Andria were married. Lord Lochlade had made no secret of his flirtation, and Beau's mother had responded in kind. What sort of people could . . . ? His train of thought was interrupted by his own emotional pain. *Andria*.

Had she carried on with Derek all that time, right under his nose? The thought made him furious, but at the same time, how could the lady he knew to be Andria act in such a way? The picture didn't fit.

Since he couldn't find an immediate answer, he pushed the thought away. Soon enough, he would know the truth, and he wasn't ready for it now.

"Blast and damn," he swore, and rifled through the stack of letters. He found some of a different paper, a faded blue with paling ink, and with a feminine slant to the writing. He looked at the signature, Isabel Saxon. Jezebel Saxon, more likely, he thought with a stab of anger.

Old Lochlade had cuckolded his own brother.

The fact was immense. Now Beau was the new lord of Lochlade. That was a real kind of revenge, Rafe thought, feeling why he could understand Beau's thirst for power— even if it was twisted. But there was never an excuse for the ill will he'd shown. There had to be more, but Rafe couldn't put the last pieces into the puzzle.

He wondered if he'd ever written any love letters to Andria. It would be easy to wax lyrical, but at this point, all he could feel was disappointment. And disgust. He knew exactly how Beau's father would've felt—that is, if he cared.

Travers entered with the dinner that Rafe had ordered. A mouth-watering stew and fresh bread invited him to a feast, and the mulled wine was superb.

The butler was about to leave when Rafe halted him. "Tell me, Travers, what is your opinion about my mother? Were my parents very unhappy? I think I was too much away from here to really notice."

Travers's eyebrows rose a notch. "Unhappy, sir?" He seemed to be looking for words. "I believe they were— mostly. I never pried into their lives."

"My father . . . say, did he often . . . stray, that you know about? You can be frank with me, Travers."

The butler shook his head. "In the . . . beginning, perhaps. Your father changed as he grew older, stayed more at home. He doted on you—until you developed a mind of your own."

"Well, be that as it may, I remember a lot of harsh arguments. I recall having many with him."

Travers smiled. "You are very much alike, if you don't mind me saying so."

Rafe snorted a laugh. "I see your point."

"Milord . . ." Travers lowered his voice to a whisper. "What about the, er, corpse? It's starting to smell bad."

Rafe thought for a moment. "I need to fetch the woman's mother from Pemberton for identification; then we'll go to the authorities so that she can be buried and the villains apprehended."

" 'Tis horrifying, milord."

"It is indeed. Do you know anything about the goings-on around here, Travers? Please, if you know *anything,* I need to hear it, as it can help us trap the killers."

"Yes, milord. There are rumors that one can't trust anyone in these parts anymore. We don't know who's involved, y'see. For all we know, Mrs. Parker could be involved in the scheme of things. That's the extreme case, if you understand. There are strangers who work with us now, and I cannot see myself trusting them."

"You're vague, Travers." Rafe set down the mug of wine and stared intently at the old butler.

"I daresay you can find answers at Lochlade. That's all I can say about that. But I have to tell you, I don't like the nursing staff here. They leave Lord Rowan too much on his own. Anything could happen, and I find myself looking in on him constantly."

"You mean Morley."

The old man nodded. "Thank you, Travers, for your loyalty. The nursing staff will go, and you can hire someone you trust, one of your relatives, perhaps, to help Father. He's getting better, isn't he?"

"Much better."

"Tomorrow will be another day, a much better day, if I have any say about it," Rafe said. "And I do."

"If I can help, milord. I'll do anything."

"You've already helped me immensely." Rafe tasted the stew. "And Mrs. Parker is not a conspirator; she's a gem."

Travers smiled. "That she is. If she would have me, I would marry her." He bowed. "Good night, sir."

"Good night."

Rafe finished his food and wine, feeling tired and lonely. Not that it was anything new. Ever since Flanders his life had been a lonely struggle, but he quite liked his own company. He hadn't before the war, so that was some kind of improvement, he thought.

He leaned his aching head back against the chair and dozed off. In his mind's eye he saw his confrontation with Andria and her shocked, pale face. Mayhap he'd been a bit too hasty. Anger was never good fuel in dealings with others.

Sleep took him deeper, and he dreamed of Nick and Serena and a little girl with curly blond hair. His eyes shot open. He'd remembered something in his sleep, but just as soon as he awakened, the image was gone.

He longed terribly for Andria. The wine soothed him as he struggled to stay awake, but within minutes he drifted into the land of sleep.

He woke up at dawn, his body stiff from sitting all night. His head ached. The lump had gone down some but was very tender. In the immense silence of the house he walked to his room, where he found a few additional hours of rest.

Awakening for the second time, he still felt exhausted, knowing that the previous day had taken a toll on him. He found Travers in the kitchen having coffee with Mrs.

Parker. They both shot out of their chairs as he entered. He chuckled.

"I'm not the Inquisition," he joked. "What I need is hot water for a bath and some shaving soap."

"Right away, milord," Travers said, and hastened to give the orders to the footmen.

In his bedroom, Rafe stood at the window in his shirt, looking at the sun climbing over the fells. The day would be glorious, with the snow glittering like diamonds and the heaven full of unseen angels, he thought. It was hard to believe such evil went on in the village when you looked at the purity of a gentle sunrise.

Soon he sat back in a large copper tub, savoring the feel of the hot water on his bare skin. A vast difference from the icy embrace of the River Fynn. A chill went through him at the memory. His head was still sore.

To his utter surprise, he heard angry footsteps in the corridor outside, and the door to his room slammed open against the wall.

Andria, a virago with eyes flashing venom and her hair curling wildly around her shoulders as if she hadn't found the patience to take the time to arrange it, stood before him.

Rafe wanted to rush out of the water and push her back out the door, but the impulse left as soon as it arrived. "Well, well. Another dawn, another fight," he drawled.

She waved a letter in her hand and stormed into the room, standing over him like an executioner. Red suffusing her cheeks and her eyes shooting blue fire, she was lovely.

"What's the matter?" he asked, soaping his arms.

She stared at his movements as if stunned. "How can you sit here and bathe as if nothing has happened?" she screamed.

Travers appeared behind her and gently closed the door to leave them in privacy.

"I haven't the faintest clue what you're talking about," Rafe said, continuing his ablutions. His heart hammered uncomfortably in his chest.

"I got this," she yelled.

He eyed the letter she was waving under his nose. "I guess it's a missive from your lover to say it's over," he said scathingly.

He knew she would slap him over the head; he put up his arm for protection, but she still clouted him good. It hurt the area where he'd been hit yesterday.

"Seems that I'm right," he goaded.

"Derek wrote me that he's left the area and won't be back for some time."

Rafe thought about that, wondering if Derek had really left or was in hiding, as he'd indicated to Rafe. The man had seemed earnest enough when he spoke about hiding until lawmen could apprehend Beau. But being a witness against a criminal had nothing to do with adultery.

"Did you chase him away from Rowan's Gate with threats?" she shouted, very close to his ear.

"I doubt I could chase Derek anywhere. He left of his own free will." Rafe lifted a foot out of the water and soaped carefully.

"I don't believe you," she said icily.

Anger clouded his vision, and he gripped the front of her cloak and yanked her forward. She tripped against the side of the tub and tumbled into the water, immediately soaking her clothes. Screaming and moaning like a large cat in pain, she twisted and fought, sputtering as water filled her mouth.

"That's your punishment for ruining my bath," he growled. Her panniers stood out like giant mushrooms, crowding him, and he wished he had a knife to cut the ties that held them up at her waist. *What a silly fashion,* he thought. They were only designed to keep the gentlemen at bay.

"You imbecile, you clod! You blasted oaf."

"Ladies don't use profanity," he chided. He caught her soaking hair and twisted it between his hands. "You know, I'm glad your lover is away. We have all the time to enjoy ourselves." He pulled her close, his mouth finding hers in a grinding kiss.

She shrieked, and he laughed. "Guttersnipe," he said, kissing her again.

She pounded at his slick, soapy chest, her fists ineffectual against his greater strength.

"I could rip your clothes and take you right here on the floor," he said. "After all, you're still my wife, and you like your male company regularly, don't you?"

"Oh-oo-yo-u-oooo," she moaned in such fury that she could barely utter the word. "I hate your arrogance." Struggling with all her might, she hauled herself out of the water and stood sodden next to the tub.

"And I hate your duplicity." He looked at her, feeling the chasm widening. Whatever progress they had made toward a new life evaporated right there.

He rinsed his limbs and got up. Toweling himself, he watched the blush rise on Andria's face as she flashed a glance at his burgeoning manhood. It was easy to tell that she felt a wild attraction to him, just as he felt one for her. In fact, he wanted nothing more than to tumble her in bed, but it would have to wait.

Andria's heartbeat escalated as she watched his splendid physique. His hard muscles glistened in the light of the morning sun, and she remembered how he felt under her hands, velvety and hard at the same time. An over-powering desire to touch him filled her, but she rapidly looked away before he could read her enchantment with his body.

Thoughts tumbled through her mind, and anger still churned in the pit of her stomach.

His voice cut through her confusion. "I had not planned on bringing you into this at this time, but it might be preferable to keeping you in the dark." He took a deep breath and continued. "We found Sally Vane—dead."

Shocked, she took a step back. "Dead? When?"

"A few days ago," he said vaguely. "Besides the killers, the only other people who know are Nick and Travers. We're working on apprehending the men who are respon-sible." He studied her carefully. "I don't know how this will affect our search for Bridget."

"Who . . . who killed Sally Vane?"

"I don't know how you'll take this. Beau and his co-horts. 'Tis only a matter of time before we confront them."

A sinking feeling went through her. "Beau . . . but—"

"Andria," he admonished, "we have proof."

He finished toweling himself off and went to his bed, where fresh clothes had been spread out. As she watched, he put on a white shirt and a cream brocade waistcoat.

"If you want, you can travel with me to Pemberton. We'll fetch Sally's mother to identify her. A necessary formality."

"I'm not needed for the trip," she said, hesitant to go but eager to see if Sally's mother knew something she hadn't told them.

"No, you don't need to go, but if you do, I can keep an eye on you." He knotted the simple cravat at his throat.

"So that you can make sure I won't see my lover behind your back?" she said scathingly.

His face darkened, and his eyes flashed fire. "If you want that . . . yes, to keep you away from adultery." He paused. "Setting that possibility aside, your life might be in danger."

"Why would my life be in any kind of danger, and why would you care, seeing as you have such a low opinion of me?" She paused, but he didn't rise to her challenge. "I don't have enemies; mostly I have friends."

He pulled on buckskin breeches and shrugged a blue coat over his shoulders. "I don't know the whole plan behind the death of Sally Vane, but I'm certain it involves you in some way, Andria."

"Beau would *never* kill me." She toweled her hair and brushed it out with her fingers. Spreading her damp cloak in front of the fire, she added, "It's hard for me to believe that Beau would kill someone."

"Beau's schemes are grandiose. Nothing and no one are allowed to stand in his way."

Andria noted that Rafe sounded cautious, as if reluctant to spread his thoughts too far and wide. His words implicated something immense, and she shuddered with apprehension. "He got Lochlade even if he didn't reckon with everyone dying. He always loved Lochlade."

"You'll have to believe me once we prove the truth."

His ominous words brought home the severity of the situation. "If Beau was involved with Sally Vane and she told you about your identity in London, besides leaving you to believe that Bridget died, he's a monster. Why would he go to such lengths?"

"Mayhap I was supposed to have died in Flanders." He pulled on his boots.

"If he knew where you were, he could've killed you

in London without anyone being the wiser," she pointed out.

"He wanted me to come back. Since I had no memory, he could pin all manner of ill deeds on me. But he doesn't know I have a great deal of memory back."

She shot him a glance to measure his level of sarcasm as to the contents of his memories but saw none. He was as caught up in the seriousness of the situation as she.

He added, "I don't grieve what happened in the past; I just want to move forward, all questions answered."

She nodded, feeling weighed down by the burden of the past. "I'll go with you."

He glanced at her quickly, all businesslike. "I'll have Travers find some dry garments for you. We'll go in the traveling chaise. No need to expose ourselves to the elements as we did last time we went to Pemberton."

Tense, and sitting at opposite ends of the carriage, they arrived in Pemberton in record time. The horses had been fresh and eager for a run. The hamlet slumbered. Only gray wraiths of smoke curled out of the chimneys, speaking of movement within the houses.

They drove to the end of the village and found Mrs. Vane's cottage. Smoke was billowing from her chimney, telling the story of wet, unseasoned wood. Mrs. Vane not only resided on the outskirts of the village; she lived on the fringes of poverty.

"You can wait here, Andria."

Andria rose, "No, I want to reassure her if she feels threatened by male arrogance."

Rafe gave her a heated look. "No need to perpetrate animosity. From now on, we're having a truce until all this is cleared up."

"Yes, as the master says," Andria replied, her head held high.

"That attitude will get you nowhere," Rafe muttered.

The gate creaked as she went through, and the path was muddy and covered with slippery dead leaves. Not looking to see if Rafe was following her, she knocked on the door. Mrs. Vane opened it a crack.

Recognition lit her eyes for a moment; then a film of mistrust covered them. "What do ye want?" she asked suspiciously. "If ye're here to cause trouble . . ."

Rafe spoke behind Andria, his arm braced against the doorjamb. "We have something serious to tell you. Would you please let us inside."

Her lips drooped downward at the corners, and she opened the door wide. A gray cat slunk outside. They went into the dark interior, smelling meat cooking and the strong odor of boiling cabbage.

Andria looked around, noting the simple rough-hewn furniture and the tatty curtains. A man sat in front of the fire, and she immediately recognized Morley, Lord Rowan's nurse. She could feel Rafe stiffen beside her.

Morley's eyes narrowed, and the skewer he was lifting stopped in midair.

"Last I saw you, Morley, you were at my father's bedside. Aren't you supposed to be there now?"

" 'Tis my half-day off," the surly nurse said. "I do what I want in my free time."

"I think you're taking too many half-days off, if the staff report is accurate. Father is alone too many hours."

"I have my schedule," Morley said, setting his skewer down. "Why are you here?"

"We've come to speak to Mrs. Vane on a matter that solely concerns her. I suggest you make yourself useful outside, Morley—or leave the village altogether." Rafe's voice held an edge of ice.

Tension filled the room as the man was reluctant to

depart. He stood slowly and turned to Mrs. Vane. "Don't let them browbeat you, Susie." With a cold look at Rafe, he left the house after shrugging on a thick coat.

"I don't like him," Andria whispered to Rafe.

"He'll be fired today," Rafe murmured in her ear. " 'Tis already settled." He raised his voice a notch. "Mrs. Vane, please sit down."

She obeyed, shoving her hands into the pockets of her apron. " 'Tis about Sally, ain't it?"

Rafe nodded. "I'm sorry to be the bringer of sad news, Mrs. Vane, but your daughter is dead."

Her eyes filled with tears, and she hunted for a rag on a wash line by the fire. "How? She went to London for a good future, not—death."

Andria looked at Rafe, curious as to the reason for Sally's death, but he answered evasively. "She had an accident of some sort. We need you to identify her so that she can have a decent funeral."

He's not telling us the truth, Andria thought, her curiosity now rampant.

Mrs. Vane's head had tilted forward, and her shoulders shook with tears. Andria stepped across the kitchen and put her hand on Mrs. Vane's arm. "I understand your distress."

Mrs. Vane was nothing but skin and bones, and her clothes smelled of old food and perspiration.

"The sooner we can deal with this, the better. We don't want many people to know about Sally's death until the militia is fully informed of everything."

"She was murdered, wasn't she?" Mrs. Vane said in a monotone. "I knew she didna keep good company even when she lived 'ere. Always wus one for adventure."

Beau, Andria thought. Maybe he was behind this atrocity as well. The idea made her recoil with fear. She felt cold in the smoky room. A sense of urgency came over her. "We'd better leave now, if you don't mind, Mrs. Vane."

The older woman nodded and rose, reaching for a woolen shawl.

But before they could reach the door, Morley came back inside, a burly stranger in tow. The man looked mean and unkempt and carried a coil of ropes.

Morley was pointing a pistol at Rafe's middle. "You're not going anywhere, mister." He indicated the rickety chairs with his head. "Sit down, you two. Hank, tie the ropes around their hands and ankles. Susie, you go outside and wait for us."

Mrs. Vane seemed to want to argue.

"Do as I say," Morley ordered through clenched teeth.

Rafe had no chance to defend himself against a pistol, Andria thought as she sat down. The stranger tied her hands together really tight, and she whimpered in pain.

Rafe had a murderous expression on his face as he stared into the dark mouth of the weapon, but he slowly sat down on the other chair and allowed his hands and feet to be tied.

"This time you're not getting away," Morley said.

TWENTY

Late that night, after having ridden relentlessly from Yorkshire, Nick Thurston stood outside Sir James's Orphanage in London, Captain Trevor Emerson beside him. Before heading out, they checked their saddlebags and ensured that the saddle straps were tight.

"We have nothing to lose," Nick said, exhausted. "If we ride hell for leather, we can get to Rowan's Gate in two days. I feel I have to get there to help Rafe even if it means sleeping in the saddle. I don't like leaving him exposed alone to evil forces like that."

"If what you said is true, we have a monumental crime on our hands," Captain Emerson said grimly. "Arresting a peer of the realm is no light matter. In fact, it's deuced difficult."

Nick twisted his mouth into a grimace. "You're right, and precious little we gleaned here, and the messenger I sent to my wife has not returned. Rafe will be disappointed by our progress."

"You're nothing if not thorough, Nick."

They swung themselves up into the saddles and swept their heavy cloaks tightly around themselves. Just as they were about to leave, a servant from Nick's estate, the Hollows, arrived, his mount foaming at the mouth.

"Lester! You're riding that horse to the ground." A fist

of fear clenched Nick's chest. "Is something the matter with my wife?"

"No, sir. She's in good health at The Hollows. She sends ye this. If I couldn't catch ye here, I had orders to ride straight to Yorkshire." The servant took a letter from the inside pocket of his coat and handed it to Nick.

Nick spread the paper quickly and read aloud:

Dearest Husband, I miss you terribly, but that is not important in the face of the serious facts I've uncovered down here in Sussex. You remember that delightful little girl Birdie Jones whom we took in after she almost died of lung fever? She's been here ever since you brought her down, learning skills in the kitchen. Well, I've found out that she's not Birdie Jones at all, but Lady Bridget, Rafe and Andria's daughter. When you think about it, Birdie has the same curly hair as Andria, the same nose and bone structure. Whatever Rafe was told by that mysterious servant at the orphanage is false information that was fed to him to lead him astray.

The head nurse at the orphanage is our cook's sister. You recall she was ill for a period of time while Rafe helped you at the orphanage. She's been visiting here for a few days, and I had a word with her as she exclaimed over Birdie's brilliant progress with her health. She said that a woman by the name of Mrs. Yarrow left the girl at the orphanage, claiming one of her servants had run away and left the child behind. It's not as the ledgers said: that Birdie's mother abandoned her at Sir James's. Sally Vane evidently made up the story about Andria and her supposed lover.

"Oliver Yarrow's wife," Nick said. "Beau's cohorts. There's more."

He turned over the paper and continued. *"The terrifying news is that Birdie has disappeared. She was last seen yesterday morning. No one knows what happened.*

"Blast and damn," Nick swore under his breath. "They've gotten to the girl." He glanced at his friend Captain Emerson. "Are you up for a wild ride? We've got to get back to Rowan's Gate *now* or we might be too late."

Emerson pressed his hat low over his eyes. "What are you waiting for?"

Nick tossed a coin to the servant and sent him home with a message of love and gratitude to Serena. Heading north, he urged his horse into a gallop.

Rafe and Andria stared at the dying fire in the cottage as night moved in. Silence hung in the room, and smoke coming from the fireplace stung Andria's eyes.

"Where are our friends now?" she said, her feet numbing from the lack of circulation.

Rafe was pale with rage. "Nick will return shortly and find out our destination from Travers. He'll be here posthaste; mark my words."

"Might be too late by then," she replied gloomily. She glared at Rafe. "I know you haven't told me everything about Sally Vane. I don't know what you're holding back."

"I seek only to protect you, Andria."

"What exactly happened to Sally?" She worked her hands behind her back as she'd been doing all day, but the knot was still as tight as ever.

She could tell that Rafe was thinking it over in his mind, but he refused to lay out the truth. "You don't need to know, Andria. Nothing will change with you knowing. You'll only have nightmares."

She wanted to insist but thought twice about it as her mind brushed against horrors that might've befallen her daughter. "Bridget's disappearance is in the middle of this," she said, her eyes filling with tears. "If they hurt her—" She choked on the last words and looked away.

The dim light entering through the dirty window did nothing to cheer her up. "I'd like to know how long they are going to keep us here," she said.

"Until they've made a decision what to do with—me. They, Beau and his cohorts, believed I was dead."

"Beau? You dead? What are you talking about?"

She was filled with terror as he told her about the blow to his head and his brush with death in the freezing river.

"I'm certain one of the attackers is Morley. He looked very surprised to see me here."

"Evidently Morley and Mrs. Vane are close," she said. "Morley is the connection with Sally Vane."

Rafe nodded, his voice icy soft. "If they did something to Bridget, I'll kill them."

"If we don't get killed first." Andria struggled with the knots, getting nowhere, her frustration rising with every moment.

"Andria, tell me about her. I've forgotten many of the details. I do know the feelings of wonder and delight that I had when she was born."

"You're only trying to distract me."

"Is that so bad?"

"No, perhaps not." Andria's mind wandered back a few years, reliving the expectation of having her baby. "She kicked ferociously, as if too eager to step into the world. I didn't sleep well for weeks because of it. There was a lot of pain during the labor, but I forgot about that once I held her in my arms. She was perfect in every way."

"Yes . . . so beautiful. I was pacing in the library at Lochlade, every step filled with the agony of waiting. I heard her first scream clear through the mansion, and how my heart welled with happiness. I raced upstairs and tore into the bedroom. I remember her tiny hands and feet and her toothless gums as she kept bellowing," he said.

"Bellowing?" She laughed despite herself. "Bulls bellow; children scream."

"She had the lungs of a bull," he insisted.

"Those were the happy days. Who could ever envision the horrors that would follow? Why didn't we speak intimately about everything? Why was there so much pride?"

He gave her a cool look. "And deceit at every corner."

She didn't take the bait right away. She needed to hold her course; be prepared for the truth, no matter how painful, and move on into a new world. Nightmarish interlude, she would call this later, she decided. Rafe still lived in her heart, but she'd grown strong, and she could move on.

"You hold back things, Rafe, so don't come to me with accusations of deceit. 'Tis too late for that. Anyhow, I'm not a hothouse flower who needs protection. All I ask is to learn the truth about Bridget." *God, please send someone to help us get out of here.*

Rafe worked on loosening the rope around his ankles by working his feet back and forth but made little progress. "It annoys me no end that I got myself into this situation."

"You couldn't very well know that Morley was involved in this."

"Being tied up reminds me of the games we used to play sometimes, Andria. Do you remember?"

Andria blushed. "You mean the silken bonds in our bedroom?" She heaved a trembling sigh. "I don't think I need to be reminded of that at this time."

His mouth tightened. "You're right."

A starless night had fallen outside. Andria felt faint with hunger and the need to relieve herself. She'd struggled with the ropes until her wrists were raw, but the knot still held strong.

Darkness moved into the room, and the embers died in the fireplace. She heard the sounds of shuffling footsteps outside. The door opened, and a man filled the opening.

"Milord?" came the shaky voice of the driver.

"Melton, whyever didn't you come to help us earlier?"

The man staggered inside. "Some'un gave me a blow to the head. I just came to in the woodshed." He moved forward cautiously, and suddenly Mrs. Vane appeared. One of her eyes looked swollen in the weak light. Hurriedly, she laid a new fire on the embers, and as flames leaped and danced, Andria saw that she'd been beaten.

"I'll help ye," she whispered between swollen lips. " 'Tis the last time I have any dealings with Morley. 'E's brought nuffin' but pain to me life."

Her cold fingers worked the knot at Andria's wrists as Melton helped Rafe.

"The carriage is gone, milord," Melton said miserably. "They took it."

No one had to ask who "they" were.

Andria could barely move her arms forward as Mrs. Vane freed her. Her whole body ached, but she struggled to stand and move around to get the circulation going.

"We have work to do," Rafe said, also stretching stiffly to regain control over his limbs. He stood before Andria as if in inner turmoil. She sensed that he needed to hold her, but she took a step back, and the fragile moment was over. She would not let him work any kind of magic on her.

"Milord, if ye don't mind, I want ye to meet some'un who'll give you information," Mrs. Vane said, pressing pale fingers to her clearly painful eye. "Come with me; 'tis urgent. Morley won't find us."

She opened the door, and Andria followed, knowing she would learn another piece of the puzzle. Rafe came closely behind her, Melton trailing behind.

They walked along a path through a thicket that lined the backs of the cottages. Mrs. Vane knew her way well in the dark. A weak moon lit their way from behind a veil of clouds.

An old cottage sat by itself in a clearing, and Mrs. Vane led them there. She knocked softly and stepped inside.

A branch of candles was the only illumination in the cramped room. It smelled of illness, a cloying stench that turned Andria's stomach. On a sagging bed lay the sick person.

Mrs. Vane waved her forward, and Andria leaned over the deteriorating woman. There was something familiar in the sunken face, and Andria remembered the fiery hair.

"Hattie Gowan, Julian's nurse," she whispered. "What in the world . . . ? I thought you moved to York."

Hattie smiled weakly. "I've come 'ome t' die. Not much left of me, milady. I'm goin' to me just rewards soon, but I 'ave to unburden meself or I'll be facin' the Devil 'isself." She took a trembling breath and coughed horribly.

Andria had to lean closer to hear her, and Rafe stood at the head of the bed so that he could listen.

"Milady, milord, I've carried a frightful secret for a long time." She paused as a spasm of pain moved over her face. "I know that . . . young Julian, bless 'is soul, was murdered. I was afraid to step forward, seein' as I might be killed as well."

"I knew it," Andria said. "Julian's death was unnatural, but there was nothing I could do." Her throat filled with tears as she again thought of the boy she'd loved as her own.

"Master Beau fed Julian some sort of concoction ever' day when 'e thought I wus prayin'. Always did me prayers afore breakfast."

"Why didn't you tell us about it, Hattie?" Andria wanted to shake the sick woman but controlled her anger.

"Me word against Mr. Saxon's?" She sounded incredulous.

"Julian was heartbroken when you left. He was very sick; he needed you."

"I couldn't bear to see 'im die, milady. Mr. Saxon discovered that I'd been watchin' 'im and threatened to kill me mother if I said a word to anyone. I knew 'e meant it."

Andria and Rafe exchanged glances across the bed. Andria could read his pain, mirroring that in her heart.

"I'll fetch the vicar as another witness," Rafe said, and hurried out the door.

"I've been full o' guilt ever since, milady. 'Tis painful to be such a coward. I should've stepped forward wi' the truth."

Andria thought about it, knowing that in the past she would've had difficulty believing that Beau would poison a little boy. She believed now.

"We could've protected your mother, Hattie, but you couldn't know that at the time. I don't blame you for what happened."

"I 'ave to set things right with God," Hattie mumbled, sweat pearling on her forehead. Her hands moved over the patched coverlet. "I've learned me lesson. The truth niver 'urt as much as the secret I've been carryin'."

Andria patted her hand. "I'm glad you stepped forward at last. 'Twill help us apprehend Beau Saxon."

"A viper, milady. Ye be careful or 'e'll sting you."

Andria went outside, trying to digest the things she'd heard. Rafe returned ten minutes later with the vicar, and they went inside the cottage.

Mrs. Vane came back outside and stood beside Andria. "For some reason, I knew this information would help ye. Revenge for me daughter's death."

"Did you know all of this?"

"No, milady. Not until 'attie came back here to die. She's been talkin' about nuffin' else. She kept askin' me to fetch ye, but then ye came without prompting." Mrs. Vane wrapped her shawl more tightly around her shoulders. "I 'ave me own shame to carry, seein' as I kept to Morley. 'Twas through him that Sally found such lucrative employment."

"She worked for the gentry in Rowan's Gate, didn't she?" Andria had expected her to say Beau's name, but the woman said, "The Yarrows—for a time."

Andria remembered the dinner party at Lochlade where Ophelia Yarrow had insulted her but could not recall that there had been any animosity between the families in the past. *I certainly didn't do anything to provoke it,* she thought.

Rafe, Melton, and the vicar joined them. Hattie had made her confession as the clergyman listened intently.

"Serious allegations indeed," the vicar said, gently pushing a hand through his white hair before putting his hat back on. "We need to rouse the militia. I'll send a note to Lord Alvondale. He's a magistrate outside of Lord Lochlade's jurisdiction. A most reliable man. I'll bring him to Hattie if there's time." He shook his head. "Most atrocious business."

"There's more," Rafe said darkly, "but we can't get into that right now. We need more proof."

"I see. Well, you have my support, and I'll have my coachman take you back to Rowan's Gate."

Rowan's Gate, Andria thought. They would be going from the ashes into the fire.

Mrs. Vane cried as she viewed Sally's eroding face in the stench-filled crypt at Rowan Hall. Rafe felt his gut clench as he thought of where he and Nick had found the young woman. How many women had served as offerings on Beau's cold altar?

"He shall pay," Mrs. Vane said through clenched teeth. "Morley did this to my daughter."

"He may have been a henchmen, but he took orders from above, Mrs. Vane. Lord Lochlade is the true culprit."

She nodded, her sobs heart-wrenching. "It frightens me to think about it."

Rafe patted her thin shoulder. "You'll stay here with us until everything has been cleared up. Travers will look after you."

Andria stood outside the crypt, hearing every word. She ached for all the lost lives and felt that she should've known Beau's true character. She'd never taken him seriously. To her he'd just been an irksome suitor and a lover of earthly wealth. How blind one could be to the people closest to oneself, she thought.

Rafe led Mrs. Vane outside, and Andria took her arm in a steadying grip. "What we need is something to warm our insides—a cup of tea and some hot soup. That'll make you feel better, Mrs. Vane."

The older woman nodded. "Thank ye kindly, milady. The man shall pay for all the evil," she muttered. "He'll burn in the fires of 'ell."

"All will come out right in the end," Andria said, not feeling at all convinced of that.

Beau looked down at the crying little girl's face. The blond hair curled just like Andria's, and the blue eyes looked at him through a film of tears.

"You've grown, wee Bridget," he said, and patted her head. "You're a young lady now. Do you remember me, Uncle Beau?"

She shook her head. "Ye're a . . . gent," she hiccuped. "I want Leddy Serena now. She's kind to me. Ye're not."

Beau looked at Morley standing by the door. "She speaks like a guttersnipe."

"She spent a couple of years in the company of orphans, milord," Morley said. "Can't 'spect her to speak like a lady."

Beau shrugged. "I suppose you're right. She's going to have a governess"—he turned toward the child—"aren't you, Bridget? Your very own governess and a lovely bedroom in this grand house."

Tears streamed down her small face. "I wants to go 'ome."

"You are home now, Bridget. You're going to meet your mother; do you remember her?"

The girl's eyes widened with surprise. "Me mum?"

"You remember her?"

"No . . ." came the trembling reply, and Bridget lowered her head, clutching a small wooden horse to her chest. "Me mum's with the angels."

Beau placed his hand over her shoulder. "No, Bridget,

your mother is nearby. Kind Mr. Morley here will fetch her shortly."

Bridget shrank back and looked at the female servant who had accompanied her in the coach on their trip. "Mr. Morley's not kind, miss. I wants to go 'ome."

Beau stalked to the spot where Morley waited patiently. "Go fetch Lady Bridget's mother—now! And don't dawdle on the road."

Morley bowed and smiled coolly. " 'Twill be an easy matter to bring her here, milord."

"This is a very important phase of our mission. If we fail, I have a lot to lose, and in my wrath, I don't know what I would do to you, Morley. So don't fail."

"I haven't failed you yet, milord. I don't think I'll meet any resistance from the young lady's mother. After all, I'll be in the position to fulfill her deepest dreams."

With a swagger in his step, Morley left the room. The sound of Bridget crying disconsolately followed him out of the house.

TWENTY-ONE

"I keep wondering how I could be so blind to the extent of Beau's evil," Andria said to Rafe after they had put Mrs. Vane in Travers's care.

Rafe closed the door to the crypt carefully. "I think Beau lives under the impression that he's invincible. His hunger for power knows no bounds."

Andria nodded, shivering in the cold air. "I'm embarrassed to have a cousin that twisted."

He reached out as if to touch her but dropped his hand as if reminded of the rift between them. "Not your fault," he said tersely. "We'll leave the rest to the law. Just as soon as Nick comes back with Captain Emerson, we'll move in to arrest Beau. We have plenty of evidence of his perfidy—and that of his cohorts."

"I know you haven't told me everything," Andria said.

"Believe me, I have a perfectly good reason for that," he replied. "First and foremost I want to protect you."

"Your thoughtfulness warms me, but it won't make up for your actions in the past," she said, turning away. She walked quickly to the waiting carriage.

He followed her, and she could feel his anguish.

She halted at the door and faced him. "None of this has brought us any closer to finding Bridget. All we have done is dig up the filthy deeds of my cousin."

He looked at her hard in the weak light of the carriage lantern. "Through Beau we'll find Bridget."

"Sounds very simple, but I want to see it first," she said, feeling desolate.

"You must be exhausted. Let me take you to Stowehurst. There's nothing we can do until Nick returns. However much I'd like to confront Beau this very minute, it would not serve a purpose."

"I doubt you can force a confession out of him." Andria felt dizzy with fatigue and a sense of defeat.

"No, I won't, but someone knows something that will help us find Bridget. As I said, cohorts. They'll talk for a price."

"As long as we learn the truth. Then we can move on with our lives—separately."

She stepped into the carriage and slammed the door shut. Rafe fetched his horse, which the stable groom had saddled for him, and escorted the carriage to Stowehurst. He was deeply saddened by the rift that kept widening between him and Andria.

As he watched her enter the mansion without a backward glance, he wondered if her past actions really mattered. Or his. *Now* was important, not the past. Still, there was no denying the damage that had been done to their emotions.

Besides, if he'd been as hard and angry in the past as she claimed, could he blame her for needing solace elsewhere? Derek had always treated her with loving concern.

However, there still remained her deceit and Derek's. He couldn't bear to think about it.

Feeling exhausted, angry, and confused, he sent the coach back to the vicar in Pemberton and headed toward Rowan Hall. If Beau found out that they'd escaped, he wouldn't wait long to come in pursuit.

"I'll be waiting unless I confront him first," Rafe said to himself. He rode along the outskirts of the village so as to stay concealed and headed down to the river path. The memories of his last ride along the path chilled him.

Heavy with exhaustion, he reached Rowan Hall unharmed and went upstairs to check on his father. Lord Rowan slept peacefully, looking better every day. Relieved, Rafe went to his bedchamber. He threw himself on the bed fully dressed and fell instantly asleep. His dreams of fires and destruction disturbed his sleep.

He woke up in the afternoon the next day, still feeling the leaden heaviness of exhaustion. Stripping off his clothes, he washed himself and looked for fresh linen. Filled with impatience, he wondered how much longer he'd have to wait for Nick.

Knowing that the only way to apprehend Beau was through the law, he still felt a powerful urge to confront the man right this morning.

Starving, he ate a hearty breakfast and looked in on his father. Lord Rowan was walking with the help of a walking stick.

"Rafe!" he called out, smiling. "I haven't had the pleasure of seeing you for a while."

"I've been extremely busy," Rafe said, and embraced his father. The frailness of the older man saddened Rafe. For how long could Rowan go on?

"Any progress with my debt?" Lord Rowan asked, his eyes heavy with guilt.

"I doubt we'll ever have to worry about it again," Rafe said as he thought of Beau's imminent arrest. "Put your worries to rest, Father. I'm dealing with everything."

The older man stared fondly at Rafe. "I want to see you happy, son, before I go. I don't think I've seen you smile once since you came back."

"Maybe I will soon, Father. Soon, when the world is rid of the monster named Lord Lochlade."

Lord Rowan squeezed Rafe's arm. "I wish I could help. I hate my weakness."

"You're the only bright promise in my world right now. I'm happy that we've made positive progress, and you *are* helping me by having accepted me back into the family. You are giving me your wholehearted support."

A tear rolled down Lord Rowan's papery cheek. " 'Tis time for some happiness in our lives."

Rafe felt his chest clench with emotion. Happiness seemed so far away at the moment. "We'll work at it. That's all we can do."

Rafe left his father eating dinner by the window. He put on his cloak and hat. Blacky stood saddled and ready to take him to Stowehurst and Andria. He hoped she'd had a restful night.

Just as he was about to leave, a servant rode up and delivered a letter. Rafe tore open the seal. The note was from the vicar at Pemberton, who had alerted Lord Alvondale of Beau's crimes and awaited further information as to the right time for the militia to march.

Rafe sent a sealed note back that Alvondale's militia could move in just as soon as they were ready. Among Julian's nurse's confession, his own and Nick's discovery in the cavern, and Mrs. Vane's, they had enough evidence to arrest Beau.

Morley must've found out by now that they'd escaped. Checking carefully for movement, Rafe rode through the woods. He went along the river path. For a moment, he stopped at the spot where he'd almost drowned and looked across the ink black water. It moved slowly in the faint sunlight. He noticed the formation of rocks on the opposite bank, and a ghost, a memory, rose from the depths of his mind.

As clearly as if it were yesterday, he remembered another struggle on the bank of the river. He'd fought for his life with Beau before leaving for the war two years ago.

He'd leaped into the defense of old Lord Lochlade, only later realizing it'd been a futile cause. If Beau's revenge was as far-reaching as he thought, Beau's pretense of caring for Andria was nothing but a sham. Beau wanted all of the Lochlades dead, just as he'd killed Lord Lochlade by the river. "With my carved knife," Rafe said to himself, finally remembering the importance of the knife that Beau had delivered back to him. Beau would've accused Rafe of killing Lord Lochlade if necessary, using the knife as evidence.

Rafe urged his horse forward. "Now I know the full motive why Beau wanted to ruin the Lochlades," he said. "Wait until I tell Andria."

He prompted his horse into a gallop as he headed toward Stowehurst, eager to share the news that would eventually draw the noose more tightly around Beau's neck.

He was breathing hard as the horse halted in front of the Stowehurst mansion. He jumped down and banged on the front door. Not waiting for someone to answer, he stormed inside. Witherspoon met him in the foyer.

"Milord!"

"I'm here to see my wife, *right now*," Rafe demanded.

"Why, that's impossible, milord. Lady Derwent left about fifteen minutes ago."

Witherspoon looked triumphant, as if finally gaining the upper hand over him.

"She said nothing about expecting you."

Rafe towered over the smaller man. "Where did she go? Tell me now."

"Lady Stowe sent word that she has the most remarkable news."

Rafe gripped the impeccable lapels of the butler's coat. *"Where* are they?"

"Lady Stowe is at Lochlade for a dinner," Witherspoon said.

Dinner? Rafe thought. He'd not heard of any dinner planned at Lochlade at this time. "Why would my wife go there? Did Lady Stowe ask for help to get back home?"

"Why, the news, milord. Evidently, Lady Bridget has been found."

Rafe could not have been more stunned if someone had hit him over the head with a rock.

"I don't know the details, milord."

Rafe loosened his grip on the other man's coat. "Who brought the message to Lady Stowe?"

"A footman, milord."

Fear rose in Rafe's heart. "When did Lady Stowe leave for Lochlade?"

"This afternoon, milord. Too early for a dinner in my opinion, but she said she wanted an early start."

Rafe turned toward the door. "Keep the fires burning, Witherspoon. We'll return soon."

Rafe raced outside and got back on his horse. He sensed that time was of the essence. Beau might have used Lady Stowe to lure Andria over to Lochlade. They could both be in danger. Whatever Beau's intentions, none of them were pure.

Andria should've known better than to ride over to Lochlade alone, but the news would've made her throw caution to the winds.

Halting at the edge of the spinney behind the Lochlade mansion, he waited. He couldn't just barge in and demand satisfaction at swords.

Andria was within those walls, and his heart turned over in despair from not knowing what was happening to her. His deep love for her contrasted sharply with the helplessness he felt this very moment.

If it took his last ounce of wit and strength, he would find a way to create a new life for Andria and himself. *Love supposedly conquers all,* he thought.

The thought of Bridget made him both happy and worried. Was she really here, or had Beau only used her name to lure Andria to the house?

Filled with ripping emotions, he remained undecided as to his next action. Minutes trickled by, and Andria and Bridget might be in graver danger with every moment.

He decided to take a closer look at the mansion, possibly finding a way to rescue the people most dear to him by stealth. And what about Rebecca? She had hardly asked to be involved in the situation, but now she was.

He tied his horse to a scraggly bush and advanced to the residence, staying hidden from view by running from one tree to another, an easy feat, as darkness was falling. He reached the terrace without raising a hue and cry. Pressing himself to the wall, he crept to the library window through which he'd once crawled when investigating with Nick.

Listening for voices, he stopped for a moment. Silence lay heavy over the mansion. Mayhap they'd left the house for some other destination, a possibility that made Rafe's blood run cold.

He glanced quickly through the window, finding the room empty. Continuing to other rooms along the terrace, he looked for movement within, but there was nothing. Even the dining room was empty. There was no formal dinner planned in this place.

His frustration level rising, he walked around to the

side, away from the domestic regions, where the servants might discover him.

He listened for voices but knew at the bottom of his heart that Beau had removed Andria and Rebecca from the premises.

As he returned to the rear of the house, he spied a young maid shaking out a rug. She saw him, and he figured he'd better give some kind of explanation.

"I'm looking for Lady Stowe and Lady Derwent. Have you seen them?"

"Aye, milord. Lady Stowe left in her carriage twenty minutes ago, and Lady Derwent went out with the master."

Ice ran through his veins. Beau had separated the ladies to suit his own purposes.

"Tell me," Rafe continued, bringing out a coin from his pocket. "Did you see a little blond girl here today, Lady Bridget?"

The maid accepted the coin and shook her head. "No, milord . . . there are no children here that I know of."

Rafe shut his eyes momentarily as acute worry flooded his senses. "Thank you. You've been most helpful."

Running back to the horse in the spinney, he suspected he would find Andria in a place much more horrifying than Lochlade. He knew Beau had taken her to the ceremonial cave.

After Beau took the blindfold off, Andria looked around the dank cave where water was dripping off the sides of the black rock. It smelled of earth, mildew, and strong incense, and she shivered in fear. She'd never felt so alone and vulnerable, and so foolish. Black candles glowed in candelabras, lighting their way.

Rebecca's message hadn't been from Rebecca at all;

she should've known better. Lady Stowe *had* been invited to a dinner at Lochlade, and she was probably even now tasting turbot in aspic and a selection of iced cakes, but Andria hadn't seen her.

Rebecca didn't know about Beau's involvement with evil, and she had written that Bridget was at Lochlade. Bridget was alive, or was she? Andria wondered if she'd come in vain, lured by a killer who would stop at nothing to get his way, including using her innocent daughter as a lure.

"Move forward, Andria," Beau said so close to her ear that she jumped with fear. "Don't dawdle."

"Where is she? Where is my daughter?" Her voice echoed in the high cave, accentuating her terror. "You promised."

Beau shoved her in the back, and she stumbled forward, stubbing her toe on a rock. Flaming and smoky flambeaux hung in intervals along the rough walls, and as she moved, she saw shadows that rose out of the darkness. Men in black shrouds soon surrounded her, soundless, faceless. Terrifying.

She tried to back away but stumbled on the uneven floor and fell. Screaming, she fought the suffocating cloth descending over her face. Someone wrapped it around her head and lifted her up.

"Let me out of here," she cried, her voice muffled. "Now!"

"Calm down, Cousin. You'll soon meet your daughter," Beau said, "but first we'll do a little ceremony. It's all to appease the powers that help us in our missions."

She made a gargantuan effort to twist free, and for a moment she could feel the grip slacken, but then arms wrapped more tightly around her. She knew she was powerless against the superior strength of her captors.

"Where's Bridget?" she shouted, tossing her head to clear the fabric off her face. "Did you just pretend to have her, Beau?"

He did not respond, and the sadness she felt was more profound than anything she'd ever experienced. Her hopes had flared so—foolishly—high. Anger blazed out of the darkness of her despair.

"You'll pay for this, Beau!" she screamed. "You'll pay for it dearly."

"Pay for what?" he asked softly. "I have done nothing, my dear. Nothing."

She felt a hard, cold surface under her body as they set her down. The cold seemed to enter the marrow of her bones immediately, and she shivered. No one removed the cloth around her face, and she was losing her breath. She smelled burning candles, and the smoke was suffocating her.

Time crept forward, or did it? For a moment, she felt warm, smoke billowing around her. Perhaps a fire . . . smoke . . . fire . . . but it *was* cold, wasn't it?

For a moment, all her thoughts floated disjointedly through her mind, and she tried to remember what had happened from the time she'd arrived at Lochlade.

Beau had met her in the foyer, all smiles and loving kindness. "Isn't it splendid?" he'd asked, beaming from ear to ear.

" 'Tis true, then? How did you find out Bridget's whereabouts? Where is she now?" She'd looked all around for her little girl but saw no one, heard no girlish voice calling her mama. "Where's Bridget?"

"Bridget is nearby."

"Take me to her now. I've waited so long for this moment." Hope had flared bright in her chest, and she'd started moving toward the stairs. "Is she in the nursery?

Let's go." She brought out the small cloth doll that she'd carried with her. "Bridget will recognize this."

He'd stepped in front of her. "All in good time, Cousin." He took a deep breath and reached out as if to touch her. She avoided his hand. "Andria . . . you know how I feel about you. I can't tell you how much I've hoped that you—"

She held up her hand to stop him. "Don't! There's no future for us, as I've told you on various occasions."

He heaved a deep sigh, and his eyes darkened with pain. "Well then, first you have to be part of a ceremony. It's the least you can do for me, since I brought back your daughter."

"Ceremony? To give thanks?"

He shook his head as if she were inexplicably obtuse. "Not what you think. We're not going to involve clergy."

"Ceremony will have to wait until I see Bridget," she said, hardening inside as she sensed Beau's deviousness behind his smiling mask.

She'd turned her back on him to move up the stairs, but he'd halted her again, this time with a loaded pistol.

"Do as I say," he'd hissed, "or you'll die right here. It doesn't matter to me."

She'd felt all her blood draining from her head. It had all been a ruse to lure her to the mansion.

"What are you gaining by doing this, Beau?"

His dark eyes had deepened with anger, and his nostrils flared. "You've always scorned me and flaunted that dark horse Rafe in front of me. All in cruelty and thoughtlessness. You were always the spoiled little girl—as long as I've known you. And your brother, how I disliked him! The spoiled heir to the Lochlade fortune who did nothing but chide me."

"I know you killed his son, Julian," she spat, instantly regretting laying herself open to more danger.

"Just a small detail." He clenched his fist in front of her face." I'm now Lord Lochlade. I have all the power of the big name that you'll never have."

Andria started, finding herself back in the cave. The cold seeped ever deeper into her body, and her mind grew hazy. The cloying smoke did something to her thoughts, but she wasn't sure what.

Her heart ached for her daughter. It ached for Rafe, for the love that she'd lost. Her body ached, and her mind cried out for help. *Rafe, where are you? I really need you.*

She heard men singing monotonously, the sound coming and going. Or was it Rafe who had arrived, singing soft lullabies to her? *Rafe,* she cried in her head, but he didn't reply.

TWENTY-TWO

Rafe rode from Lochlade to the cave, slowing down in the passage between the rocks that led to the entrance. He slid out of the saddle and walked cautiously to the black opening. As that night when he'd been here with Nick, he saw the horses tied up inside. The men were here.

What about Andria and Bridget? Cold sweat ran down his spine, and for a moment he felt powerless against the dark forces moving through his life.

If he made one wrong step, he might jeopardize the only chance he had to bring Beau to justice. Not to mention endangering the lives of the people he cared the most about.

He walked slowly forward, feeling his way along the chilly wall. The sound of chanting came to his ears, and he clenched his fist in defense. The voices had that hypnotic quality he remembered, and he shivered, feeling the evil.

His eyes adjusted to the darkness, and he rounded the bend that opened up into the main cave. Pressing himself close to the wall, he tried to make out what was going on in the swirling smoke of the burning torches. He saw the shapes of the men dancing and noticed the bundle wrapped in a black shroud on the stone altar. He knew it was Andria.

Anger boiled in the pit of his stomach. He had to get help—now—or it would be too late. He couldn't take on five men alone, especially since he only had one sword at his side and one loaded pistol in his hand and one in the saddlebag.

Fighting an urge to storm forward, he retreated. Just as he neared the mouth of the cave, someone stepped into his path. It was Beau. He must've been hiding behind one of the rocky outcrops.

"I knew you would come looking for her," he said, and laughed. "I was waiting." The hood of his robe was thrown back, and his eyes shone diabolically. "I shall have the pleasure of putting an end to you myself. That's why I waited when I heard you'd survived in Flanders, but I almost lost my patience a few times. When you survived the attack by the river, I knew I had to deal with you myself. Hired help can't be trusted with these important missions."

Rafe looked at the barrel of the pistol pointed at him and knew only caution would save him from now on.

"Don't tell me you hired a horse to kick me in the head in Flanders," Rafe said sarcastically.

Beau smirked. "There was no horse, Rafe. You were supposed to die that day, but my henchman bungled the assignment. The battlefield would've been a convenient place to get rid of you. However, luck ran your way, not mine."

"Luck still runs my way, Beau," Rafe said with more conviction than he felt. "You knew about my presence in London, so why wait all this time?"

"Seeing as you had no memory, you were harmless—until you got involved with the orphanage. Funny coincidence that you should find yourself in the same orphanage as Bridget, but you didn't know that. 'Twas easy to plant the idea that your daughter died in your arms. After that, I wanted you back here to finish off what we started before the war. Beyond anything, I wanted you gone." He stepped closer to Rafe. "You always were a difficult hurdle in my path."

"In your path to power."

"And to Andria. If she hadn't met you, she would've married me, you know."

Rafe laughed. "Hardly. She never liked you. Told me as much herself."

"That's why she has to go. We could've built a dynasty, but she's too stubborn for her own good." He waved his pistol. "Turn around and walk into the cave, and don't make any sudden moves or I'll shoot you in the back."

"Your specialty," Rafe muttered. He obeyed. Staying cool and collected would be the only qualities that might extend his life and give him a chance to save Andria. *Nick, where are you?* he thought.

Nick and Captain Emerson rode into the courtyard of the inn at Rowan's Gate. Deliriously tired, they got off their equally exhausted mounts that they had changed at a posting inn two hours ago and led them to the stables. Stable grooms took charge of the horses, and the men went inside the warm taproom to eat and rest.

"We don't have much time, I think, but let's get something in our stomachs before we continue," Nick said, warming himself by the fire.

Mr. Brown, the landlord, greeted them warmly and offered tankards of mulled wine. He looked thoughtful as he took in Emerson's red militia uniform.

"Bring in a hearty meal, my dear man," Nick said. "We

have traveled without rest. Has anything of importance happened since I left Rowan's Gate?" he added casually.

"Some unfortunate events, sir. Lord Derwent was set upon by villains and almost drowned in th' river. Mr. Guiscard 'as disappeared, but on a good note, Lord Rowan's 'ealth is improving steadily."

Nick furrowed his brow, feeling an urgency that he couldn't explain. "Have you seen Lord Derwent since the river incident?"

The landlord shook his head. "No, but there are rumors flying that there's a bitter feud between Lord Lochlade and Lord Derwent and that it's comin' to a 'ead. People are saying there's a corpse at Rowan Hall, but no one knows who it is."

Sally Vane, Nick thought, unless another corpse had appeared since he left.

"I think we'll just have to eat some bread and cheese, Trev," Nick said to Captain Emerson. "There's no time to waste if we're going to be of any help to Rafe."

Captain Emerson nodded. "Yes, let's continue. There's much at stake here."

As they pulled on their muddy cloaks anew and walked toward the door chewing on hunks of bread and cheese, the door opened. In walked a man who looked familiar, hollow-eyed, his face worried.

Nick remembered his name, Derek Guiscard.

Derek spoke, "Gentlemen, I'm back; you don't know all the details about what's going on, but I'm a key witness. I couldn't sit and wait for developments to occur with Beau's arrest. I want to help, to take part; 'tis the least I can do. You are Rafe's friends and so am I."

Nick nodded. "Yes, and we're going to find Rafe now. You're welcome to join us, and we're grateful for your offer to help."

They left the inn, and the icy cold of the day folded around them as they headed back toward the stables.

"I found out from the Rowan Hall butler that Lord Alvondale has raised the militia and they are marching down here to arrest Lochlade," Derek said. "Much has happened since I left, but I realize there have to be more witnesses to Beau's crimes if the militia is marching."

"I have a grave feeling that Rafe is in over his head," Nick said.

"And I worry about Andria," Derek said. "I stopped at Stowehurst along the way, and Witherspoon said that everyone had gone to Lochlade. According to him, Bridget has been found."

Nick grimaced and swore under his breath. "So that's where she is. I suspected as much. We never had the chance to get the upper hand on Beau, but it's not over yet."

"So you know about Bridget?"

"She was right under our noses at the Hollows, my estate in Sussex, but we thought she was someone else. She disappeared a couple of days ago."

"If they aren't at Lochlade now, I know where they are," Derek said grimly.

"The cave," Nick said. "Blast and damn."

Derek nodded. "The cave."

They got back on their horses and headed along the river path toward Lochlade as fast as they could. Nick turned to Derek behind him.

"How far away is the militia in your estimation?"

"They should be here within the hour if they keep marching."

"We doubt we have time to await their arrival before we strike. At least we have the element of surprise."

They rode in silence along the river. Nick felt worry

clench his stomach, and he shivered in the cold. He prayed he wouldn't be too late. Rafe had only him to count on.

They halted at the top of the path that led down to Lochlade. Smoke rose from the chimneys in the great mansion, and they could see movement outside the kitchen area.

"This is where the militia is heading?" Captain Emerson asked.

"Yes," Derek replied. "This is Lord Lochlade's residence."

"Do we ride down there or head toward the cave you mentioned?" Emerson asked, giving Nick a questioning glance.

Nick rubbed his jaw. " 'Sfaith, there are times when I wish I had the sight of a seer."

Derek said, "If Beau has Andria and Rafe, he's taken them to the cave. I've no doubt about that. It would be Beau's way of putting an end to the rest of the Lochlade family members."

"Which means he took Bridget there as well," Nick said.

"That's more than likely. I'd give my eyeteeth to save her," Derek said fervently. "As long as they are alive, there's hope that we can save them."

"You're right on that score," Nick said.

"Let's head down to the cave and examine the situation," Derek said. "One of us can always ride back to Lochlade and lead the militia here."

Feeling grim, Nick followed Derek's mounts down the steep path, and Emerson was swearing softly behind him. "How many men can we expect to fight us?" the captain asked.

"Five, six, possibly more," Nick said. "We're well

armed, and as I said, we have the element of surprise on our side."

"You always were the optimist," Emerson said, smiling.

"And you never avoided a fight," Nick said, and dug his heels into the flanks of his horse. "Let's move on."

Rafe watched the bundle on the stone slab. It didn't move. Had they already . . . ? In fury, he turned on Beau, but only faced down the barrel of a pistol. He was losing his promise to himself to stay calm.

"Where is Andria?" he asked, playing innocent. "I don't see her anywhere. And where's Bridget?"

"Don't bother yourself with things that don't concern you anymore. I have everything under control."

Under control. Rafe's eyes watered from the smoke in the cave, and he felt slightly dizzy. He watched the men move around the stone slab, and the long bundle lay completely still. Beau poked him in the back with the pistol, and Rafe moved forward.

Fear curled through Rafe as he looked for signs of life from the black bundle. He couldn't see any blood.

One of the men separated from the group and walked toward them. He picked up a rope from a chair and motioned to Rafe to sit down. Unable to fight them all and hope to win, Rafe had to obey.

He threw himself down, unable to take his eyes off the shrouded figure on the table. The man who tied him had no face. It was concealed behind the voluminous hood and mask.

"I know who you are," Rafe said. "Crisp, you never liked to cut your fingernails."

"They make great scratches," Crisp replied. In a fit of

anger, he tightened the cords more, cutting off most of the circulation to Rafe's hands.

"No reason to take out your rage on me," Rafe said. "The one you're angry at is Beau; he's ruining your life. You'll eventually hang for your crimes. Do you want my blood on your hands as well?"

"You should never have come back home, Rafe. If you'd had any sense, which you don't, you should've stayed away and left us alone."

"And you should've found something better to do with your life than killing and offering up young women to the Devil."

Crisp backhanded him across the face, and Rafe's neck snapped back. Pain blossomed, and his skin burned. He kicked out, catching the other man in the knee.

Crisp howled with pain and aimed another blow at Rafe's head, but before he struck, Beau shouted from the altar.

"Halt your idiocy and come back to the group. We're not here to desecrate the space with a silly brawl."

Rafe watched in helpless rage as the men continued their chanting. They were walking around the stone slab, waving torches in their hands with hypnotic coordination.

Rafe thought he would suffocate on the smoke that grew thicker by the moment. He worked on the knots around his wrists, knowing it was futile.

Beau came to stand over him. "I have gained much power by the support of the supernatural, but also by the support of my loyal men. You realize that we cannot be stopped. This has been set into motion for a long time, and Andria will be the last offering. Only women have that privilege."

"You're completely insane, Beau. And how do you plan

to kill me if I'm not good enough for an offering to the dark forces?"

"You'll be dealt with in due course."

"You'll have to let Bridget live. No child should suffer from the sins of her father—or her mother. Not that Andria ever did anything to you."

"I like to see you grovel, Rafe. A very humbling experience, don't you agree?"

"Tell me, Beau, how are you going to explain the death of Andria and me to our relatives? You know Lady Stowe won't let this go without an investigation."

"You forget that *I am* the law in these parts."

"Even lawmen can be persecuted, no matter how high your status. No, Beau, you won't be able to ride through this unscathed. Let's say we make a deal instead."

Beau laughed. "What do you have that I would need? Compared to me, you are a pauper."

"But I have peace of mind. I never intentionally killed anyone. No matter how much wealth you acquire, you'll never be happy or have peace of mind."

Beau's handsome face twisted in an ugly grimace. "Peace of mind is a myth. No one has peace of mind. Everything in life is an exchange of power. The most powerful always get their way."

"For a while, perhaps, but even Caesar's Roman Empire crumbled. In the end, your little empire will crumble, and your house will be filled with sickness."

"Is that a prophesy?" Beau's voice had turned icy cold.

"No, just history repeating itself. There's no mystery here. How many people are you going to sacrifice to quench your desire for power?"

"With you, all the naysayers will be gone. That's when I'll have peace of mind."

Rafe laughed at the absurdity of the situation. He could

never reason with Beau, only buy time. *Nick! Where are you?*

"Beau, I'm not a very religious man, but I know there's mercy. When I had nothing and knew nothing, I was still blessed with life and the support of caring people. As long as you believe in goodness, there's a solution for every situation."

"I never saw any goodness, Rafe. It's only in children's stories that angels and fairy queens exist."

"Be that as it may. Darkness destroys, never builds."

Beau stared at him long and hard, then turned toward the altar where the men waited to go on with the ceremony. One of them held a huge silver dagger with a jewel-encrusted handle in one hand.

Rafe froze, knowing that the dagger would soon be applied to the motionless body on the altar. *Dear God, if you can hear me, please help us now,* he prayed, relying on the power of goodness.

The man raised his hand, and the dagger glittered in the light from the torches. Beau was praying something in a guttural tongue, and Rafe wanted to close his ears to the grating sound.

They slowly circled the altar once, then halted, everyone raising their arms toward the jagged rock ceiling with a keening cry.

In a flurry of movement, men shouted at the opening of the cave and stormed into the chamber.

"Nick," Rafe said, "at last." He raised his voice. "On the stone slab, Nick!"

To Rafe's surprise, there were only three men: Nick, Captain Emerson, and Derek. Where was the militia? Derek and the captain stood back, pistols in each hand, aiming at the robed men. "Drop your dagger," Emerson ordered, "or I'll shoot."

The dagger clattered to the floor. Beau shouted a string of obscenities.

Nick had one pistol and a sword at his side. He moved fast to the table and, after ordering the nearest men away from the body, tore the shroud off Andria. She lay very still.

Rafe filled with unspeakable anguish. If he'd lost her, there'd be nothing to live for. He shouted, and Nick came over and pulled a knife from his waistband.

"Got yourself in a pickle, didn't you, old fellow?" Nick said, sawing away at the rope awkwardly, since he wouldn't let go of his pistol.

The robed men were gliding silently toward the far end of the cave, and Captain Emerson ordered them to stand still in the name of the law.

Nick managed to free Rafe, who rubbed his aching wrists and rolled his shoulders to get his mobility back. As soon as he could move, he rushed to Andria's side. She still wasn't showing any signs of life.

He put his ear to her chest, and to his immense relief noted that her heart was beating strongly. She was only sedated. He gave her a quick kiss on the forehead and went to join Nick, pulling Nick's sword to take part in the arrest.

Captain Emerson's voice boomed out. "I am a militia captain, and I arrest you for the murder of young Julian and Sally Vane."

Silence. No one moved until Rafe went to the group of men and pulled off their hoods with the tip of his sword. He recognized them all: Oliver Yarrow, Crisp and Cupid, his childhood friend Cunningham, and Beau.

Rafe felt the hatred of the leader. "You'll never see Bridget alive now," Beau spat.

"You certainly won't ever see her again," Rafe said, sick inside at the possibility Beau presented.

Tension rose in the room as the captain ordered the men to separate. At first, nothing happened, but then Crisp and Cupid moved to one side.

"We had nothing to do with the murders," Crisp said. " 'Twas all Beau's master plan."

"Be that as it may, you were still present, aiding him in his schemes," Nick said. "The law does not look upon that lightly."

He stepped up with the length of rope that had been used to tie Rafe. It was frayed and in two shorter pieces, but enough to use as cuffs. He motioned for Crisp to stand aside and handed the pistol to Rafe. With quick movements, he tied up the man's hands behind his back. He continued with Cupid, who was now whimpering in fear.

"Stop that mewling," Beau snarled. "You cowards. I always knew you had no real backbone."

"What in the world made you think you could get away with acts like this? And with the blood of several bodies on your hands," Rafe asked.

No one answered until Nick said, "No fear of retribution. Success always brings a great amount of recklessness." He tied up Oliver Yarrow and said, "Rafe, not only was Mr. Yarrow here involved. His wife was the woman who brought Bridget to the orphanage and left her there. My wife found all this out through a woman who used to work there."

Startled by the news, Rafe stared at Oliver, seeing only the coldness and the calculation on the other man's face.

"The cruelty behind such action is beyond reason," Nick continued.

Rafe said, "Their perfidy doesn't end there. The Yarrows stood to gain all the profits from the Bostow farm after they ruined Phoebe Bostow."

Nick turned to Beau. "And you—there isn't enough time to outline all the crimes you've perpetrated."

"I can attest to that," Derek said quietly. "You all have to admit that Beau possesses an appeal, a way of seducing you into believing that power and possessions are the ultimate happiness no matter how many lives you have to ruin to get to that goal."

"You sniveling little worm," Beau shouted as Nick moved behind him with another length of rope.

"At least I saw the light and left the group." He raised his mangled hand. "And paid dearly for it. But I would do it again if I had to. I finally have peace."

As Derek said the last words, Beau whirled around, gripped a burning torch from the wall, and flung it into a large vessel of oil sitting by the altar. It immediately caught fire. He swung his arm like a cudgel and hit Nick on the side of his head. Nick went down, and a shot rang out.

Captain Emerson had shot Beau in the leg, and with a howl, the criminal crumpled beside Nick.

Shaking his head, Nick got back on his feet. For a moment, he swayed. He rubbed the area where the blow had landed. "That was a devilish punch."

"Watch it! Fire!" Emerson shouted. "We'll be suffocated by the smoke if we don't get out of here now."

Huge billows of smoke and flames rose from the oil vessel, and Rafe looked desperately for something to smother it with. There were no lids or metal vessels large enough to cover the boiling inferno.

Acrid smoke rapidly filled the cave, and Rafe struggled to see where Andria lay. He gathered her into his arms and started toward the opening of the cave, where he could

see torches still flaring on the walls. Black smoke made
his eyes tear, and he lost his breath.

"Rafe!" Nick cried. "Let's go. Now."

Rafe followed Nick's voice and stumbled into the passage that led to freedom. He staggered forward, concentrating only on Nick's retreating back. Within minutes,
he'd carried his precious burden outside, and he fell to
the ground, coughing violently.

For one terror-filled moment he thought he might not
find his breath, but then his lungs filled with the sweet,
crisp air of the mountains.

Confused horses milled around him. Someone had
managed to untie them and let them loose.

He looked at Andria's pale face. Nick knelt beside them
and patted Andria's cheeks; he lifted her torso and shook
her gently. She coughed once and opened her eyes. They
were huge and vacant, as if she still walked in the land
of dreams.

"Andria," Rafe called hoarsely. "Can you hear me?"

Life came back to her eyes, and she looked from Nick
to Rafe. "What . . . happened?"

"You were drugged with something, Andria," Rafe
said, and gathered her body close to his own as Nick re-
linquished his hold. "I thought you were dead." Rafe buried his face against her smoke-filled hair and breathed
with relief.

He was vaguely aware of men coughing around him.
Nick said, "Trevor, where's Beau?"

Rafe looked up and saw Derek and Captain Emerson
bent over, coughing. There was no sign of the other men.

"We left them all inside," Captain Emerson said when
he could find his voice.

Billows of smoke came out of the cave. No one could

breathe that kind of air for any length of time, Rafe thought.

Derek's cough calmed down, and he went to fetch his cloak for Andria. She was sitting on the ground, still dazed.

"The ending was unexpected," Captain Emerson said. "I feel as though we failed. I wanted to see justice done, not mass suffocation."

Just as he finished speaking, they heard a moan coming from the mouth of the cave. Out of smoke crawled Beau, dragging a sack on the ground. Nick rushed forward and pulled the man out. Beau collapsed on the ground, wheezing.

Although Beau didn't seem to have any strength left to move, Captain Emerson hurried to tie him up.

The sack kicked, and a child started crying desperately. Rafe rushed forward and struggled with the knot at the top of the sack. Nick pulled out his knife and helped to open it.

"Birdie," he said.

"Bridget," Rafe said, and choked up. He gathered the child into his arms. She seemed unharmed, if dirty. Clearly she'd been drugged as well. She stared at him vacantly, and he hugged her fiercely. Staggering, he brought Bridget to the spot where Andria was still sitting, propped against Derek.

Rafe placed Bridget in Andria's lap and found a horse blanket to wrap around them both.

"Bridget," she whispered, and pushed the golden hair away from the child's brow. "My darling Bridget."

Bridget's face tightened into a coughing fit. Andria soothed her back until the fit subsided. The little girl started crying, and Andria crooned to her.

"The militia brought by Lord Alvondale should be at Lochlade by now," Rafe said.

"I'll fetch them," Nick said. "We'll have to go back into the cave once the smoke evaporates."

Rafe gave Nick a hug and a handshake. "Thank you for all you've done. I'll never forget your kindness."

Nick smiled. "Don't mention it." He gathered the reins of his horse. "I'll be back shortly with reinforcements."

Rafe sat down next to Andria, speechless with delight that both she and his daughter were safe.

TWENTY-THREE

Andria felt the fog lifting from her mind. Looking into her daughter's soot-streaked face, she experienced the fullness of a perfect dawn opening up a new day. She cried with happiness and held the child tightly. "My darling daughter."

"Mama?" Bridget's quavering voice said. "Ye was with th' angels. Am I wi' th' angels now?"

Andria shook her head, unable to speak at once.

Bridget's attention was drawn to Nick as he swung himself into the saddle of his horse. "Mr. Nick, are ye leavin' me?"

Nick looked down at the child. "No, Birdie, my sweet, I'll be back shortly. You rest with your mother and father now. They are so happy to see you, and so am I."

Birdie studied Rafe's and Andria's faces, then moved to Derek, right beside her. "You're Uncle Derek. You're wi' th' angels, too?"

"No, Bridget, we're all alive here in Lochlade. You're back home with your parents. You stayed with Mr. Nick at the orphanage for a while, but that time is over now."

Bridget's face lit up. "Mum," she said, and cuddled closer to Andria.

"She learned a new language in London, I think," Derek said.

Andria nodded, her heart too full for her to speak.

Rafe said, "We need to get out of the cold."

Derek glanced at the horses standing aimlessly on the muddy lane leading from the cave. "I'll get the horses ready. We'll ride directly to Lochlade. 'Tis the closest. From there we can use a carriage to take Andria and Bridget to Stowehurst."

Rafe wanted to object but said nothing. He watched as Derek spoke with Captain Emerson and handed him two blankets for himself and the prisoner. Beau looked as if he were about to expire. He hung his head, his complexion gray and pasty.

Captain Emerson had tied a rag around Beau's bleeding leg, but Rafe could see a lot of blood still trickling into the muddy snow.

Andria looked at Rafe. "You came to save me."

"You don't know, but I was tied up, too. Beau was going to sacrifice you on the altar, then kill me. I had no idea he'd brought Bridget here, as there was not any sign of her."

"The madness of that man chills me beyond anything," Andria said.

"We're safe now."

"Why would Beau go to such lengths to destroy us all?" Andria looked at her cousin and shuddered. She could feel nothing but deep fear when she thought of Beau.

"I remembered the whole truth earlier this morning. You recall that Beau's mother had written a bundle of love letters to your father? She was the woman he called Bijou. Well, I read those, and it's clear that there was a full-blown love affair between your father and Beau's mother. That's a known fact."

Andria said, "Yes, Father was not a discreet man by any means."

"Beau took this very heavily I'm sure, especially when your father killed his father in a duel over the mother." He threw an appraising glance at Beau. "I'm sure it festered for a long time, and combined with his madness, Beau stopped at nothing to avenge his father."

"You remember all of this now?"

"Yes. I was riding down by the river and recalled an incident before the war when Beau tried to kill me and almost succeeded. I stepped in to defend your father as he struggled with Beau on the riverbank. Lord Lochlade died that day, and it was said that he drowned. For a fact, I know that Beau killed him to avenge his father."

Andria sighed, tears running down her cheeks. "I never suspected that Beau had anything to do with Father's death. The terror has continued for a long time. Beau's only redeeming grace was that he brought Bridget out of the cave. She would surely have died otherwise."

She looked at her cousin and noted across the clearing that he was staring straight at her in the gathering gloom. He raised his hand feebly as if in a gesture of peace. "I did truly love . . . you . . . once," he said, his voice weakening with every word. "For that . . . Bridget lives." His head sank toward his chest in a faint, and Andria cried for all the people who had lost their lives to Beau's madness.

"If he survives his wound, he'll hang," Rafe said.

Bridget struggled to sit up, content to cuddle in Andria's lap.

Rafe stroked Andria's tangled hair. "I love you. I've always loved you, and I fear the chasm that still is between us. But I ask you, can we start a new life together? I realize the preciousness of being alive after everything that has happened. I ask your forgiveness for my past behavior."

Andria's voice took on a hard edge. "You don't mind what happened in the past?"

"You mean between you and Derek?" He paused for a moment, staring from her to Derek. "Let bygones be bygones. Nothing matters after what we went through today, and I don't hold a grudge against Derek. I will call him my friend if he's willing."

"I'm willing," Derek said with a grin.

Andria looked at Rafe for a long time, chewing on her bottom lip. "I was full of pride, Rafe, angry that you would think the worst of me without the benefit of the doubt."

"You mean the reason I left Lochlade—you and Derek."

She nodded. "You never gave me a chance back then to explain, and you never gave me one this time. You jumped to conclusions, and you were ready to call out Derek to pay for his 'sins.' "

Rafe hung his head, and Andria could read the remorse on his face. Love sprang like a new blade of grass toward the light of the sun.

"I was volatile and selfish," Rafe said. "I don't think that what you'd said back then would've mattered to me. I would've refused to believe you. 'Twas all wounded male pride. I'm deeply sorry that you had to live through the horrors of the last two years."

Andria placed her hand on his arm. "I'm sorry, too. There was something wrong that we could not speak intimately with each other."

"I've changed; I've learned my lesson. I'm ready to speak of anything you like, and most of all, I'm ready to listen."

Andria took a deep breath. "Derek and I did not commit adultery—as we've claimed before. You did see Derek in bed with a blond woman. It was my cousin Georgina. Derek fell madly in love with her when she visited Lochlade. I don't know what perversion brought them into *our"*—she glanced at Bridget, who was curled up with her thumb in her mouth—"boudoir, but Georgina always flaunted her daredevil attitude."

"Well, it's evident that Derek didn't make an honest woman out of her."

"He proposed, and she played him along, then decided to marry into a title and great wealth. Derek had neither. He was devastated."

"I'm sure she discovered the hard way that nothing but love can make you happy. In the long run, Derek was lucky to get out of her clutches."

"Yes, I was," Derek said vehemently.

Andria nodded. "So there you have it, Rafe. You left Lochlade due to a complete misunderstanding."

Derek nodded. "Everything she said is true. Georgina broke my heart, but I later saw her true, selfish character. I was relieved to find that I'd escaped a marriage destined to fail."

Rafe blew his breath hard through his nose. "I was an arrogant bastard. I want to make up for what we lost."

She looked deeply into his eyes, knowing that this time, they would get it right. "I do, too. I love you, Rafe."

EPILOGUE

Nick and Serena visited Rafe and Andria the following summer, at the festivities celebrating Rafe and Andria's eleventh wedding anniversary. Nick held Serena protectively around the shoulders.

" 'Twill be a boy, of course," he said, touching Serena's swelling stomach.

"Don't be so sure of that," Serena said. "I would welcome a daughter."

Nick laughed and turned to Rafe. "I always told you she was the most stubborn woman I've ever known."

Rafe smiled. "A perfect match for you, then." Filled with love, he glanced at Andria, who looked beautiful in a cream embroidered silk gown and a wide straw hat tied with a wide blue silk ribbon under her chin.

The tables on the lawn had been decorated with masses of flowers, and the canopy over their heads fluttered in the light breeze.

Bridget sat between them in a tiny replica of her mother's dress and hat, clutching her favorite old cloth doll. Rafe's heart overflowed with happiness. On Andria's other side sat Derek, handsome in a blue silk coat over white breeches. He looked content and relieved.

"Rowan Hall is a happier home than Lochlade ever was," Rafe said. "Travers is spoiling Bridget rotten, and my father dotes on the girl. He's doing so much better. He truly recovered once he discovered that his debt to Beau was wiped out at Beau's arrest. He's even riding again."

"You don't miss Lochlade?" Serena asked.

Rafe shook his head. "The Crown has still to decide what to do with it, but we won't ever live there again."

"Anyhow, it would remind me too much of Beau and the bad blood that ran between the males in that household," Andria said. "Rowan Hall is a happy home. We're free here."

"What about Rebecca? Does she resent your reunion?" Nick asked.

"No, at first she held a grudge against me," Rafe said, "but she's come around. She now spends more time at Rowan Hall than at Stowehurst, always urging us to create more great-nieces and nephews."

"She has a point," Serena said, and patted her stomach.

"Peace is finally ours," Andria said. "We've been following the trial of Beau's crimes, and it's finally coming to an end. Despite his brilliant defense, the evidence was stacked against him."

"He'll hang, just as we predicted," Rafe said.

"Justice is served," Nick said. "The other men should've been tried as well, but you can't try dead men. Justice will be served on the other side, I have no doubt."

"All that matters to me is that I have Andria and Bridget back in my life," Rafe said.

Nick laughed. "The Midnight Bandit's last mission was a huge success."

Embrace the Romances of
Shannon Drake

__**Come the Morning** $6.99US/$8.50CAN
   0-8217-6471-3

__**Blue Heaven, Black Night** $6.50US/$8.00CAN
   0-8217-5982-5

__**Conquer the Night** $6.99US/$8.50CAN
   0-8217-6639-2

__**The King's Pleasure** $6.50US/$8.00CAN
   0-8217-5857-8

__**Lie Down in Roses** $5.99US/$6.99CAN
   0-8217-4749-0

__**Tomorrow the Glory** $5.99US/$6.99CAN
   0-7860-0021-4